SPECIAL MESSAGE TO READERS

Karen Thompson Walker is a graduate of UCLA and the Columbia MFA programme. A former book editor, she wrote *The Age of Miracles* in the mornings before work. Born and raised in San Diego, California, she now lives in Brooklyn with her husband. This is her first novel.

THE AGE OF MIRACLES

What if our twenty-four-hour day grew longer, first in minutes, then in hours, until day became night and night became day? What effect would this slowing have on the world? On the birds in the sky, the whales in the sea, the astronauts in space, and on a family and a young girl, who is already coping with the normal disasters of everyday life? Julia's account of how lives can be knocked unexpectedly out of kilter begins on one seemingly ordinary Saturday morning in a California suburb — when she and her parents wake to discover that the rotation of the earth has suddenly begun to slow. No one knows why, no one knows how to deal with it. The enormity of this change is almost beyond comprehension . . .

KAREN THOMPSON WALKER

THE AGE OF MIRACLES

Complete and Unabridged

CHARNWOOD
Leicester

First published in Great Britain in 2012 by
Simon & Schuster UK Ltd.
London

First Charnwood Edition
published 2013
by arrangement with
Simon & Schuster UK Ltd.
London

A catalogue record for this book is available
from the British Library.

ISBN 978–1–4448–1559–7

Published by
F. A. Thorpe (Publishing)
Anstey, Leicestershire

Set by Words & Graphics Ltd.
Anstey, Leicestershire
Printed and bound in Great Britain by
T. J. International Ltd., Padstow, Cornwall

This book is printed on acid-free paper

For my parents
and
for Casey

Here in the last minutes, the very end of the world, someone's tightening a screw thinner than an eyelash, someone with slim wrists is straightening flowers . . .

Another End of the World,
JAMES RICHARDSON

1

We didn't notice right away. We couldn't feel it.

We did not sense at first the extra time, bulging from the smooth edge of each day like a tumor blooming beneath skin.

We were distracted back then by weather and war. We had no interest in the turning of the earth. Bombs continued to explode on the streets of distant countries. Hurricanes came and went. Summer ended. A new school year began. The clocks ticked as usual. Seconds beaded into minutes. Minutes grew into hours. And there was nothing to suggest that those hours, too, weren't still pooling into days, each the same fixed length known to every human being.

But there were those who would later claim to have recognized the disaster before the rest of us did. These were the night workers, the graveyard shifters, the stockers of shelves, and the loaders of ships, the drivers of big-rig trucks, or else they were the bearers of different burdens: the sleepless and the troubled and the sick. These people were accustomed to waiting out the night. Through bloodshot eyes, a few did detect a certain persistence of darkness on the mornings leading up to the news, but each mistook it for the private misperception of a lonely, rattled mind.

On the sixth of October, the experts went public. This, of course, is the day we all remember. There'd been a change, they said, a slowing, and that's what we called it from then on: *the slowing*.

'We have no way of knowing if this trend will continue,' said a shy bearded scientist at a hastily arranged press conference, now infamous. He cleared his throat and swallowed. Cameras flashed in his eyes. Then came the moment, replayed so often afterward that the particular cadences of that scientist's speech — the dips and the pauses and that slight midwestern slant — would be forever married to the news itself. He went on: 'But we suspect that it *will* continue.'

Our days had grown by fifty-six minutes in the night.

At the beginning, people stood on street corners and shouted about the end of the world. Counselors came to talk to us at school. I remember watching Mr. Valencia next door fill up his garage with stacks of canned food and bottled water, as if preparing, it now seems to me, for a disaster much more minor.

The grocery stores were soon empty, the shelves sucked clean like chicken bones.

The freeways clogged immediately. People heard the news, and they wanted to move. Families piled into mini-vans and crossed state lines. They scurried in every direction like small animals caught suddenly under a light.

But, of course, there was nowhere on earth to go.

2

The news broke on a Saturday.

In our house, at least, the change had gone unnoticed. We were still asleep when the sun came up that morning, so we sensed nothing unusual in the timing of its rise. Those last few hours before we learned of the slowing remain preserved in my memory — even all these years later — as if trapped behind glass.

My friend Hanna had slept over the night before, and we'd camped out in sleeping bags on the living room floor, where we'd slept side by side on a hundred other nights. We woke to the purring of lawn-mower motors and the barking of dogs, to the soft squeak of a trampoline as the twins jumped next door. In an hour we'd both be dressed in blue soccer uniforms — hair pulled back, sunscreen applied, cleats clicking on tile.

'I had the weirdest dream last night,' said Hanna. She lay on her stomach, her head propped up on one elbow, her long blond hair hanging tangled behind her ears. She had a certain skinny beauty that I wished I had, too.

'You always have weird dreams,' I said.

She unzipped her sleeping bag and sat up, pressed her knees to her chest. From her slim wrist there jingled a charm bracelet crowded with charms. Among them: one half of a small brass heart, the other half of which belonged to me.

'In the dream, I was at my house, but it wasn't my house,' she went on. 'I was with my mom, but she wasn't my mom. My sisters weren't my sisters.'

'I hardly ever remember my dreams,' I said. Then I got up to let the cats out of the garage.

My parents were spending that morning the way I remember them spending every morning, reading the newspaper at the dining room table. I can still see them sitting there: my mother in her green bathrobe, her hair wet, skimming quickly through the pages, while my father sat in silence, fully dressed, reading every story in the order it appeared, each one reflected in the thick lenses of his glasses.

My father would save that day's paper for a long time afterward — packed away like an heirloom, folded neatly beside the newspaper from the day I was born. The pages of that Saturday's paper, printed before the news was out, report a rise in the city's real estate prices, the further erosion of several area beaches, and plans for a new freeway overpass. That week a local surfer had been attacked by a great white shark; border patrol agents discovered a three-mile-long drug-running tunnel six feet beneath the U.S./Mexico border; and the body of a young girl, long missing, was found buried under a pile of white rocks in the wide, empty desert out east. The times of that day's sunrise and sunset appear in a chart on the back page, predictions that did not, of course, come to pass.

Half an hour before we heard the news, my mother went out for bagels.

4

I think the cats sensed the change before we did. They were both Siamese, but different breeds. Chloe was sleepy and feathery and sweet. Tony was her opposite: an old and anxious creature, possibly mentally ill, a cat who tore out his own fur in snatches and left it in piles around the house, tiny tumbleweeds set adrift on the carpet.

In those last few minutes, as I ladled dry food into their bowls, the ears of both cats began to swivel wildly toward the front yard. Maybe they felt it somehow, a shift in the air. They both knew the sound of my mother's Volvo pulling into the driveway, but I wondered later if they recognized also the unusually quick spin of the wheels as she rushed to park the car, or the panic in the sharp crack of the parking brake as she yanked it into place.

Soon even I could detect the pitch of my mother's mood from the stomps of her feet on the porch, the disorganized rattle of her keys against the door — she had heard those earliest news reports, now notorious, on the car radio between the bagel shop and home.

'Turn on the TV right now,' she said. She was breathless and sweaty. She left her keys in the teeth of the lock, where they would dangle all day. 'Something God-awful is happening.'

⋆ ⋆ ⋆

We were used to my mother's rhetoric. She talked big. She blustered. She overstated and oversold. *God-awful* might have meant anything.

5

It was a wide net of a phrase that scooped up a thousand possibilities, most of them benign: hot days and traffic jams, leaking pipes and long lines. Even cigarette smoke, if it wafted too close, could be *really and truly God-awful*.

We were slow to react. My father, in his thinning yellow Padres T-shirt, stayed right where he was at the table, one palm on his coffee cup, the other resting on the back of his neck, as he finished an article in the business section. I went ahead and opened the bag of bagels, letting the paper crinkle beneath my fingers. Even Hanna knew my mother well enough to go right on with what she was doing — hunting for the cream cheese on the bottom shelf of the refrigerator.

'Are you watching this?' my mother said. We were not.

My mother had been an actress once. Her old commercials — mostly hair-care and kitchen products — lay entombed together in a short stack of dusty black videotapes that stood beside the television. People were always telling me how beautiful she was when she was young, and I could still find it in the fair skin of her face and the high structure of her cheekbones, though she'd gained weight in middle age. Now she taught one period of drama at the high school and four periods of history. We lived ninety-five miles from Hollywood.

She was standing on our sleeping bags, two feet from the television screen. When I think of it now, I imagine her cupping one hand over her mouth the way she always did when she worried,

6

but at the time, I just felt embarrassed by the way the black waffle soles of her running shoes were twisting Hanna's sleeping bag, hers the dainty cotton kind, pink and polka-dotted and designed not for the hazards of campsites but exclusively for the plush carpets of heated homes.

'Did you hear me?' said my mother, swinging around to look at us. My mouth was full of bagel and cream cheese. A sesame seed had lodged itself between my two front teeth. 'Joel!' she shouted at my father. 'I'm serious. This is hellacious.'

My father looked up from the paper then, but still he kept his index finger pressed firmly to the page to mark his place. How could we have known that the workings of the universe had finally made appropriate the fire of my mother's words?

3

We were Californians and thus accustomed to the motions of the earth. We understood that the ground could shift and shudder. We kept batteries in our flashlights and gallons of water in our closets. We accepted that fissures might appear in our sidewalks. Swimming pools sometimes sloshed like bowls of water. We were well practiced at crawling beneath tabletops, and we knew to beware of flying glass. At the start of every school year, we each packed a large ziplock bag full of non-perishables in case The Big One stranded us at school. But we Californians were no more prepared for this particular calamity than those who had built their homes on more stable ground.

When we finally understood what was happening that morning, Hanna and I rushed outside to check the sky for evidence. But the sky was just the sky — an average, cloudless, blue. The sun shone unchanged. A familiar breeze was blowing from the direction of the sea, and the air smelled the way it always did back then, like cut grass and honeysuckle and chlorine. The eucalyptus trees were fluttering like sea anemones in the wind, and my mother's jug of sun tea looked nearly dark enough to drink. In the distance beyond our back fence, the freeway echoed and hummed. The power lines continued to buzz. Had we tossed a soccer ball into the air, we might not have even noticed that it fell a little faster to the earth, that it hit the ground a little harder than before. I was eleven years old in the suburbs. My best friend was standing beside me. I could spot not a single object out of place or amiss.

★   ★   ★

In the kitchen, my mother was already scanning the shelves for essentials, swinging cupboards on hinges and inspecting the contents of drawers.

'I just want to know where all the emergency supplies are,' she said. 'We don't know what might happen.'

'I think I should go home,' said Hanna, still in purple pajamas, her arms wrapped around her tiny waist. She hadn't brushed her hair, and hers was hair that demanded attention, having grown uncut since second grade. All the Mormon girls I knew had long hair. Hanna's dangled near her waist and tapered at the end like a flame. 'My mom is probably freaking out, too,' she said.

Hanna's house was full of sisters, but mine was the home of only one child. I never liked it when she left. The rooms felt too quiet without her.

I helped her roll up her sleeping bag. She packed her backpack.

Had I known how much time would pass before we'd see each other again, I would have said a different goodbye. But we just waved, Hanna and I, and then my father drove her back to her house, three streets over from ours.

There was no footage to show on television, no burning buildings or broken bridges, no twisted metal or scorched earth, no houses sliding off slabs. No one was wounded. No one was dead. It was, at the beginning, a quite invisible catastrophe.

I think this explains why what I felt first was not fear but a thrill. It was a little exciting — a sudden sparkle amid the ordinary, the shimmer of the unexpected thing.

But my mother was terrified. 'How could this happen?' she said.

She kept clipping and reclipping her hair. It was dark and lovely, thanks in part to a deep brown dye.

'Maybe it was a meteor?' I said. We'd been studying the universe in science, and I'd memorized the order of the planets. I knew the names of all the things that floated out in space. There were comets and black holes and bands of giant rocks. 'Or maybe a nuclear bomb?'

'It's not a nuclear bomb,' said my father. I could see the muscles clenching in his jaw as he watched the television screen. He kept his arms crossed, his feet spread wide. He would not sit down.

'To a certain extent, we can adapt,' a scientist on the television screen was saying. A tiny microphone had been pinned to his collar, and a newscaster was plumbing him for the darker possibilities. 'But if the earth's rotation continues to slow — and this is just speculation — I'd say we can expect radical changes in the weather. We're going to see earthquakes and tsunamis. We might see mass plant and animal die-outs. The oceans may begin to shift toward the poles.'

Behind us, our vertical blinds rustled in the breeze, and a helicopter buzzed in the distance, the thrumming of its blades wafting into the house through the screens.

'But what could possibly cause something like this?' said my mother.

'Helen,' said my father, 'I don't know any more than you do.'

We all forgot about that day's soccer game. My uniform would remain folded in its drawer all day. My shin guards would lay untouched at the bottom of my closet.

I heard later that only Michaela showed up at the field, late as usual, her cleats in her hands, her long hair undone, her red curls flying in and out of her mouth as she ran sock-footed up the hill to the field — only to find not a single girl warming up, not one blue jersey rippling in the wind, not one French braid flapping, not a single parent or coach on the grass. No mothers in visors sipping iced tea, no fathers in flip-flops pacing the sideline. No ice chests or beach chairs or quarter-sliced oranges. The upper parking lot, she must have noticed then, was empty of cars. Only the nets remained, billowing silently in the goals, they the only proof that the sport of soccer had once been played on this site.

'And you know how my mom is,' Michaela would tell me days later at lunch, slouching against a wall in imitation of the sexier

11

seventh-grade girls. 'She was gone by the time I got back down to the parking lot.'

Michaela's mother was the youngest mother. Even the most glamorous of the other mothers were at least thirty-five by then, and mine had already turned forty. Michaela's was just twenty-eight, a fact that her daughter denied but we all understood to be true. Her mother always had a different boyfriend at her side, and her smooth skin and firm body, her high breasts and her slim thighs, were together the source of something shameful we only dimly perceived but which we most certainly *did* perceive. Michaela was the only kid I knew who lived in an apartment, and she had no father to speak of.

Michaela's young mother had slept right through the news.

'You didn't see anything about it on television?' I asked Michaela later that week.

'We don't have cable, remember? I never even turn the TV on.'

'What about the car radio?'

'Broken,' she said.

Even on ordinary days, Michaela had a continuous need for rides. On that first day of the slowing, while the rest of us watched the news in our living rooms, Michaela, stranded at the soccer field, fiddled for a while with an ancient, out-of-service pay phone, long forgotten by its maker — all the rest of us had cell phones — until finally the coach drove up to tell anyone who had shown up that the game was canceled, or at least postponed, and he gave Michaela a ride home.

By noon on that first day, the networks had run out of new information. Drained of every fresh fact, they went right on reporting anyway, chewing and rechewing the same small chunks of news. It didn't matter, we were mesmerized.

I spent that whole day sitting on the carpet only a few feet from the television with my parents. I still remember how it felt to live through those hours. It was almost physical: the need to know whatever there was to know.

Periodically, my mother went around the house checking faucets one by one, inspecting the color and clarity of the water.

'Nothing's going to happen to the water, honey,' said my father. 'It's not an earthquake.'

He held his glasses in his hands and was wiping the lenses with the bottom of his shirt, as if ours were a problem merely of vision. Bare of the glasses, his eyes always looked squinty to me, and too small.

'You're acting like this isn't a big deal,' she said.

This was a time when the disagreements between my parents were still minor.

My father held his glasses up to the light, then carefully set them on his face. 'Tell me what you want me to do, Helen,' he said. 'And I'll do it.'

My father was a doctor. He believed in problems and solutions, diagnosis and cure. Worry, to his mind, was a waste.

'People are panicking,' said my mother. 'What about all the people who run the water systems

13

and the power grid? What about the food supply? What if they abandon their posts?'

'All we can do is ride this thing out,' he said.

'Oh, that's a good plan,' she said. 'That's a really excellent plan.'

I watched her hurry out to the kitchen, her bare feet slapping the tile. I heard the click and creak of the liquor cabinet, the clinking of ice in a glass.

'I bet things will turn out okay,' I said, gripped by an urge to say some cheerful thing — it rose up from my throat like a cough. 'I bet it will be fine.'

Already the crackpots and the geniuses were streaming out of the wilderness and appearing on talk shows, waving the scientific papers that the established journals had declined to publish. These lone wolves claimed to have seen the disaster coming.

My mother returned to the couch with a drink in her hand.

At the bottom of the television screen, a question blared in red block letters. This was the question: IS THE END NEAR?

'Oh, come on,' said my father. 'That's just pure sensationalism. What are they saying on public television?' The question dissolved in the air. No one changed the channel. Then he looked over at me and said to my mother, 'I don't think she should be watching this. Julia,' he said, 'you want to go kick the ball around?'

'No, thanks,' I said. I didn't want to miss a single piece of news.

I had pulled my sweatshirt down over my

14

knees. Tony lay beside me on the rug, his paws outstretched, his breathing wheezy. His body was so bony, you could see the knobs in his spine. Chloe was hiding under the couch.

'Come on,' said my father. 'Let's go kick the ball around for a while.' He dug my soccer ball out of the hall closet and pressed it between his hands. 'It feels a little low,' he said.

I watched him handle the pump as if it were a piece of his medical equipment, inserting the needle into the opening with a surgeon's precision and care, then pumping methodically, like a respirator, always waiting for the last gasp of air to pass into the ball before forcing the next one through.

I tied my shoes reluctantly and we went outside.

We kicked back and forth in silence for a while. I could hear the newscasters chattering inside. Their voices mingled with the clean thud of foot against ball.

The neighboring backyards were deserted. Swing sets stood still as ruins. The twins' trampoline had ceased to squeak. I wanted to be back inside.

'That was a nice one,' said my father. 'Good accuracy.'

But he didn't know much about soccer. He kicked with the wrong part of the foot. I hit the next one too hard, and the ball disappeared into the honeysuckle in the corner of our yard. We stopped kicking then.

'You're okay, right?' he said.

Large birds had begun to circle the sky. These

were not suburban birds. These were hawks and eagles and crows, birds whose hefty wings spoke of the wilder landscapes that persisted east of here. They swooped from tree to tree, their calls drowning out the twitter of our usual backyard birds.

I knew that animals often sensed danger where humans did not, and that in the minutes or hours before a tsunami or a wildfire strikes, the animals always know to flee long before the people do. I had heard that elephants sometimes snapped their chains and headed for higher ground. Snakes could slither for miles.

'Do you think the birds know?' I asked. I could feel the muscles in my neck tensing as I watched them.

My father studied their shapes but said nothing. A hawk landed at the crown of our pine tree, flapped his wings, then took off again, heading farther west toward the coast.

From inside, my mother called to us through the screen door, 'Now they're saying it might be affecting gravity somehow.'

'We'll be there in a minute,' said my father. He squeezed my shoulder hard, then tilted his head up to the sky like a farmer on the lookout for rain. 'I want you to think how smart humans are,' he said. 'Think of everything humans have ever invented. Rocket ships, computers, artificial hearts. We solve problems, you know? We always solve the big problems. We do.'

We walked inside after that, through the French doors and onto the tile, my father insisting that we wipe our feet on the doormat as we crossed — as if remembering our rituals could ensure our safe passage — back to the living room to my mother. But I felt as he spoke and as we walked that although the world remained intact for now, everything around me was about to come apart.

★ ★ ★

In the hours that followed, we would worry and wait. We would guess and wonder and speculate. We would learn new words and new ways from the scientists and officials who paraded in and out of our living room through the television screen and the Internet. We would stalk the sun across our sky as we never had before. My mother drank Scotch over ice in a glass. My father paced in the living room. Time moved differently that Saturday. Already the morning felt like yesterday. By the time we sat waiting for the sun to drift down behind the hills to the west, it seemed to me that several days had passed inside the skin of just this one, as if the day had ballooned by much more than a single small hour.

In the late afternoon, my father climbed the stairs to my parents' bedroom and then reappeared transformed in a collared shirt and dark socks. A pair of dress shoes was swinging from two of his fingers.

'Are you going somewhere?' asked my mother.

'I'm on at six, remember?'

My father delivered babies for a living, and he specialized in high-risk births. He was often on call, and he sometimes worked the overnight shift at the hospital. He frequently worked weekends.

'Don't go,' said my mother. 'Not tonight.'

I remember hoping she could convince him not to leave, but he continued to tie his shoes. He liked the loops in his bows to be exactly the same size.

'They'll understand if you don't show up,' said my mother. 'It's chaos out there, with the traffic and the panic and everything.'

Some of my father's patients had spent months in the hospital, trying to hold their babies in their wombs until the babies were strong enough to survive the world.

'Come on, Helen,' he said. 'You know I can't stay.'

He stood up and patted his front pocket. I heard the muted jingle of keys.

'We need you here,' my mother said. She rested her head sideways against my father's chest — he was over a foot taller. 'We really don't want you to go, right, Julia?'

I wanted him to stay, too, but I'd grown expert at diplomacy as only an only child can.

'I wish he didn't have to go,' I said carefully. 'But I guess if he *has* to go.'

My mother turned away from me and said to him more softly, 'Please. We don't even know what's happening.'

'Come on, Helen,' he said, smoothing her hair. 'Don't be so dramatic. Nothing's going to happen between now and tomorrow morning. I'm betting this whole thing will blow over.'

18

'How?' she said. 'How could it?'

He kissed her on the cheek and waved to me from the entry hall. Then he stepped outside and shut the door. Soon we heard his car starting up in the driveway.

My mother flopped down next to me on the couch. 'At least *you*'re not abandoning me,' she said. 'We'll have to take care of each other.'

I felt like escaping to Hanna's house right then, but I knew it would upset my mother if I left.

From outside, the voices of children floated into the living room. Through the blinds, I could see the Kaplan family walking down the sidewalk. Saturday was their Sabbath day, which meant they didn't drive all day. There were six of them now: Mr. and Mrs. Kaplan, Jacob, Beth, Aaron, and the baby in the stroller. The kids went to the Jewish day school up north, and they dressed mostly in black, in a way that reminded me of characters in old movies, a flutter of long skirts and black pants. Beth Kaplan was my age, but I didn't know her well. She kept to herself. She wore a long-sleeve shirt and a long rectangular black skirt with stylish red patent-leather shoes. I figured that footwear was her one place to shine. As the Kaplans glided past our house, the littlest one picking dandelions from the edge of our lawn, I realized that they might not yet know about the slowing.

I found out much later from Jacob that I was right: The Kaplans did not discover until sundown — when their Sabbath was over and their religion once again allowed them to flip light switches and watch TV — that this world was any different from the one they'd been born into. If you didn't hear the news, the landscape looked unchanged. This was not true later, of course, but for now, on this first day, the earth still seemed itself.

★   ★   ★

We lived on a cul-de-sac in a neighborhood of tract houses built in the 1970s on quarter-acre lots with stucco exteriors and asbestos in the ceilings and the walls. An olive tree twisted up from every front yard unless it had been torn out and replaced with some trendier, thirstier tree. The yards on our street were well kept but not obsessively so. Daisies and dandelions were scattered amid the thinning grass. Pink bougain-villea bushes clung to the sides of almost all the houses, shaking and shimmering in the wind.

In satellite maps from that era, our row of cul-de-sacs looks neat and parallel, each with a fat bulb at the end, like ten thermometers hanging from a string. Ours was one in a web of modest streets carved into the less expensive side of a coastal California hill whose pricier slope faced the ocean.

Our mornings were bright back then. Our kitchens faced east. Sun streamed through windows as coffeepots gurgled and showers ran, as I brushed my teeth or chose an outfit for school. Our afternoons were shady and cool because each evening, the sun dropped behind the nicer houses at the top of the hill a full hour before it slipped into the ocean on the other side. On this day, we waited for sunset with new suspense.

'I think it moved a little,' I said, squinting. 'I mean, it's definitely going down.'

All along the street, garage doors cased open on electric tracks. Station wagons and SUVs emerged, loaded with kids and clothes and dogs. A few neighbors stood clustered, arms crossed, on their lawns. Everyone was watching the sky as if waiting for a fireworks show to begin.

'Don't look directly at the sun,' said my mother, who was sitting beside me on the porch. 'It'll ruin your eyes.'

She was peeling open a package of double-A batteries she'd found in a drawer. Three flashlights lay on the cement beside her, a mini arsenal of light. The sun remained high in the sky, but she had grown obsessed already with the possibilities of an extra-long night.

In the distance at the end of the street, I spotted my old friend Gabby, sitting alone on her roof. I hadn't seen her much since her parents had transferred her to a private school in the next town over from ours. As usual, she was dressed in all black. Her dyed black hair stood out against the sky.

'Why did she dye it like that?' said my mother.

'I don't know,' I said. Not visible from this distance were the three tiers of earrings that hung from both of Gabby's ears. 'She just felt like it, I guess.'

A portable radio chattered and buzzed beside us. We were gaining more minutes with every

21

hour. Already, they were arguing about the wheat point — I've never understood if this was a term that had been buried for decades in the glossaries of textbooks, or if it was coined on that day, a new answer to a new question: How long can major crops survive without the light of the sun?

My mother switched the flashlights on and off, one by one, testing their beams in the cup of her hand. She dumped the old batteries out of each barrel and replaced them with new ones, as if arranging ammunition in a set of guns.

'I don't know why your father hasn't called me back,' she said.

She'd brought the cordless phone out to the porch, where it sat silent beside her. She took quick soundless sips of her drink. I remember the sound of the ice clinking in the glass, the way the water dripped down the sides, leaving intersecting rings on the cement.

Not everyone panicked. Sylvia, my piano teacher, who lived across the street, went right on tending her garden as if nothing at all had happened. I watched her kneeling calmly in the dirt, a pair of shiny shears in one hand. Later, she took a slow walk around the block, her clogs tapping the sidewalk as she went, her red hair falling from a hasty braid.

'Hi, Julia,' she said when she reached our yard. She smiled at my mother but did not say her name. They were about the same age, but Sylvia still seemed girlish somehow, and my mother did not.

'You don't seem very worried,' said my mother.

'Que será, será,' said Sylvia. Her words were one long sigh. "That's what I always say. Whatever will be, will be.'

I liked Sylvia, but I knew my mother didn't. Sylvia was cool and wispy and she smelled like lotion. Her limbs were lanky, like the branches of eucalyptus trees, and were often encircled in chunky turquoise jewelry, which she removed at the beginning of each of my piano lessons in order to commune more closely with the keys. She always played piano barefoot.

'Or maybe I'm just not thinking straight,' Sylvia said. 'I'm in the middle of doing a cleanse.'

'What's a cleanse?' I said.

'It's a fast,' said Sylvia.

She bent toward me to explain, and I heard my mother slide her flashlights behind her back. I think she was suddenly embarrassed by her fear.

'No food, no alcohol, just water. For three days. I'm sure your mother has done one before.'

My mother shook her head. 'Not me,' she said. I was aware of my mother's drink, sweating on the pavement beside her. For a moment nothing else was said.

'Anyway,' said Sylvia, beginning to walk away, 'don't let this stop you from practicing, Julia. See you Wednesday.'

Sylvia would spend the next few afternoons pruning roses in a sun hat and casually pulling up weeds.

'You know, it's not healthy to be that skinny,' said my mother after Sylvia had gone back to her gardening. (My mother kept a closet full of dresses one size too small, all waiting in plastic, for the day when she lost the ten pounds she'd been complaining about for years.) 'You can see her bones,' said my mother. And it was true: You could.

'Look,' I said. 'The streetlights came on.'

Those lights were set to a timer, designed to ignite at dusk. But the sun continued to shine.

I imagined people on the other side of the world, in China and in India, huddling now in the darkness, waiting, like us — but for dawn.

'He should let us know he got to work safely, at least,' said my mother. She dialed again, waited, set the phone down.

I'd gone with my father to work once. Not much had happened while I was there. Pregnant women watched television and ate snacks in bed. My father asked questions and checked charts. Husbands milled around.

'Didn't I ask him to call?' she said.

She was making me nervous. I tried to keep her calm.

'He's probably just busy,' I said.

In the distance, I noticed that Tom and Carlotta, the old couple who lived at the end of the street, were sitting outside, too, he in a faded tie-dyed T-shirt and jeans, she in Birkenstocks, a long gray braid resting on her shoulder. But they were always out there at this time of night, beach chairs in the driveway, margaritas and cigarettes in their hands. Their garage door stood open behind them, Tom's model train tracks exposed like guts. Most of the houses on our street had been remodeled by then, or fixed up, at least, given fresh veneers like old teeth, but Tom and Carlotta's house remained untouched, and I knew from selling Girl Scout cookies that the original burgundy shag still lined their floors.

Tom waved at me, his hand thick with a drink. I didn't know him well, but he was always friendly to me. I waved back.

It was October, but it felt like July: The air was summer air, the sky a summer sky, still light past seven o'clock.

'I hope the phones are working,' said my mother. 'But they must be working, right?'

In the time since that night, I've developed many of my mother's habits, the persistent churning of her mind on a single subject, her low tolerance for uncertainty, but like her wide hips and her high cheekbones, these were traits that would sleep dormant in me for some years to come. That night I could not relate to her.

'Just calm down,' I said. 'Okay, Mom?'

Finally, the phone did ring. My mother answered it in a rush. I could tell she was disappointed by the voice she was hearing. She passed the phone to me.

It wasn't my father. It was Hanna.

I stood up from the porch and walked out into the grass with the phone to my ear, squinting at the sun.

'I can't really talk,' said Hanna. 'But I wanted to tell you that we're leaving.'

I could hear the voices of Hanna's sisters

25

echoing in the background. I could picture her standing in the bedroom she shared with them, the yellow-striped curtains her mother had sewn, the stuffed animals crowded on her bed, the hair clips spread out across the dresser. We had spent hours together in that room.

'Where are you going?' I asked.

'Utah,' Hanna said. She sounded scared.

'When are you coming back?' I asked.

'We're not,' she said.

I felt a wave of panic. We'd spent so much time together that year that teachers sometimes called us by one another's names.

As I would later learn, thousands of Mormons gathered in Salt Lake City after the slowing began. Hanna had told me once that the church had pinpointed a certain square mile of land as the exact location of Jesus' next return to earth. They kept a giant grain silo in Utah, she said, to feed the Mormons during the end times. 'I'm not supposed to tell you this stuff because you're not in our church,' she said. 'But it's true.'

My own family's religion was a bloodless breed of Lutheranism — we guarded no secrets, and we harbored no clear vision of the end of the world.

'Are you still there?' said Hanna.

It was hard to talk. I stood in the grass, trying not to cry.

'You're moving away for good?' I finally said.

I heard Hanna's mother call her name in the background.

'I have to go,' Hanna said. 'I'll call you later.'

She hung up.

'What did she say?' called my mother from the porch.

A hard lump had formed in my throat.

'Nothing,' I said.

'Nothing?' said my mother.

Tears rushed into my eyes. My mother didn't notice.

'I want to know why Daddy hasn't called us,' she said. 'Do you think his phone is dead?'

'God, Mom,' I said. 'You're making everything worse.'

She stopped talking and looked at me. 'Don't be a smartaleck,' she snapped. 'And don't say *God*.'

A slight static crackled through the radio speakers, and my mother adjusted the dial until it cleared. An expert from Harvard was talking: 'If this keeps up,' he said, 'this could be catastrophic for crops of all kinds, for the whole world's food supply.'

We sat in silence for a moment.

Then from inside the house, we heard a quick thud, the wet smack of something soft striking glass.

We both jumped.

'What was that?' she said.

The unimaginable had been imagined, the unbelievable believed. Now it seemed to me that dangers lurked everywhere. Threats seemed to hide in every crack.

'It didn't sound good,' I said.

We hurried inside. We hadn't put anything away, and the kitchen was a mess. My bagel from the morning lay half eaten on a plate, exactly where I'd left it nine hours earlier, the cream cheese crusting at the edges. A container of yogurt had been overturned by the cats, its insides licked clean. Someone had left out the milk. I noticed that Hanna had left her soccer sweatshirt on a chair.

The source of the sound turned out to be a bird. A blue jay had struck a high window in our kitchen, then dropped to the back deck, its narrow neck apparently snapped, its wings spread asymmetrically around its body.

'Maybe it's just stunned,' said my mother.

We stood at the glass.

'I don't think so,' I said.

The slowing, we soon came to understand, had altered gravity. Afterward, the earth held a little more sway. Bodies in motion were slightly less likely to remain in motion. We were all of us and everything a little more susceptible to the pull of the ground, and maybe it was this shift in physics that had sent that bird straight into the flat glass of our windowpane.

'Maybe we should move it,' I said.

'I don't want you touching it,' said my mother. 'Daddy will deal with it.'

And so we left the bird exactly as it lay. We kept the cats inside for the rest of the night.

We left the kitchen as we'd found it, too. We'd remodeled it recently, and you could smell the paint in the air, but that chemical scent was mixing with the tinge of soured milk. My mother poured a fresh drink: Two new ice cubes cracked and resettled beneath a stream of sparkling Scotch. I'd never seen her drink so much in one day.

She headed back out to the front porch. 'Come on,' she said.

But I was tired of being with her. I went up to my room instead and lay flat on my bed for a while.

Twenty minutes later, the sun finally did slip behind the hill, proof at last that the earth, however slowly, continued to turn.

★   ★   ★

The wind reversed in the night and turned hard, blowing in from the desert instead of up from the sea. It howled and shrieked. Outside, the eucalyptus trees struggled and heaved, and the glittering stars showed that the sky was clear of clouds — this was an empty, stormless wind.

At some point, I heard the creaking of cabinets in the kitchen, the soft squeak of hinges. I recognized the shuffling of my mother's slippered feet, the uncapping of a pill bottle, and a glass of water slowly filling at the sink.

I wished my father were home. I tried to picture him at the hospital. Maybe babies were being born into his hands right at that moment. I wondered what it might mean to come into the world on this of all nights.

Soon the streetlights flashed off, sucking the low glow from my room. This should have marked dawn, but the neighborhood remained submerged in the dark. It was a new kind of darkness for me, a thick country black, unseen in cities and suburbs.

I left my room and crept into the hall. Through the crack beneath my parents' door, I could see the sickly blue light of the television leaking onto the hall carpet.

'You're not sleeping, either?' said my mother when I opened the door. She looked slouchy and worn in an old white nightgown. Bouquets of fine wrinkles fanned out from her eyes.

I climbed into bed beside her. 'What's all that wind?' I asked.

We spoke in low tones as if someone were sleeping nearby. The television was on mute.

'It's just a Santa Ana,' she said, rubbing my back with the palm of her hand. 'It's Santa Ana season. It's always like this in the fall, remember? That part, at least, is normal.'

'What time is it?' I asked.

'Seven-forty-five.'

'It should be morning,' I said.

'It is,' she said. The sky remained dark. There was no hint of dawn.

We could hear the cats, restless in the garage. I could hear a scratching at the door and Tony's persistent, uncertain wailing. He was nearly blind from cataracts, but I could tell that even he knew something was wrong.

'Did Daddy call?' I asked.

My mother nodded. 'He's going to work another shift because not everyone showed up.'

We sat for a long time in silence while the wind blew around us. The light from the television flashed on the white walls.

'When he gets home, let him rest, okay?' said my mother. 'He's had a very rough night.'

'What happened?'

She bit her lip and kept her eyes on the television.

'A woman died,' she said.

'Died?'

I'd never heard of such a thing happening under my father's care. To die in childbirth seemed to me a frontier woman's death, as impossible now as polio or the plague, made extinct by our ingenious monitors and machines, our clean hands and strong soaps, our drugs and our cures and our vast stores of knowledge.

'Daddy feels it never would have happened if they were working with a full staff. They were stretched too thin.'

'What about the baby?' I asked.

'I don't know,' she said. There were tears in her eyes.

For some reason, it was right then and not earlier that I really began to worry. I rolled over in my parents' bed, and the scent of my father's earthy cologne wafted up from the sheets. I wanted him home.

On the television screen, a reporter was standing in a desert somewhere, the sky pinkening behind her. They were charting the sunrise as they would a storm — the sun had reached the eastern edge of Nevada, but there was no sign of it yet in California.

Later, I would come to think of those first days as the time when we learned as a species that we had worried over the wrong things: the hole in the ozone layer, the melting of the ice caps, West

Nile and swine flu and killer bees. But I guess it never *is* what you worry over that comes to pass in the end. The real catastrophes are always different — unimagined, unprepared for, unknown.

4

At last, like a fever, the night broke. Sunday morning: The sky glowed a delicate blue.

Our backyard was littered in pine needles from the wind. A pair of potted marigolds lay overturned on the patio, the soil spilling from the pots. The umbrella and the lawn chairs had been strewn around the deck. Our eucalyptus trees stood listing and windblown. The dead blue jay remained unchanged.

In the distance, a wisp of smoke was puffing up from the horizon, floating quickly westward with the wind. I remembered then that this was fire season, too.

A news helicopter circled the plume like a fly. And it was reassuring to know that at least one crew had been assigned to cover this most ordinary of disasters.

After breakfast, I tried Hanna's cell phone, but it just rang and rang. I knew it was different for her: Hanna's life was noisy with sisters, her house a maze of bunk beds and shared sinks where the washing machine ran perpetually just to keep up with the dresses that piled each night in the laundry basket. It took two station wagons to carry her family away.

In my house, I could hear the floors creak.

★   ★   ★

By the time my father came home from the hospital in the late afternoon, the winds had calmed, and a low fog was rolling in from the coast, obscuring the slow motion of our sun across the sky.

'Had my headlights on the whole way home,' said my father. 'Couldn't see five feet in front of me in that fog.'

He looked exhausted, but it was a relief to see him standing in our kitchen.

He ate half a sandwich standing up. Then he cleared the counters of the dishes we'd left out the day before and wiped everything down with a sponge. He watered my mother's orchids, and then he stood at the sink, washing his hands for a long time.

'You should get some sleep,' said my mother. She was wrapped in the same gray sweater she'd worn the day before.

'I'm too wired,' he said.

'You should lie down, at least.'

He looked out the window and surveyed the back deck. He pointed at the dead bird. 'When did that happen?'

'Last night,' I said.

He nodded and slid open the drawer, where he kept a supply of surgical gloves for use in household jobs. I followed him outside.

'It's a shame,' he said, crouching low near the bird.

A troupe of ants had discovered the body and were marching back and forth from the edge of the deck, descending deep into the feathers, and emerging with tiny bits of the bird on their backs.

My father flapped a white trash bag in the air until it snapped open and inflated.

'Maybe it's because gravity changed,' I said.

'I don't know about that,' he said. 'Birds have always had trouble with our windows. Their eyesight isn't very good.'

He stretched a surgical glove over each of his hands. A wave of rubbery dust floated off the wrist cuffs. I could smell the latex where I stood.

He closed one gloved palm over the bird's rib cage, the wings sagging like tree branches as he lifted it into the air. Two black eyes the size of peppercorns remained motionless in its head. A few lost ants ran in frantic circles across my father's wrist.

'Sorry about what happened at work,' I said.

'What do you mean?' said my father. He let the bird slip from his hand and into the bag. The sound was wet and echoey against the plastic. He blew on his wrist to get rid of the ants.

'A woman died, right?' I said.

'What?'

He looked at me, surprised. I understood then that it was a mistake to mention it.

My father was quiet. I could feel my cheeks turning hot and red. He used two fingers like tweezers to pick up the last stray feather from the deck and drop it into the sack. Then he rubbed his forehead with the back of one bent wrist.

'No, sweetheart,' he said. 'No one died.'

This was the first lie I ever heard my father tell — or the first time I knew that he was lying. But it would not be the last. And not the boldest, either.

On the deck where the bird had lain, a hundred ants ran in circles, in search of their lost feast.

My father pulled the trash bag's drawstring shut and tied it firmly at the top.

'You and your mom worry too much as it is,' he said. 'I told you two that nothing would happen overnight, and see? Nothing did.'

We took the bag to the garbage cans on the other side of the house. The bird's dark silhouette showed through the white plastic as we walked, the body folding in on itself as the bag swung in time to my father's quick paces.

He pulled the hose out to the deck and washed away the ants and the blood, but a spot of grease would remain on the window for weeks, like skid marks after a car accident.

Finally, he went upstairs to sleep, and my mother went with him.

I sat alone in the living room for a long time, watching television, while my parents murmured together through the closed door of their bedroom. I heard my mother ask a question. My father raised his voice: 'What is that supposed to mean?'

I turned the television down and strained to hear the rest.

'Of course I was at work,' he said. 'Where the hell else would I be?'

*   *   *

We were living under a new gravity, too subtle for our minds to register, but our bodies were already subject to its sway. In the weeks that followed, as the days continued to expand, I would find it harder and harder to kick a soccer ball across a field. Quarterbacks found that footballs didn't fly as far as they used to. Home-run hitters slipped into slumps. Pilots would have to retrain themselves to fly. Every falling thing fell faster to the ground.

And it seems to me now that the slowing triggered certain other changes too, less visible at first but deeper. It disrupted certain subtler trajectories: the tracks of friendships, for example, the paths toward and away from love. But who am I to say that the course of my childhood was not already set long before the slowing? Perhaps my adolescence was only an average adolescence, the stinging a quite unremarkable stinging. There *is* such a thing as coincidence: the alignment of two or more seemingly related events with no causal connection. Maybe everything that happened to me and to my family had nothing at all to do with the slowing. It's possible, I guess. But I doubt it. I doubt it very much.

5

New minutes kept flooding in with every hour. Two days had passed. Now it was Monday. There was no new news.

I'd been hoping that school would be canceled — all the kids were. Instead, school was simply delayed. A hasty plan had been devised to push back our start time by ninety minutes, roughly the amount by which we were running behind.

We'd been asked by the government to carry on as usual. This was not true later, obviously, but for now our leaders stood before microphones, dressed in dark suits and red ties, American-flag pins glinting from navy blue lapels. Mostly, they talked economics: Go to work, spend money, leave your cash in the banks.

'They're definitely not telling us everything,' said Trevor Watkins at the bus stop that Monday morning. More than half the kids who usually waited there had stayed home or left town with their families.

I missed Hanna like a phantom limb.

'It's just like Area 51,' said Trevor, chewing the frayed black straps of his backpack. 'They never tell the public the truth.'

Our lives were mild back then. We were girls in sandals and sundresses, boys in board shorts and surf shirts. We were growing up in a retiree's dream — 330 days of sunshine each year — and

38

so we celebrated whenever it rained. Catastrophe, too, like bad weather, was provoking in all of us an uneasy excitement and verve.

From the other side of the lot came the echo of a skateboard striking the curb. I knew who it was without looking, but I wanted to look: Seth Moreno — tall and quiet and always on his own, now stepping carefully off of his skateboard and into the dirt, his dark hair falling into his eyes as he moved. I had never spoken much to Seth Moreno, but I had perfected a way of watching him that didn't look like I was watching.

'Trust me,' Trevor went on. Trevor was skinny and friendless, and his enormous green backpack was so heavy that it forced him to hunch forward, like an old man, for balance. 'The government knows a lot more than they're saying.'

'Shut up,' said Daryl. Daryl was the new kid, the bad kid, the kid who left fourth period every day to go to the nurse's office to swallow a dose of Ritalin. He was the kid we all tried to avoid. 'No one's listening to you, Trevor.'

The bus stop was the hard ground where our school days always began, where insults were slung and secrets spilled or spread. We were standing where we always stood, in the same patch of dirt beside the same empty lot, the morning sun slanting at roughly the same slant. Our watches were useless, but the light felt right.

'I'm serious, you guys,' said Trevor. 'This is the end of the world.'

'If that bus doesn't show up in the next two minutes,' said Daryl, 'I'm leaving.'

Daryl slouched against the chain-link fence that surrounded a neighboring vacant lot. Years earlier, the house that used to sit on that lot had slipped into the canyon along with a section of limestone cliff. You could still find remnants of the house below, splinters of wood tangled in the brush, shards of tile in the dirt. Not much was left of the property. A cracked driveway led nowhere. Weeds grew where the lawn once was. Yellow signs warned of the instability of the bluff.

'Here's how it's going to happen,' said Trevor. 'First the crops are going to die. And then all the animals are going to die. And then the humans.'

But at that moment, my own anxieties were closer at hand: Without Hanna, I felt awkward standing alone on that curb. Even on a normal day, the bus stop was a bad place to be without a friend. Bullies reigned. No supervisor supervised here.

I decided to stand beside Michaela because we'd been elementary school friends, but those bonds had worn thin.

'Hey, Julia,' she said when she saw me. 'You're smart. Do you think this earth thing could screw up my hair somehow?' She was redoing her red ponytail. 'Because my hair is going crazy today.'

She looked ready for the beach, in miniskirt and baby tee. Sequined flip-flops clung to her feet. My mother never would have let me wear flip-flops to school.

'I don't know,' I said, regretting my practical outfit, white canvas tennis shoes double-knotted beneath plain jeans. 'Maybe.'

40

These days, Michaela's lips perpetually shimmered with gloss. Her hips perpetually swayed. Mascara streaked her cheeks at every soccer practice, and she spoke of boys in multitudes — it was hard to keep track of all her Jasons and Brians and Brads. How could I admit to her my own modest desire? How could I explain to her that for months I'd hoped to talk to just one boy who right then was waiting with us at the bus stop, slowly rolling his skateboard back and forth on the other side of the lot? Seth Moreno: like a blinking light in my head.

'Seriously,' said Michaela, holding up the ragged tip of her ponytail. 'Look at all this frizz.'

A fruity shampoo scent wafted up from her hair whenever she moved.

'Ouch,' said Michaela, whipping around as if stung by a bee. There was Daryl, snapping the strap of her bra. 'Quit it, Daryl,' she said.

That bra wasn't supporting much. Michaela was as flat as I was. But she wore it anyway, a racy symbol of things to come. Visible through the white cotton of her tank top, those two empty cups held at least the possibility of breasts, if not the real things, and I guess just the expectation, just the idea, the mere dream of a female body was enough to lure the boys to her side.

'I mean it,' she said as Daryl snapped it again. I could hear the quick slap of the elastic landing on her skin. 'You're annoying me.'

In the distance, I watched Seth Moreno throw a rock over the chain-link fence and into the canyon. I had the feeling that he cared about important things. His sadness was always apparent. It was in the angry whip of his wrist as he let the rock go. It was in the tired motion of his head. It was in the way he squinted at the sky but would not look away.

Seth already knew about disaster: His mother was sick, and she'd been sick for a while. I'd seen him with her once or twice at the drugstore, a red bandana wrapped around her head where her hair once was, her skinny legs planted in a pair of chunky orthotic shoes. Breast cancer: She'd had it for years already, forever, it seemed, but I'd heard that now she was really dying.

Suddenly, I felt a hard pinch through the back of my T-shirt. I turned. Daryl was behind me. He was laughing at me.

'Gross!' he said, turning his head toward the rest of the kids. 'Julia's not even wearing a bra!'

My cheeks turned hot.

Hanna would have known what to do. She was the leader between the two of us, the talker, the boss. She could be mean when she needed to be. Maybe having sisters had trained her. She would have stepped in at that moment and said to Daryl the exact right thing.

But I was on my own that day and unaccustomed to getting teased.

A few months earlier, I'd passed through the lingerie section of a department store with my mother. A salesclerk had asked if we'd like to see the training bras. My mother looked at the clerk as if she'd said something about sex. I looked at the department store floor. 'Oh,' said my mother. 'I don't think so.'

42

Daryl was staring at me. He had the palest white skin, the sharpest, freckliest nose. I could feel the eyes of the other kids on my face, attracted to cruelty like flies to meat.

A lie formed in my mouth. It tumbled out like a broken tooth. 'I am too wearing one,' I said.

A silver minivan came around the corner, kept moving, and was gone.

'Oh yeah?' said Daryl. 'Then let's see it.'

Everyone but Seth was watching us. The older boys, the eighth-graders, had stopped their shoving matches to see what would happen. Even Trevor had stopped talking. Diane watched, too, rubbing with two fingers the silver cross that always hung around her chubby neck. The Gilbert twins stared their silent stare. Seth was the only one who stayed apart. I hoped he hadn't noticed what was happening. He was standing on his skateboard, facing the other way, the wheels crunching the dirt, as he rolled back and forth on the other side of the lot.

'If you're wearing a bra,' said Daryl, leaning toward me, 'then prove it.'

I longed for the sounds of the school bus to rescue me but heard nothing — only the faint murmur of insects, busy among the flowers in the canyon, and the dull ring of Seth's skateboard striking the curb again and again. The power lines were humming above us as usual, the flow of electric current uninterrupted by the slowing. I would later hear that all our machinery would keep working for a while even if all the humans were gone.

I fiddled with my necklace. Suspended from a

delicate chain around my neck was a tiny gold nugget, unearthed sixty years earlier by my grandfather's hands when he worked in the mines of Alaska. It was the one artifact of his that I treasured.

'Leave her alone,' Michaela finally said, but her voice was too thin and too late.

What I understood so far about this life was that there were the bullies and the bullied, the hunters and the hunted, the strong and the stronger and the weak, and so far I'd never fallen into any group — I was one of the rest, a quiet girl with an average face, one in the harmless and unharmed crowd. But it seemed all at once that this balance had shifted. With so many kids missing from the bus stop, all the hierarchies were changing. A mean thought passed through my mind: I didn't belong in this position; it should have been one of the uglier girls, Diane or Teresa or Jill. Or Rachel. Where was Rachel? She was the nerdiest one among us. But she'd been kept home by her mother to prepare and to pray — they were Jehovah's Witnesses, convinced that this was the end of days.

Another car floated around the corner. This time it was my father in the green station wagon, on his way to work. He waved as he passed. I wished I could flag him down, that he could rescue me. But he could not have read in that plain scene the signs of any trouble.

'Either you show it,' said Daryl, 'or I'll do it for you.'

As has been well documented, rates of murder and other violent crime spiked in the days and

44

weeks following the start of the slowing. There was something in the atmosphere. It was as if the slowing had slowed our judgment too, letting loose our inhibitions. But I've always felt that it should have produced the opposite effect. This much is certainly true: After the slowing, every action required a little more force than it used to. The physics had changed. Take, for example, the slightly increased drag of a hand on a knife or a finger on a trigger. From then on, we all had a little more time to decide what *not* to do. And who knows how fast a second-guess can travel? Who has ever measured the exact speed of regret? But the new gravity was not enough to overcome the pull of certain other forces, more powerful, less known — no law of physics can account for desire.

I finally heard the bus rumbling around the corner toward us, its brakes squeaking, its engine rattling. Daryl heard it too, and that's when he grabbed hold of the front of my shirt and pulled up. I twisted away from him, but I was too late.

Here's what I remember next: the white of my T-shirt over my face, the whoosh of damp air on my bare breastbone and bare ribs, over the whole flat plane of my chest. The excited squeals of the other kids. As I turned, I saw Seth, his long limbs swinging as he walked, heading in our direction, just in time to see my bare chest. Daryl held me that way for a few long seconds while I twisted and turned, the two of us locked in a perverse dance. I could feel the cold air on my skin and the chain of my necklace digging into the back of my neck.

Finally, Daryl let the edge of my shirt drop.

'Liar,' he said. 'I knew you weren't wearing a bra.'

The bus stopped at the curb and began to idle there. The light sweet smell of diesel filled the air. I felt faint. I was blinking back tears.

'Jesus, Daryl,' said Seth, coming up and shoving him in the shoulder. 'What the hell?'

Months later, Michaela's mother would spread a star chart before us and explain to me that the slowing had shifted everyone's astrological signs. Fortunes had changed. Personalities had rearranged. The unlucky had turned lucky. The lucky had turned less so. Our fates, so long written in the stars, had been rewritten in a day.

'Don't worry,' whispered Michaela as we climbed up the steps and into the bus. 'No one saw anything.'

But I knew that this was just something you said when the exact opposite was true: Everyone saw everything.

Seth was the last one onto the bus. He smiled a weak smile as he passed me, heading as usual for the back rows. What I saw in his face was more alarming than what I'd seen in Daryl's. In Seth's dark eyes and his thick, pressed lips, I saw something different, something worse: I saw pity.

I considered running off the bus right then, but it was too late. The doors were closing.

'I bet they're already sending the president and the smartest scientists to the space station, where they'll be safe,' said Trevor from the front seat, as if his stream of theories had never been interrupted. For once, I was glad that he was talking.

The bus jerked away from the curb. The driver, a fat man in a thick black belt, looked rattled and distracted. He kept glancing up through the windshield at the sun.

I reached for my necklace, and that was when I noticed it was gone, my grandfather's tiny gold nugget, flung somewhere in the dirt.

I turned to Michaela, panicked. 'My necklace,' I said. 'Where's my necklace?'

But Michaela didn't hear me. She was already involved in a conversation on her phone.

'I'm telling you,' said Trevor. 'This is Armageddon.'

* * *

At school, we were told to disregard the bells, now rogue, the whole bell system having come unhooked from time.

Without the morning bell to prod us, we turned aimless and imprecise. Kids floated this way or that, a shifting flock of birds. The crowd was wilder than usual, harder to herd. We were loud and wound up. I hid out at the edge of the group while teachers tried in vain to corral us. Their thin voices were drowned out by the ocean of our own.

This was middle school, the age of miracles, the time when kids shot up three inches over the summer, when breasts bloomed from nothing, when voices dipped and dove. Our first flaws were emerging, but they were being corrected.

47

Blurry vision could be fixed invisibly with the magic of the contact lens. Crooked teeth were pulled straight with braces. Spotty skin could be chemically cleared. Some girls were turning beautiful. A few boys were growing tall. I knew I still looked like a child.

By now, the fog had burned away, leaving a bright, clear sky in its place. The flags on the school's flagpole were snapping and fluttering in the wind.

Through the crowd of kids out front, a potent rumor was wafting. These same channels had previously carried news of the illicit explorations of Drew Costello's fingers and of the acrobatics of Amanda Cohen's tongue, of the ziplock bag of marijuana found stashed in Steven Galleta's backpack and, later, of the details of Steven Galleta's life at the Mount Cuyamaca Camp for Troubled Boys. Amid this usual bilge now floated a different kind of gossip, its sources equally dubious: In 1562 a scientist named Nostradamus had predicted that the world would end on this exact day.

'Isn't that creepy?' said Michaela, nudging me with her shoulder.

I was eager to escape. I wanted to burrow into the crowd, but I was afraid to leave Michaela's side.

'I guess he was some kind of psychic or something,' she said.

You could still see the stretch marks on my T-shirt from the bus stop.

'Hey,' she said, looking around. 'Where's Hanna?'

'Utah,' I said. I could barely say the words. 'Her whole family left right away.'

I pictured dozens of cousins sleeping in cars in the Utah desert, encircling a giant grain silo.

'Holy crap,' said Michaela. 'Like forever?'

'I think so.'

'Weird,' she said.

Then Michaela asked to copy my history homework.

'I didn't think we'd have school today,' she said. 'So I didn't do it.'

But I knew that Michaela had stopped doing her homework earlier that year. She was developing a different set of skills. There was a lot to learn about the care of hair and skin. There was a proper way to hold a cigarette. A girl wasn't born knowing how to give a hand job. I let her see my homework whenever she asked.

★   ★   ★

In science, we made new sundials to replace the ones we'd made the first week of school. I was glad to be sitting in a classroom full of kids who had none of them been at the bus stop.

'Adaptation is a necessary part of nature,' said Mr. Jensen after he handed out the new calibrations for the sundials. He was folding and unfolding his hands as he talked. 'This is all perfectly natural.'

We were struggling to jam toothpicks into mounds of wet clay. The trick was to insert the toothpick at exactly the right angle. It was already clear that most of our sundials would tell a useless, sloppy sort of time.

'Think of the dinosaurs,' he continued. 'They died out because they couldn't adapt to a changed environment.'

Mr. Jensen had a ponytail and a beard. He wore a lot of tie-dye. He rode a bike to school, and it was rumored that he cooked his meals on the Bunsen burners in the back of the classroom and slept in a sleeping bag under his desk. He wore hiking boots to school every day. He looked like he could live for many months in the desert with only a compass and a pocketknife and a canteen.

'But of course,' he added, clasping his hands together, 'we're very different from the dinosaurs.' I could tell he was hoping not to scare us, but that was the thing: We kids were not as afraid as we should have been. We were too young to be scared, too immersed in our own small worlds, too convinced of our own permanence.

Competing rumors held that Mr. Jensen was actually a millionaire or that he'd invented something important for NASA and taught science only for the love of teaching. He was my favorite teacher that year. I knew he liked me, too.

He set up a question-and-answer box that day so that we could ask anonymous questions about what was happening.

'There's no such thing as a stupid question,' he said as he collected our scraps of paper in a converted Kleenex box.

This was the same box we had used on the day they separated the girls from the boys, and the nurse came to tell the girls about our futures. 'Something very special is going to happen to you,' she had said slowly, like a fortune teller reading palms. 'It comes from the Greek word for *month*, because it's going to happen once a month, just like the lunar cycle.' Only Tammy Smith and Michelle O'Connor had sat apart, shifting knowingly in their seats, their bodies already in tune with the moon.

Now Mr. Jensen reached into the box and pulled out a question. He unfolded the piece of paper with great care: ' "Is it true,' he read, 'that a scientist predicted that the world would end today?" '

'Nostradamus wasn't exactly a scientist,' said Mr. Jensen. He had evidently heard the rumor circulating the halls. 'You all know that no one can predict the future. No one can say what will happen tomorrow, much less five hundred years from now.'

The school bell buzzed. But we all stayed put on our lab stools. The lunch bell was out of sync with us now.

Outside, the sky remained bright. Sunlight was pouring in through the windows, catching on the rows of clean beakers and clean test tubes, glittering like wineglasses on the shelves.

Mr. Jensen pulled another question from the box. Someone asked if the slowing might be caused by pollution.

This question seemed to depress him. 'We don't know yet why this is happening,' he said.

He took off his glasses and rubbed his

forehead with the back of his hand. He paused near the fish tank, empty since September, when the filtration system abruptly stopped working. It happened on a weekend. We had returned Monday morning to find five fish floating like leaves on the surface. You could see the blood beneath the scales on their little bodies. The water looked clear to our eyes, but it had turned toxic for fish.

'Human activity has done a lot of damage to this planet,' said Mr. Jensen as we continued to work on our sundials. 'Humans are responsible for global warming and the thinning of the ozone layer, and for the extinction of thousands of plant and animal species. But it's too early to say yet if we've caused this change, too.'

Before the end of the period, Mr. Jensen updated our solar system wall, where outer space was neatly represented by six yards of black butcher paper and eight butcher-paper planets. There was also a sun on our map and a tinfoil moon. Scattered in the corners were rainbow-colored pushpins that stood in for all the planets we had not yet discovered. There were supposed to be thousands of them out there. Millions, maybe. It still astounds me, how little we knew about the universe.

On the sign above the Earth, Mr. Jensen replaced *24 Hours* with *25:37*, but he wrote the new figure on a Post-it note so we could update it if we needed to.

★ ★ ★

Classrooms were half empty all day or, depending on your outlook, half full. Dozens of desks stood unused, attendance sheets went largely unchecked. It was as if certain kids really had been sucked up from the earth to the heavens, the way some Christians were expecting, leaving the rest of us behind, we the children of scientists and atheists and the simply less devout.

Our teachers discouraged us from following the news during class, but one kid had a radio and we all had cell phones.

The first outbreaks of gravity sickness were already popping up around the globe. Hundreds of people were experiencing symptoms of dizziness, faintness, and fatigue. In PE, some kids got out of running the mile by clutching their stomachs, complaining of nausea and mysterious pains. 'I can't help it,' they'd say. 'It's the sickness.'

Our teachers pretended not to worry. But at lunch, they all watched the news in the teachers' lounge. We could see their expressions as they watched, their tired eyes, their wrinkled foreheads, the naked fear in their faces.

⋆   ⋆   ⋆

I didn't see Seth Moreno again until fifth period. We had math together. His assigned seat was directly in front of mine, and I looked forward every day to being near him. I knew everything about the back of that head — the swirl of his hair, the curve of his ear, the straight, sharp line

53

of his jaw. I liked the way he smelled like soap even late in the afternoon.

We never talked to each other. I had never even said his name out loud, not even to Hanna. 'Come on,' she used to whisper in the dark of my living room, both of us curled deep inside sleeping bags. 'There must be *someone*,' she'd say. But I'd always shake my head and lie. 'Nope,' I'd whisper back. 'There's no one.'

For weeks I'd been hoping that Seth might look my way, but not today. I was too embarrassed about what had happened that morning.

Mrs. Pinsky was trying to make a lesson out of the slowing. On the chalkboard, she'd written the Daily Math Brain Teaser: *The length of a day on earth has increased by ninety minutes in two days. Assuming a steady rate of increase, how long would a day on earth be two days from now? What about three days from now? A week?*

'Do we have to do this?' asked Adam Jacobson, slouching in his chair. He was always asking this question.

'The only thing you *have* to do in this life is die,' said Mrs. Pinsky. This was one of her favorite sayings. 'Everything else is a choice.'

Mrs. Pinsky was morbid and intimidating. If ever a kid got the hiccups in her class, she called the kid up to her desk. By the time you reached the front of the classroom, the hiccups were always gone; it was as sure a cure as any other sudden fright.

'Don't just write the answer, show your work,' she said, walking up and down the aisles, the folds of her orange dress swishing against the chrome-colored legs of our chairs. 'And no guesswork. Use your algebra.'

The walls of her classroom were lined with encouraging posters: NEVER SAY NEVER, EXPECT THE UNEXPECTED, THE IMPOSSIBLE IS POSSIBLE.

Mrs. Pinsky called a few of us up to the board to show our answers. Seth and I were among the chosen, and we stood side by side, transcribing our work from our notebooks to the board. I remember being aware of his right arm beside me, stretching up to write his answers, his numbers slanting down and to the right as his chalk scraped the board. The hard brown carpet felt worn out beneath my feet. Thirty years' worth of sixth-graders had worked out solutions in these exact same spots.

Seth clapped two erasers together. The dust made him sneeze. Even his sneeze was endearing. He had wonderful hands. You could see the strength in his wrists, right in the veins, and in the tendons that traversed the backs of his hands. Seth's mother was at home, dying. But here Seth was, growing stronger every day.

As I checked my work, I noticed that Seth's answer was wrong, and I felt a sharp protective stab for him. I wanted to fix it or say something, but he'd already dropped his chalk in the tray and was walking back to his seat.

Through the open windows of the classroom, we heard the screech of a fire truck racing away somewhere. A moment later, a second one set off in the same direction. But these were the ordinary sounds of our school days. There was a fire station across the street. Sirens rang out all day. The sounds had bothered me at first, all the emergencies of strangers, but I'd grown used to them. We all had.

★　★　★

The shift in the air was barely perceptible at first: a fading. It was the feeling you get when a cloud moves across the sun.

'Something weird is happening outside,' said Trevor from the back of the classroom. He'd been playing with a metal compass but now dropped it on his desk with a clink. 'Something really weird.'

'If you have something to say, Trevor, please raise your hand,' said Mrs. Pinsky. She was preparing the rest of our lesson on a transparency. I could hear the squeak of her pen on the plastic, the hum of the projector's fan. She preferred the old technology over the computers that all the other teachers were using by then.

'Holy crap,' said Adam Jacobson, whose desk was closest to the windows. 'Holy shit.'

'Adam, watch your language,' said Mrs. Pinsky.

We could hear voices rising in the neighboring classrooms, too. A cooler breeze had begun to blow.

'Come look,' said Adam. 'It's getting dark.'

The windows were on one side of the classroom, and we all rushed to that side like objects sliding across the deck of a listing ship. I couldn't see much over the heads of the taller kids, but I sensed the changing light. A strange gloom was moving in like a storm, but this was no storm. The sky was cloudless. The sky was clear.

The rest happened quickly — thirty seconds.

'Return to your seats,' said Mrs. Pinsky. But no one did. 'I said return to your seats.'

She stepped outside to see for herself what was happening. Back in the classroom, she snapped into emergency mode. 'Okay,' she said. 'Okay. Stay calm. Everyone just stay calm.'

She grabbed the whistle and the bullhorn, the master keys and the walkie-talkie. These were the supplies for fire drills and earthquake drills and drills to practice what to do if a shooter started shooting at our school.

All the colors of the spectrum had collapsed to a few dusky grays. There was a paleness in the classroom. That light was the light of the last small moments of a day, the thin wedge of time just after the sun has set but just before you reach for a lamp. A sudden sunset at high speed. It was 1:23 in the afternoon.

Kids began to leak out of classrooms, a trickle at first, then a flood.

Someone grabbed my wrist. I looked up. I was shocked to see that it was Seth, his sharp features even more lovely in the half light.

'Come on,' he said. His palm on my wrist felt electric. Even then I noticed it, the sweaty warmth of his hand on my arm.

We burst outside together.

57

'Come back here,' said Mrs. Pinsky, but no one was listening. She said it again, this time shouting it through the bullhorn. Not a single kid turned her way. We were running in every direction, most of us rushing up the grassy hill behind campus.

Within a few seconds, it was as dark as dusk outside and growing darker. The sky turned a brackish evening blue. An orange glow ringed the whole horizon.

Seth and I threw ourselves on the grass, sensing it was safer to lie low.

'This might be it,' he said. I thought I heard a thrill in his voice.

All around us, kids were screaming. I heard someone sobbing in the dark. Camera phones were clicking and flickering in the blackness. We could see the stars in the sky.

On the road beside campus, dozens of cars had stopped. Drivers stood in the streets, car doors flung open like wings, headlights flipped on in the dark. Every eye was on the sky. A cool night wind was blowing across the grass.

At the bottom of the hill, Mr. Jensen was yelling from the doorway of the science lab. He was waving his hand. I could not hear him over the screams of the crowd, but I could see that he was frantic. If even Mr. Jensen was panicked, what chance was there for the rest of us to stay calm?

Seth reached for my hand, our fingers interlaced. I'd never held hands with a boy this way. I almost couldn't breathe.

My cell phone buzzed in my pocket. I knew it was my mother. I didn't answer.

'What if this is how we die?' whispered Seth. He sounded serious. He did not seem afraid.

We all grew quieter as the seconds passed, hushed by the darkness and the chill in the air. I became aware that dozens of dogs were barking, howling, from their yards. Minutes passed. The temperature continued to drop.

A vague prayer slipped out of my mouth: *Please, please let us be okay.*

We were, on that day, no different from the ancients, terrified of our own big sky.

★　★　★

We know now that the darkness lasted four minutes and twenty-seven seconds, but it seemed to stretch much longer. Time felt loose in those first few days. If it weren't for the records — hundreds of people filmed the event — I'd still swear that at least an hour passed before the first glint of light reappeared in the sky.

'Look,' I heard Seth saying. 'Look. Look.'

A bleed of brightness was spreading directly overhead, a sliver of sun returned to us, as if by miracle. Now we could see the outline of the whole thing, a thin circle of light with a blinding bulge on one side, like a diamond on a ring.

I saw Mr. Jensen hurrying through the crowd. When he reached us, we finally heard what he'd been shouting.

'Listen to me,' he said. 'This is just an eclipse. It's harmless. It's just the moon's shadow passing in front of the sun.'

As we would learn in the coming hours, Mr. Jensen was right: A total solar eclipse had been anticipated for the middle of the Pacific Ocean. It was to be visible only from the decks of passing ships and from a handful of thinly populated islands. But the slowing had shifted the coordinates of all predicted eclipses — they used to have them all figured out, every future eclipse charted to the minute and the decade. This one had caught us by surprise. It was seen from a thick swath of the western United States.

Relief passed through my whole body. We were fine. And there I was, lying on a hill with Seth Moreno.

Seth seemed disappointed by the news.

'That's it?' he said. 'It was just an eclipse?'

We remained on the hill together, watching the sun re-emerge. We squinted side by side, our backs on the grass. I was so close to him I could see the hairs on his forearm.

'Do you ever wish you could be a hero?' he said.

'What do you mean?' I said.

'I want to save someone's life someday.'

I thought of his mother. My father had explained to me once how cancer worked, how it almost never gave up, how you had to kill every single cell of it. And you were never completely sure that you had won. It could always come back, and mostly, it *did* come back.

'I might want to be a doctor,' I offered. This was only half true. I didn't really know then if I could do what my father did. I didn't know then if I could stomach all that blood and sadness.

'Whenever I'm in a bank,' said Seth, 'I kind of hope that a robber will come running in with a gun and that I'll be the one who tackles him and saves everyone else.'

From a distance, it had seemed that Seth's mother was not going to die of her disease. The year before, she was still bringing brownies for bake sales and raising money for Mrs. Sanderson's Christmas gift. She'd remained so active that it had looked like her cancer would be merely a trait she lived with, like being overweight or going gray. But I hadn't seen her in a while.

The color was returning to the sky, slowly but surely, the way a person's face recovers after fainting.

'I'm going to be an Army Ranger when I'm older,' he said. 'That's the most elite branch of the military.'

'That's cool,' I said.

People were climbing back into their cars. Horns were honking. Dogs continued to bark. Some kids were heading back to their classrooms. Others were drifting away, off campus and into the world, too jittery to obey any rules or routine.

Seth and I stayed where we were on the hill. A silence stretched between us, but it was an easy silence. We were alike, I thought, the quiet, thinking kind.

I watched him watching the sky. A frail-looking cirrus was gliding in from the west, the first and only cloud of the day. I wanted to say something important and true.

'I'm really sorry about your mom,' I said.

'What?' he said. He turned toward me. He looked surprised.

It was suddenly hard to look him in the eye. So I didn't. Instead, I looked back up at the sky.

'I'm just sorry that she's sick,' I said. 'That must be really hard.'

Seth sat up and brushed his palms on the front of his jeans.

'What the hell do you know about it?' he said.

He was standing now. The sun was nearly full again, and it was too bright to look up; it was hard to see his face in the light.

'You don't know anything about my mom,' he said. His voice cracked. 'Don't talk about her. Don't ever talk about my mom. Never talk about her again.'

I felt each word sting a separate sting.

I tried to apologize, but Seth was already walking away, hurrying off campus and out into the world. I watched him cross the street, looking angry and reckless, dodging traffic as he walked, moving farther and farther away from me.

By then the sky had turned to its afternoon self, its boldest, bluest blue. I sat up and discovered that I was the only one left on the hill.

I began to walk slowly back toward math. I passed Michaela on the way. She was heading toward the campus gate with a group of older kids I didn't know.

'We're going to the beach,' she said as she passed me.

'What about next period?' I said. I regretted these words as soon as they left my mouth.

Michaela laughed. 'Oh, God, Julia,' she said. 'Have you ever done one bad thing in your life?'

★　★　★

That afternoon soccer practice was canceled. My mother picked me up from school. She was furious.

'Why didn't you answer your phone?'

I climbed into the passenger side of the car and slammed the door shut behind me, hushing in an instant the giddy voices ringing from the bus lines.

'It was just an eclipse,' I said. I clicked my seat belt and leaned back as my mother pulled away from the curb.

'You should have answered your phone,' she said. 'You should have called me back.'

The air conditioner was blasting in the car. News about the eclipse was streaming from the car radio.

'Are you listening to me?' my mother said, her voice rising as we waited in a line of slow-moving cars, waiting for the crossing guards to wave us out of the school parking lot.

I was watching a swarm of kids through the window. They seemed suddenly distant out there on the quad. I traced my finger on the glass.

'Hanna moved to Utah,' I said. I had known for two days, but this was the first time I mentioned it to my mother.

She turned toward me. Her expression softened. A red Mercedes squeezed past our car.

'She moved?'

I nodded.

'Oh, Julia,' said my mother. She reached over and squeezed my shoulder. 'Really? Are you sure it's permanent?'

'That's what she said.'

We headed toward the freeway. I could feel my mother glancing at me as she drove. She turned the radio down.

'I think they'll come back,' she said.

'I don't,' I said.

'People are scared right now,' she said. 'You know? They're not thinking straight.'

When we got home, we discovered that the garbage cans my father had wheeled out to the curb that morning were still heaping with trash. The garbageman had not shown up to collect, but the ants and the flies were busy. The bird was still in there. We rolled the garbage back into our side yard and unloaded the groceries from the car. My mother had bought several boxes of canned food, six jugs of bottled water. She suspected that shortages were on the way — and she wasn't the only one who thought so.

★   ★   ★

That night my father claimed he'd understood right away that the eclipse was an eclipse and nothing more.

'You're telling me that you weren't afraid even for a single second?' asked my mother.

'Not really,' he said. 'I knew what it was.'

The nightly news was dominated by the story and featured a handful of eclipse enthusiasts who, before the slowing started, had traveled to a remote Pacific island, one of the few specks of dry land from which it was supposed to be possible to view the total solar eclipse. These people had packed expensive camera equipment in their luggage, special filters designed for capturing pictures of vanishing suns. But their tools sat unused in cushioned cases. Their special filters were unnecessary, their protective glasses remained folded in chest pockets, never used — the eclipse struck the West Coast instead.

That night the baseball playoffs went on without interruption. To play on in the face of uncertainty seemed the only American thing to do. But that night's game was terrible. It was harder than ever to defy gravity. Seven pitchers were pulled. No one could hit. With each new hour, every bit of matter on the earth was more and more fettered by gravity.

It seemed the stock market, too, was subject to the same downward pull, having plunged to a record low. The price of oil, on the other hand, was shooting upward.

By the time I climbed into bed that night, we'd gained another thirty minutes. All the television stations had added perpetual crawls to their screens, which reported, instead of stock prices, the changing length of a day on earth: twenty-six hours, seven minutes, and growing.

6

The days passed. More and more people drained away from our suburb. They fled to wherever they were from, and this was California — almost everyone had migrated here from someplace else. But my family stayed. We were natives. We were home.

On the third day, my mother and I drove out to my grandfather's house after school.

'He says he's okay,' my mother said as she drove. 'But I want to make sure.'

He was my father's father, but it was my mother who worried over him most. I had begun to worry about him, too — he lived all alone out east.

We stopped at a gas station on the way and discovered a long line of cars, waiting for the pumps. Dozens of minivans and SUVs formed a chain that overflowed the parking lot and wrapped around the street corner.

'Jesus,' said my mother. 'This line looks like something out of a war zone.'

A woman in a pink-floral-print dress hurried between the cars, slipping orange flyers beneath windshield wiper blades as passengers looked away: *The end is now! Repent and save yourself!*

I avoided her eyes as she passed, so frantic and so sure, but she sought out mine and paused at my window to shout through the glass: 'And the Lord God said, 'On that day, I will make the sun go down at noon and darken the earth in broad daylight.' '

My mother flicked the lock on the doors.

'Is that from the Bible?' I asked.

'I can't remember,' my mother said.

We inched forward slightly. I'd counted nineteen cars ahead of ours.

'Where is everyone going?' asked my mother. She rubbed her forehead and exhaled. 'Where is there to go?'

★　★　★

My grandfather lived in the middle of a luxury housing development. His old house was a holdout against the new surroundings. Once off the freeway, we drove through a network of fresh black streets, sliced at every corner by a shimmering white crosswalk. The stop signs were new. The speed bumps were new. Everything here was new. Curbs remained sharp and unscuffed. Fire hydrants stood gleaming and rust-free. Rows of saplings grew at evenly spaced intervals along the sidewalks, and the sidewalks literally sparkled. All the houses had lawns like thick heads of hair.

Amid all this newness, my grandfather's dusty acre persisted, invisible, like a patch of dark matter: You could tell it existed from the way the roads curved around it, but you couldn't see it from the outside. You only sensed it. The developer of the neighboring community had planted thick pine trees on every side of my grandfather's lot, so the neighbors could avoid looking at it.

We drove through my grandfather's open wooden gate, where the smooth asphalt turned to chunky gravel beneath our tires and the carefully planned green spaces of the development gave way to the region's natural landscape: scraggly and dry, barren and brown and unlovely. My father had grown up on this land in an age when there were chickens and horses here. But the last horse had long since died, and now the stable stood like a relic of an ancient era. The wooden fence posts and crosspieces lay bleaching in the sun. The chicken coop was empty of chickens. My grandfather was eighty-six years old. All his old friends were dead. His wife was dead. He had grown bitter about his own longevity.

'Just hope you didn't inherent my genes, Julia,' he said to me often. 'It's a curse to live too long.' I liked the way he always said exactly what he thought.

Years earlier, the developers had tried to buy my grandfather's property. But he refused to sell. 'Dammit,' he said, 'I got things buried in this land.' I knew that at least two cats had been interred out behind the woodpile, and I suspected he had also buried certain other valuables over the years. The developers went ahead without him, laying roads and foundations around him, erecting houses and street signs on every side of his property. The new neighborhood rose up around my grandfather's land like flood-water surrounding high ground.

My mother and I walked into the kitchen

without knocking. When you moved around in this house, the shelves rattled slightly, knickknacks teetering on every surface. My grandfather was sitting at the table in a red sweatshirt, the news-paper and a magnifying glass in front of him.

'Hi, Gene,' my mother said. 'How are you doing?'

'I told you on the phone I'm fine,' he said without looking up. 'Chip's been here.'

Chip was a neighbor of his, a teenager who helped keep the house going. Chip wore black T-shirts and black jeans every day, and a lip ring was responsible for the slight drooping of his lower lip. They were an unlikely pair, but I think Chip hated the development as much as my grandfather did, though he lived with his parents in one of the new houses.

'This is bullshit, anyway,' said my grandfather.

'What is?' asked my mother.

'I figure it's all a trick to take our minds off the Middle East.'

He had the palest blue eyes, like my father's but lighter, and they seemed to be fading as he aged, like fabric left too long in the sun. A few wisps of white hair fell now and then on his forehead.

'Come on, Gene,' said my mother. 'How could someone rig all this?'

'I'm just saying, how do you know it's true? Have you measured it? They can do anything these days.'

'Gene — '

'You just wait. They've got something cooked up. That's all I know. They're messing with the

70

clocks or some damn thing. I'm just saying I don't believe it. I don't believe it for a second.'

My mother's cell phone buzzed, and I could tell from the way she answered that it was my father on the other end. She stepped outside to talk. I sat down at the table — this was the same table where my grandfather and I used to play hours of Old Maid together, but his eyesight had grown too poor to see what kind of cards he held. I missed how he used to be.

'So, Julia,' said my grandfather. 'You see anything around here you want?'

He waved at his shelves of antique glass, his rows of weathered hundred-year-old Coke bottles, my grandmother's silver tea service, her collections of decorative thimbles and tiny silver spoons, the pewter and porcelain figurines she had arranged on lace doilies in some different, better decade.

'I can't take it with me, you know,' he went on. 'You should take what you want now, because when I'm dead, Ruth is going to try to get her hands on everything.'

Ruth was my grandmother's younger sister. She lived on the East Coast.

'No, thanks, Grandpa,' I said. I hoped he wouldn't notice that I wasn't wearing my gold nugget necklace. 'You should keep your stuff.'

Before the arthritis, he used to spend his mornings at the beach running a metal detector over the sand, hunting for coins and treasure in the dunes. But now he'd grown eager to hand off his things, as if the weight of his possessions kept him tethered to this earth and, by giving them

71

away, he could snip those strings.

He stood up from his chair and shuffled to the counter for another cup of coffee. He stood at the window. My mother was pacing out there, making hand motions while she talked on the phone. The wind was blowing her hair all to one side, and she kept brushing it out of her face.

'Did I ever tell you that I seen a guy killed out there in that yard once?'

'I don't think so,' I said.

'He wasn't more than seventeen,' he said, shaking his head. 'A horse trampled right over top of him.'

'That's terrible,' I said.

'It sure was.'

My grandfather nodded slightly as if to underline the thought. He had a vast memory for awful things. Somewhere farther back in the house, I could hear a faucet dripping.

'This whole thing reminds me of when I worked in Alaska,' he said. Alaska was one of his favorite subjects. 'We had sun all day and all night in the summer. We had sun at two in the morning. The sun never went down. Not for weeks. And then in the winter, it was pitch-dark all day every day for two or three months.'

He trailed off. I noticed a television satellite wobbling on a nearby roof, barely visible through the pine trees. I could smell a hint of smoke in the air.

'This whole thing is bullshit, believe me,' he said. 'I just can't figure how.'

'You really think so?'

He looked at me with a serious, steady gaze.

'Do you know that in 1958 the United States government began running a secret nuclear test program right here in this county?' he said. 'They were testing the effects of nuclear substances on regular people. They were putting uranium in the water and then monitoring the cancer rates. Have you ever heard that?'

I shook my head. Somewhere under his backyard, a bomb shelter lay abandoned. My grandfather had built it himself in the sixties.

'Of course you haven't,' he said. 'That's the way they like it. That's exactly how they like it.'

A gust of wind whooshed past the back of the house, carrying a paper bag past the window.

'Have your mother and dad been taking you to church?' he asked.

'We go sometimes,' I said.

'You should go every week,' he said. 'Especially now.' He picked up a pair of tiny boots encased in a skin of tarnished silver. 'You want these?'

'That's okay,' I said.

'These were my shoes when I was four years old. Don't you want anything around here?'

I could hear the labor of his lungs as he breathed, the sound of his air whistling through narrowing passageways.

'Wait a minute. I know what you'd like.' He pointed to a low cupboard on the far side of the kitchen and instructed me to kneel down on the floor. 'Now reach all the way inside,' he directed. 'Feel that?'

'What?'

I was up to my shoulder in the cupboard. The

73

linoleum was pressing its paisley pattern uncomfortably into my kneecaps. But I wanted to please him, so I kept going.

'It's a false back, see?' he said. 'Slide it to the right.'

In my grandfather's house, a cereal box was never full of cereal; soup cans almost always contained a substance more precious than soup. It's no wonder he believed so fiercely in forces unseen. Behind the false back of the cupboard stood a row of coffee cans, so old I didn't recognize the labels.

'The Folgers can,' he said. 'Give it here.'

He pulled at the lid, wincing.

'Let me do it,' I said.

The lid came off easily in my hands, but I tried, for his sake, to make it look like a harder task than it was. The can was stuffed with layers of crumpled newspaper. At the bottom was a small silver box, inside of which, on a bed of stiff velvet, lay a tarnished gold pocket watch, its chain snaking around behind its face.

'This was my father's,' he said. 'You wind that up, and it'll tell the time. It'll last forever. Them gears are good quality. That's how they used to make things, good quality, you know? I'll bet you never even seen something as well made as that.'

I did not want the watch. I would only add it to the stack of other objects my grandfather had given me, all of them ancient and obscure: uncirculated commemorative silver dollars pack-ed in plastic, four pairs of my grandmother's clip-on earrings, framed maps of our city as it was a hundred years ago. But he insisted, and I couldn't admit to him that I had lost the one heirloom of his that I really loved. That morning I had searched the dirt for my gold nugget necklace, but I couldn't find where it had flung.

'Thanks,' I said, holding the watch in my hand. 'It's pretty.'

'Be even prettier once you shine it up,' he said. He rubbed the face with the cuff of his sweatshirt. 'You take good care of that, Julia.'

The screen door slammed, and my mother came into the kitchen. She noticed the pocket watch in my hand. 'Oh, Gene, don't give away all your things.'

'Let her keep it,' he said. 'I can't take it with me.'

'You're not going anywhere,' she said.

He waved her off.

'Take this, too,' he whispered to me as we were leaving. He handed me a ten-dollar bill. A quick smile flashed across my grandfather's face, a rare and precious sight. I could see the outline of his false teeth against his gums.

'Do something fun with it,' he said.

I squeezed his hand and nodded.

'And Julia,' he said. 'Don't believe everything you hear, okay? You're a smart girl. You can read between the lines.'

* * *

We took what we always referred to as the scenic route home, back roads with less traffic. We listened to the news on the radio as we drove.

75

Reporters from around the world were describing local reactions. From South America streamed more reports of gravity sickness. The Centers for Disease Control were investigating.

'Jesus,' said my mother. 'Tell me if you start to feel sick.'

At that moment, I did begin to feel a little dizzy.

'This disease seems to be affecting some people more than others,' said one official on the radio. 'And the name of this disease is paranoia.'

In our own country, according to the radio, clusters of born-again Christians were making their final arrangements, hoping at any moment to be summoned from their beds, leaving behind empty houses and piles of crumpled clothing where their bodies once stood.

'I don't get it,' I said. 'Why wouldn't your clothes come with you?'

'I don't know, honey,' said my mother. 'You know we don't believe in that stuff.'

We were a different kind of Christian, the quiet, reasonable kind, a breed embarrassed by the mention of miracles.

They were interviewing a televangelist on the radio. 'The signs of the revelation have been in place for years,' he said. 'We've known it was coming ever since the restoration of Israel.'

As the road turned, I could see a sliver of shining ocean through a gap in the hills ahead. All the beachfront homes had been evacuated by then — no one knew what might happen to the tides.

Outside, housing developments streaked past

the window, the homes and the lots shrinking in size as we neared the coast. The land was so valuable near the ocean that some houses hung out over the edges of canyons, supported on one side by giant stilts.

We came to a stop sign, and as my mother turned her head from right to left to check for traffic, I noticed the skinny path of gray that sometimes ran along the part in her hair where the roots showed through the dark dye. She'd gone gray at thirty-five, and I never liked seeing it, that earliest sign of her physical decline.

I felt a wave of loneliness. It occurred to me for perhaps the first time, as the car lurched forward, that if anything were to happen to my family, I'd be all alone in the world.

We were passing the fairgrounds now. The county fair was scheduled to open its gates in a week. Hanna and I had been planning to go on opening day.

Usually, the construction workers worked nonstop to get the rides up and running. But I saw as we passed that the construction had ceased. I imagined the workers and the carnies had fled to their hometowns, too — everyone wanted to be close to their families. The roller coasters stood half built, colored skeletons in the wind. The log ride, incomplete, was a suicide leap. The Ferris wheel stood only partially erect: A single red bucket dangled from a single spoke like the last fruit of summer, or like autumn's final leaf.

7

For a while the days still felt like days. The sun rose and the sun also set. Darkness was followed by light. I remember the cool swell of morning, the slow burn of afternoon, the sluggishness of dusk. Civil twilight stretched for hours before fading finally into night. Time slunk lazily by, slower and slower as it passed.

With each new morning, we fell further out of step with the clocks. The earth still turned and the clocks still ticked, but they now kept different times. Within a week, midnight no longer necessarily struck at some dark hour of night. The clocks might hit nine A.M. in the middle of the day. Noon sometimes landed at sunset.

Those were chaotic, makeshift days.

Every morning officials announced the minutes gained overnight, like raindrops collected in pans. The totals varied wildly, and we never knew what to expect. Our school start time was decided at sunrise each day — it was always different, and I remember watching the local news channel with my mother in the mornings, waiting to hear what time they'd choose.

More and more kids stopped coming to school.

Extra hours emerged between the cracks in workers' shifts. Planes were grounded for days, and trains were halted on tracks until new scheduling schemes could be invented and put into place. Timetables had to be tossed out and reimagined every day.

We improvised. We adapted. We made do.

My mother slowly packed our cupboards full of emergency supplies. She accumulated them gradually, a rising tide of condensed milk and canned peas, dried fruit and preserves, four dozen cans of soup. She never returned to the house anymore without a package of batteries under her arm, or a box of tapered candles, or more dehydrated food sealed in plastic or aluminum — the unperishable, the unending, the never-ever-to-expire.

Meanwhile, my soccer team practiced mostly as usual, and my mother's drama students continued to rehearse their production of *Macbeth*. All across the country, events like these were held as planned. Shows *had* to go on. We clung to anything previously scheduled. To cancel seemed immoral, or it might mean we'd given up or lost hope.

New minutes surfaced everywhere. Time was harder to waste. The pace of living seemed to slow.

Some say that the slowing affected us in a thousand other unacknowledged ways, from the life expectancy of lightbulbs to the rate at which ice melted and water boiled and human cells multiplied and human cells died. Some say that our bodies aged less rapidly in the days immediately following the start of the slowing, that the dying died slower deaths, that babies took longer to be born. There *is* some evidence that menstrual cycles lengthened ever so slightly in those first two weeks. But these effects were the stuff of anecdote, not science. Physicists will tell you that if anything, the opposite should have been true: It's the man on the speeding train who experiences time more slowly, and not the other way around. As far as I could tell, the grass grew as it always had, the bread in our bread box molded at the usual pace, and the apples on Mr. Valencia's apple tree next door ripened as they did every fall, then dropped to the ground, rotting among the weeds at what seemed the traditional speed.

All the while, the clocks continued to tick. Wristwatches went right on beating faint beats. My grandfather's antique clocks chimed their ancient chimes. Church bells rang every hour on the hour.

A week passed, then two. Every time the phone rang in our house, I hoped it would be Hanna. She still hadn't called.

The stream of new minutes continued to flow. Our days were soon approaching thirty hours.

How quaint the old twenty-four-hour clock began to look to our eyes, how impossibly clean-cut, with its twin sets of twelve, as neat as walnut shells. How had we believed, we wondered, in such simplistic things?

8

In the second week after the start of the slowing, something began to happen to the birds.

You'd find pigeons scrambling on sidewalks, wings dragging, feathers scraping the pavement as they walked. Sparrows were dropping on lawns. Flocks of geese were seen traveling great distances on foot. The bodies of seagulls were washing up on the beaches. Birds were found dead on our streets and our rooftops, on our tennis courts and our soccer fields. The fowl of the air were falling to the earth. It was happening all over the world.

No one knew why.

You were supposed to call animal control whenever you found a dead one, but my father refused. There were too many, he said, so we just threw them away, like that first dead bird on our deck.

I remember those birds as well as anything else from that time: the rotting feathers and the raisin eyes, the fluids staining our streets. And there were rumors even then that the affliction might soon spread to us.

*   *   *

Sylvia, my piano teacher, kept finches. They were small and fat, and they lived in a bell-shaped metal cage in the corner of her living room. Here

81

was where I spent half an hour every Wednesday afternoon, learning — or failing to learn — to play the piano. And here, just minutes after me, was where Seth Moreno sat as well, his lesson always immediately following mine, his fingers brushing the same keys mine had, his feet pressing the same pedals that my feet had so recently pressed. Often the idea of him hung over my whole lesson. But on this day, it was the finches that distracted me: I was listening for signs of the sickness in every sound they made.

'You haven't been practicing, have you?' said Sylvia. I'd made a slow, pecking attempt at 'Für Elise.'

Sylvia sat beside me on the glossy black bench, her slim bare feet resting near the brass pedals below. She wore a white linen dress and a string of large wooden beads around her neck. I liked the way she looked. She was two kinds of teachers: She also taught yoga down at the Y.

'I practiced a little,' I said.

That was how my lessons always began. Maybe if I had known that this was one of the last times I would ever sit on that bench, I would have tried a little harder.

'How are you ever going to improve if you don't practice?'

One of Sylvia's finches cried out from the cage in the corner. They did not sing so much as squeal, each chirp like the squeak of a rusting hinge.

Officials were reluctant at first to connect the deaths of the birds to the slowing. There was no evidence, they said, that the two phenomena

82

were linked. Experts pointed instead to more familiar causes, like disease: avian flu, a worldwide pandemic. But tests had come back negative for all the known strains.

However, we, the people, did not need more proof. We did not believe in spurious correlation. We rejected random chance. We knew the birds were dying because of the slowing, but as with the slowing itself, no one could explain why.

'You should be practicing now more than ever,' said Sylvia, gently pressing her palm to my lower back to make it straight. My posture always melted as the lesson wore on. 'Art thrives in times of uncertainty.'

Piano lessons had been my mother's idea. I didn't like the piano much, but I liked Sylvia and I liked her house, which was the same model as ours but unrecognizable to me on the inside. Hardwood floors instead of carpet fanned out across the rooms. Leafy houseplants thrived in every corner. Sylvia didn't believe in chemicals or air-conditioning. Her house smelled like tea and birdseed and incense.

'I'm going to play it through once,' she said. 'And I want you to close your eyes while I'm playing, and memorize how it's supposed to sound.'

She set the metronome to a certain speed, releasing a smooth stream of tick-tocks. I could never learn to properly knit my notes to those clean, steady beats.

She began to play.

I tried to listen, but I couldn't concentrate. I was worried about the finches. They seemed quieter than usual, and they looked a little less fat. They were named for musical terms, and the one called Forte seemed to be teetering on his perch, his corny orange feet unstable and unsure. The smaller one, Adagio, was hanging around on the newspaper on the floor of the cage.

Doomsdayers were reading the bird die-off as one more harbinger of doom. I'd seen a heavyset televangelist discussing it that morning on a talk show. To his mind, the bird pestilence was a warning from God, and it was only a matter of time before the disease would spread to humans.

'Your eyes are open,' said Sylvia. She was always genuinely surprised when I failed her. This was part of her charm.

'Sorry,' I said.

She caught me staring at the birdcage.

'Don't worry,' she said. 'It's not affecting domesticated birds, just wild ones.'

At the time, this was true, though the nation's poultry farmers had been advised to watch their flocks for strange symptoms.

Experts disagreed about what was causing the syndrome. Some blamed the slight alteration in gravity. Perhaps it was interfering with balance and thus hampering flight and navigation. Or else it was a problem with circadian rhythms; the birds' sense of day and night had been disrupted by the change, sending metabolisms awry. They'd lost track of when to sleep and when to eat. They were starving or they were sleep-deprived, confused and less alert.

But the real bird experts, the ornithologists,

kept quiet. It was too soon to say.

'They're fine,' said Sylvia. 'Right, guys?'

The finches were silent. The only sound was the faint tapping of a tiny talon poking through a layer of newspaper.

Something similar had happened once to the bees. This was only a few years before the slowing began. Millions of honeybees had died. Hives were found abandoned, inexplicably empty. Whole colonies had vanished in the breeze. No one ever did conclusively pinpoint the cause of that collapse.

'Do you want to know what I think?' said Sylvia.

She had dark, serious eyes, and she never wore makeup. Her skin was smooth and tanned, her limbs dotted with freckles, the kind that seem submerged beneath skin, like crumbs sinking into milk.

'I think the slowing of the earth is just the last straw for the birds. We've been poisoning the planet and its creatures for years. And now we're finally paying for it.'

I'd heard this argument on television, that the causes of the bird die-off were multiple, long-standing, and our fault: pesticides and pollution, climate change and acid rain, the radiation emanating from cell phone towers. The slowing, some said, had simply tipped the balance in exactly the wrong way, leaving the birds more vulnerable to all the man-made threats they'd been battling for years.

'I believe the planet has been out of balance for a long time, and this whole thing is its way of

85

correcting itself,' continued Sylvia. She was a woman who grew her own wheat grass in a greenhouse out back and then squeezed her own wheat grass juice. 'All we can do is give in to it. We have to let the *earth* guide *us*.'

I didn't know what to say next. But the slow turn of the doorknob let in another awkwardness — the next student was arriving, and I knew who it would be. Seth Moreno hadn't spoken to me since the eclipse.

A wind chime made of seashells rang and echoed from the porch and was followed by the soft clench of the door meeting the doorframe. I could hear my heart pounding in my head. Usually, Seth and I overlapped for only a moment or two, slipping quickly past each other in the entry hall, letting small nods of the head stand in for hellos.

'I wasn't sure when to come,' said Seth. His tennis shoes squeaked on the wooden floor. He flicked his head to the right to clear his shaggy bangs from his eyes. His hair was damp, fresh from a shower and, I happened to know, from soccer practice before that. 'Because of the clocks and everything.'

A walnut grandfather clock in the living room reported a nonsensical time — ten o'clock — but it was midafternoon.

'So I just sort of guessed,' he said, shifting his music books from one arm to the other.

'This is fine, Seth,' said Sylvia. 'We'll only be a few more minutes.'

He sat down on a worn leather armchair in the corner beside the birdcage. A potted fern hung from the ceiling above his head, suspended from a ropy net of macramé. There must be certain details that I no longer recall about the interior of that house, but when I close my eyes, it seems to me that the entire house and its contents remain to this day intact in my memory, preserved like a crime scene, exactly as it was.

Sylvia cleared her throat, and we were back in the lesson. ''Für Elise,' ' she said, resetting the metronome. 'One more time through.'

I'd played only the first few notes when the telephone rang in the kitchen. Sylvia ignored the phone, but it rang again. The ringing seemed to aggravate the finches, who screeched and called out from their cage. Sylvia stood to answer, but the machine caught the call and then projected through the house the first scratch of a man's voice.

Sylvia picked up the phone and shut off the machine. She seemed to know who it would be.

'I'm teaching,' she said, as if annoyed. 'Remember?'

But she looked pleased and embarrassed, her face the face of a woman much younger. Sylvia was about forty at the time.

I'd never seen her with a man. I imagined a dusty outdoorsman with a ponytail and beard, calling on a cell phone from a pickup or a van.

Sylvia laid the phone on her shoulder and motioned to Seth and me that she would be right back. Then she went upstairs, the phone pressed to her ear, the hem of her white linen dress brushing the backs of her legs as she moved.

Seth and I were alone in the living room.

Neither of us moved. He rearranged his music books on his lap, letting the pages slide against one another. I stayed on the piano bench and studied the keys, too nervous to look in his direction.

Eventually, Seth fished his cell phone from his pocket and began to play a game with his thumbs. Tinny music radiated out from the phone like the sounds of a distant carnival. I wondered if this was how he passed his time in hospitals while doctors operated on his mother or injected toxic chemicals into her blood.

I pulled the rubber band from my hair and remade my ponytail, smoothing out the tangles. I was breathing fast, but I tried to conceal it.

In the distance outside, I could hear the shouts of younger children. A cherry ball was smacking the pavement. Through the window, I thought I saw something dark fall from the sky.

One of Sylvia's finches let out a loud screech. Seth turned toward the cage. He studied the birds for a few seconds. The music from his game played on.

Finally, I spoke: 'Do they look okay?'

Seth shrugged his shoulders and said nothing.

I slid off the piano bench to see for myself.

Inside the cage, a bowl of chopped apples sat untouched, the fruit flesh browning in the air. Two mealworms, which I knew from Sylvia were also part of the finch diet, wiggled freely in the bowl.

'They're not eating,' I said.

'Maybe she just fed them,' said Seth.

'Or maybe it's the sickness.'

Up close, Seth smelled like detergent, but his T-shirt was badly wrinkled — as if, in his home, the folding of laundry had become a lost art, an outmoded custom turned obsolete by suffering.

I heard the creak of Sylvia's footsteps moving back and forth upstairs. The metronome continued to click, segmenting time in its ancient way.

Adagio was sitting like a miniature hen on the newspaper that lined the bottom of the cage.

'That one looks really bad,' I said.

Seth tapped on the bars with one finger. 'Hey, little guy,' he said. 'Over here. Hello?'

The tapping upset the healthier bird, whose head darted toward the noise, but Adagio did not react.

Seth glanced behind his shoulder, checking for Sylvia. Then he unlatched the cage door and swung it open. Slowly, he reached inside, touching Adagio lightly on the back. The bird wobbled like an egg under his finger, and Seth pulled his hand away.

'Shit,' he said. 'It's dead.'

'Are you sure?' I said.

'Definitely.'

'It *is* the sickness,' I said.

'Maybe,' he said. 'Or maybe not. Maybe it just got sick with something normal and died.'

We heard the upstairs bedroom door snap open. Seth shut the cage door. We looked at each other but said nothing. We made a sudden silent agreement.

The other bird remained at the top of the cage, uselessly flapping his wings. I felt sorry for that bird, all alone in his world.

We heard Sylvia's feet on the stairs, her hand on the banister, the cordless phone landing in its cradle on the kitchen counter.

'What's wrong?' she said when she appeared, unclipping her hair and then tying it up again.

'Nothing,' said Seth. He sat down in the old leather chair, his long arms dangling on the sides.

'We were just looking at your birds,' I said.

'Stop worrying about them,' she said. She waved her hand as if shooing an insect. 'They're fine.'

Sylvia apologized for cutting my lesson short, but she thought she'd better start Seth's.

As I packed up my things, I tried to catch Seth's eyes, but he wouldn't look in my direction. I gathered up my books and left the house, not knowing then that I would cross that threshold only a few more times in my life.

I was getting used to the sight of lifeless things. I'd been learning, since the slowing, about the qualities of the dead, the way a bird's body deflates after a few days, the way it drains, growing flatter and flatter until only the feathers and the feet remain.

Outside, the sky was a pure, flinty blue, streaked by two delicate clouds. In science, we'd begun to study the atmosphere, and I'd memorized the names of all the different types of clouds. These two were cirrus, the highest, finest kind.

Higher still than the clouds, two hundred miles above my head, I knew that six astronauts

— four Americans and two Russians — were stranded at the space station. The shuttle launch that had been planned to retrieve them had been postponed indefinitely. The complex calculation, the giant cosmic slingshot, that for decades had brought our astronauts back and forth from space, was judged, for the time being, too dangerous to attempt. Whenever I looked at the sky during that time, I thought of them up there, stranded so far from earth.

As I crossed the street, an ocean breeze washed through the eucalyptus and the pines. A single sparrow sailed across the sky. I picked a dandelion from the yard and shook it in the wind while our cat Tony slept, belly up, on the porch. The sidewalks shimmered in the sun. Somewhere a dog was barking. I wondered what Hanna was doing in Utah right then. This was one of the last real afternoons.

9

There had always been regions of the earth where the sun could not be trusted, where the days were never measured by the rising and setting of our star. At certain remote coordinates, the sun had always set in December and then failed to rise all season. There, every summer had always been one continuous loop of daylight, the sun relentless in the June night sky.

These were difficult places. Trees refused to grow. They were the ancient fishing settlements of northern Scandinavia, the icy slopes of Siberia, the Inuit villages of Canada and Alaska. For the inhabitants of these places, *night* and *day* had always been abstract. Morning did not necessarily bring with it the light. And not all nights were dark.

Those of us living in the lower latitudes were about to experience a lifestyle strange to us but long familiar in the land of the midnight sun.

★   ★   ★

The announcement was made at night, fourteen days after the start of the slowing. Broadcasts were interrupted. Newscasters broke in with a special message. I remember the blare of the trumpets — the network's emergency intro music — slicing through the crowd noise of Game 7 of the World Series.

92

'Jesus,' sighed my mother. 'What now?'

We'd been watching the game over dinner, plates of Bellisario's cheese pizza steaming on our knees. It had been a good day: that afternoon I had finally heard from Hanna — she'd written me a cheerful postcard with a picture of the desert on the back. My mother had relaxed a little. My father was drinking a beer. A quart of cookies and cream was waiting in the freezer. A stranger passing our window that night could have detected our moods from the sounds: the clean crack of bat striking ball and the synchronized cheers of my parents. We were happy.

But now my mother lifted her dinner plate from her lap and set it on the coffee table. She pulled her hair away from her face, as if to better hear the news. I was sure her roots were turning grayer every day. She'd skipped her monthly salon appointment — and the slowing of the planet had interfered not at all with the speed at which human hair grew.

My father sat on the couch beside her, his mouth tight. I could see him chewing the inside of his cheek. He took one slow sip of beer.

Outside, the sky was bright — the days had swelled beyond thirty hours, and the slowing was showing no signs of letting up.

'Maybe they figured out how to fix things,' I said from the floor, where I'd stretched out on my stomach with the cats.

No one said anything.

Rumors must have surged through certain circles before the official announcement was made. There must have been some early, unconfirmed reports. Doesn't big news always leak before it's meant to? Aren't secrets usually spilled? Anonymous sources love to talk. But if there was any chatter about this development, we hadn't heard it.

The network took us live to the White House, where the president was waiting behind an enormous polished desk, his hands folded stiffly on its surface. A large American flag hung in folds beside him.

A series of meetings between congressional leaders, White House officials, and the secretaries of Commerce, Agriculture, Transportation, and the Interior had produced a radically simple plan: in the face of massive global change, we, the American people, would be asked to carry on exactly as we always had.

In other words, we would remain on the twenty-four-hour clock.

My first response was disbelief. The cable box glowed a green 11 A.M., but it was the end of the day. We had learned, by then, to disregard the clocks.

'I don't get it,' I said. 'How can we?'

The Chinese government had taken the same sweeping step. The European Union was expected to follow suit. The alternative, we were told, would be disastrous.

'Markets need stability,' said the president. 'We can't continue this way.'

It requires a certain kind of bravery, I suppose, to choose the status quo. There's a certain boldness to inaction.

But it seemed to me that we were being asked to perform the impossible, as unlikely a strategy as if they'd proposed strapping ropes to the sun and dragging it across the sky.

I waited for my mother to react, but she only sighed a loud sigh. I turned to look at her and saw her as she was: a woman on a couch, looking weary. There's a limit to shock, I suppose, even for her.

'This is never going to work,' she said.

My father said nothing. That was one of his specialties, I was learning, the ability to remain silent at all the crucial junctures, to meet each crisis with a simple, stalwart quiet. I can see now that I inherited a bit of that habit from him.

My father went back to his dinner. He ate his pizza with a knife and a fork, a paper napkin spread neatly across his knees.

The green of the infield snapped back onto the television screen.

As obvious as the implications would be later, the effects of the plan were not immediately clear to me. What would become apparent soon enough was this: We would fall out of sync with the sun almost immediately. Light would be unhooked from *day*, darkness unchained from *night*. And not everyone would go along with the plan.

10

It was voluntary, of course. We were not *required* to squeeze our days into twenty-four little hours. No new law was passed or put into place. This was America. The government could not dictate the way we lived our lives. But in the week following the president's announcement, as the natural days swelled to a record thirty-two hours, officials of various levels and types of expertise went to work convincing us of the virtues of the plan — and the urgency with which we needed to launch it. Clock time, they called it, the only practical solution. It was a matter of economic stability, said the politicians, of competitive advantage, and even, some insisted, national security.

I know now that clock time ignited a complex national debate — with just as many dissenters shouting from the far left as from the far right — but in my memory, it happened all at once, a clean tidal shift, abrupt and complete.

The public schools jumped on board right away. Government offices, too. The television networks all decided to comply. The corporations were *definitely* doing it — they'd been losing millions every week in inefficiency and overtime pay.

But any American could choose to forgo clock time, to remain instead on daylight time, or what some were already referring to as real time. We were still free to arrange our lives around the sun's comings and goings if we wished, but soon those who did risked losing their jobs or having to quit. Their children could no longer practically attend public school. They'd be perpetually out of time with society. To hesitate would have been like choosing to linger in some evacuated city where the buildings and the streets remain, but the city, let's face it, has disappeared.

★ ★ ★

And so it was: We reclaimed the clocks. Wristwatches returned to wrists. Batteries were replaced. I cleared my nightstand of books so that I could once again see my alarm clock from my bed. I pulled my grandfather's pocket watch out of a drawer and set it on my desk.

Clock time began at two A.M. on a Saturday night, like daylight saving time. They'd chosen a day when the sun rose more or less in tune with the clocks. In that era, synchronized days like these rolled around every few weeks like full moons. The gap would widen as the day passed, but the idea was to transition us slowly.

The sun rose that morning at clock time 7:02 A.M. The Sunday paper landed in the driveway with a thud. My father ground the coffee early, toasted toast. The sun shone as usual on the eastern side of the house. We would feel the real differences only the next day, when we, like the clocks, would fall completely out of sync with the sun.

'This can't be healthy,' said my mother, squinting in her green terry-cloth bathrobe. Her hair was wild from sleep.

I was sitting beside her in flannel pajamas, weaving a friendship bracelet for Hanna. Her birthday was a few weeks away.

'This is the best of bad options,' said my father from the table.

The cats paced at my feet, hungry for milk. Tony's bony tail flicked my shins as he passed. The sun was shining in the kitchen, catching on the copper pots that dangled, sparkling, above the steel sink.

'What are the other bad options?' I asked.

My mother was filling a copper can with water for the two milky white orchids that lived in the kitchen window. Her attention to her plants had increased since the start of the slowing, as if our survival somehow hinged on theirs. Or maybe it was something else entirely. Beauty can be a very reassuring thing.

'You know what I think?' said my mother. 'I think this whole clock thing is a crock of shit.'

Tony jumped on the counter, paws first. I swooped him up and set him down on the tile.

'We'll survive,' said my father.

As a doctor, he was already a night worker, a day sleeper, a deliverer of babies in the middle of the night. He was a creature whose body had grown accustomed years ago to ignoring its circadian rhythms.

'What about the real problem?' said my mother. We'd gained more than thirty minutes the night before. 'What is anyone doing about that?'

98

My father continued reading the paper, slowly shuffling the pages. Missing from that day's paper were the details of an even more audacious plan, still top-secret at the time but being furiously plotted by scientists and engineers in the government labs of this country. We would soon learn the details — and the hubris — of the infamous, ill-fated Virginia Project. Absurd as it was, you have to admire the spirit of the endeavor, the wild sense of possibility, the cowboy optimism required to imagine that a bit of human ingenuity might actually control the turning of the earth.

'Wait a minute,' said my mother. She waved a jar of peanut butter in my father's direction. 'You opened this?' In her other hand, she held the evidence, the knife. Its sharper side glistened with a coat of extra-crunchy.

My father, at the table, took a giant bite of wheat toast.

'Goddammit, Joel,' she said. 'Goddammit. I was saving this.'

I kept my eyes on the bracelet I was weaving and waited for the fight to pass. I focused on the complicated pattern I'd chosen, using Hanna's favorite colors. There was something calming about the tying of those knots, one after another, the way the design emerged from the tips of my fingers, so orderly and so slow.

My father chewed, swallowed, took a careful sip of coffee.

'Helen,' he said. 'We have six jars in there.'

He was against my mother's hoarding.

'Do you think this is a joke?' she said. 'A guy

on CNN said we might only have a few weeks left before everything falls apart.'

In her fury, my mother tripped over the blue ceramic water bowl we kept on the floor for the cats. 'Shit,' she said. A miniature tide rolled across the tile.

'Until what falls apart?' I asked.

'I haven't heard anything like *that*,' said my father.

My mother's voice took on a low, serious register: 'Well, then, maybe you're not listening.'

If my father responded, I didn't hear it. I slipped upstairs. Most likely, he simply returned to the paper.

What went on in that head of his? I would soon come to understand that he gave voice to only a fraction of the thoughts that swam behind his eyes. It was not nearly so clean and smooth in there as it seemed. Other lives were housed in that mind, parallel worlds. Maybe we're all built a little bit that way. But most of us drop hints. Most of us leave clues. My father was more careful.

When I think now of that moment in the kitchen, an almost unbelievable thought comes to my mind: There was a time when those two people — that man hunched at the table and that woman shouting in a bathrobe — were young. The proof was in the pictures that hung on the living room walls, a pretty girl and a bookish guy, a studio apartment in a crumbling Hollywood building overlooking a courtyard and a kidney-shaped pool. This was the mythical period before I was born, when my mother was not a mother and was instead an actress who might make it someday, any day, maybe soon, a serious girl with a lovely face. How much sweeter life would be if it all happened in reverse, if, after decades of disappointments, you finally arrived at an age when you had conceded nothing, when everything was possible. I like to think about how my parents' lives once shimmered in front of them, half hidden, like buried gold. Back then the future was whatever they imagined — and they never imagined this.

But doesn't every previous era feel like fiction once it's gone? After a while, certain vestigial sayings are all that remain. Decades after the invention of the automobile, for instance, we continue to warn each other not to *put the cart before the horse*. So, too, we do still have *day*dreams and *night*mares, and the early-morning clock hours are still known colloquially (if increasingly mysteriously) as *the crack of dawn*. Similarly, even as they grew apart, my parents never stopped calling each other *sweetheart*.

★ ★ ★

I'll tell you one thing about that first Sunday on the clock: Time flew. We'd grown quite accustomed to those long, lazy days. But now the morning zoomed. Midday zipped by at an inhumane speed. The hours tumbled quickly after one another, as if sliding downhill — and there were suddenly so few!

My parents avoided each other all afternoon.

A muggy quiet settled over the house. On any other Sunday, I would have escaped to Hanna's.

Instead, I walked over to my old friend Gabby's. Her house was three houses down from mine, and we'd grown up together, but I hadn't seen her much lately.

'I think clock time's gonna be cool,' Gabby said once we were upstairs in her bedroom. She was sitting on her unmade bed, painting a second coat of black polish on her fingernails. She waved the bottle at me, but I shook my head. It was a glossy, grim black. A few drops had landed on the plush cream-colored carpet. 'I like going out in the dark,' she said.

Her dyed black hair kept falling into her face. Charcoal eyeliner ringed her eyes. Silver studs shaped like human skulls glinted from her ears. I hardly recognized her anymore.

'I wish I still went to your school,' she said.

'You hated our school,' I said. When she started smoking and skipping classes, her parents had transferred her to a strict Catholic school.

'Yeah, but all the girls at my school are anorexic bitches,' she said.

We used to swim in her pool every summer and eat potato chips on lawn chairs while our ponytails drip-dried on our backs. But now Gabby never wore a swimsuit; she'd gained a lot of weight. She was always in trouble these days. Hanna hadn't been allowed to come to her house.

'My mom's afraid we're all going to die,' I said.

The room smelled like nail-polish remover and

vanilla; a fat white candle was burning on the desk. Two pleated plaid skirts, Gabby's school uniform, hung over the edge of a chair.

'We are going to die,' said Gabby. 'Eventually.'

She was playing music I didn't recognize: The thin crystal voice of a woman, enraged, shot through the room from two big black speakers.

'But she thinks we're going to die from this,' I said. 'And soon.'

Gabby blew on her fingernails and held up one hand for inspection. A can of diet soda popped and fizzed on the rug.

'Do you believe in past lives?' she said.

'I don't think so.'

She'd draped a crimson scarf over the only lamp, and the room was dim and stuffy. She'd pulled the vertical blinds shut, but stripes of sunlight glowed through the cracks.

'I'm pretty sure I've lived past lives,' she said. 'I have this feeling that in every one of them, I die young.'

Lately, I'd begun running out of things to say to other kids. I'd stopped knowing how to respond.

'Hey,' she said. 'Want a tattoo? I learned how on the Internet.' She pointed to a sewing needle and a tiny jar of black ink laid out beside the candle on the floor like primitive surgical equipment. 'You just run a needle through the flame, then scratch your skin in the shape you want and pour ink into the cut.'

Gabby's house was the same model as ours but reversed. Her bedroom was the same bedroom as mine, the dimensions exactly equal.

For twelve years, we'd slept between walls erected by the same construction crews and looked out on the same fading cul-de-sac through identically sized windows. Grown under similar conditions, we had become very different, two specimens of girlhood, now diverging.

'I'm going to do an outline of the sun and moon on my wrist,' she said. 'I'll do one on you, too, if you want.'

The album came to its end. Silence filled the room.

'I don't think so,' I said. 'I should probably go home.'

Maybe it had begun to happen before the slowing, but it was only afterward that I realized it: My friendships were disintegrating. Things were coming apart. It was a rough crossing, the one from childhood to the next life. And as with any other harsh journey, not everything survived.

★   ★   ★

That night, while the sun continued to shine, my father came home with a telescope.

'It's for you,' he said as he unpacked it in my bedroom, tissue paper crinkling. 'I want you to know more about science.'

The telescope came in a shiny mahogany box, inside of which lay a silver tube and a trio of titanium legs that glittered in the sunlight. The telescope looked expensive. He set it up in my bedroom and pointed it at the still-bright sky. My mother watched him from the doorway, arms crossed. She was often annoyed with my

104

father these days, and it seemed that even this offering — in the encrypted language that traveled between them — was in some way an affront to her.

'There's Mars,' said my father, squinting one eye while he aimed the other through the telescope. He motioned for me to look. 'You'll be able to see it even better when it gets dark.'

Mars had shown up in the news lately, after draft plans for something called the Pioneer Project had surfaced on the Internet. Privately funded by a group of secretive billionaires, it was a plan for a human settlement on Mars, complete with temperature-controlled biospheres and a self-cleaning water supply. The Pioneer Project was an evacuation plan from Earth. If necessary, a cluster of humans could supposedly survive up there on Mars, the whole settlement like a time capsule, like a living, breathing souvenir of life as we once knew it on Earth.

Through the telescope, Mars didn't look like much to me, a fat red dot, hazy at the edges.

'Some of the stars you'll see out there don't exist anymore,' said my father, gently turning the knobs of the telescope with his thumb. The gears squeaked softly. 'Some of the stars you'll see have been dead for thousands of years already.'

'Are you two going to be up here all night?' asked my mother.

My father wiped the lens with a black strip of felt that had come in the box.

'What you'll see with this telescope are not the

stars as they are today but how they were thousands of years ago,' he went on. 'That's how far away they are; even the light takes centuries to reach us.'

'If we're ever going to have dinner,' said my mother from behind us, 'we should eat.'

My father didn't answer, but I was eager to calm her. 'We'll be ready soon,' I said.

I liked the idea, how the past could be preserved, fossilized, in the stars. I wanted to think that somewhere on the other end of time, a hundred light-years from then, someone else, some distant future creature, might be looking back at a preserved image of me and my father at that very moment in my bedroom.

'Couldn't that be true?' I said to my father. 'Like a hundred light-years from now?'

'Could be,' he said.

But I wasn't sure he was listening.

I would spend a lot of hours watching the stars that year, but I used my telescope to spy on nearer bodies, too. I soon realized I could see into the other houses on the street. I could watch the Kaplans, all seven of them, sitting down to dinner. I could see Carlotta at the end of our cul-de-sac, drinking tea on her porch, her long braid dangling like macramé, its every strand apparent through my lens; and there was Tom behind her, dumping a bucket of slop onto their compost pile.

But my clearest view was of Sylvia's house. Hers faced ours like a mirror image, and I could see right into her living room — to the keys of her piano, to the wood boards of her floor, right to the pages of the newspaper that lined the birdcage, now empty.

★ ★ ★

That night we slept in sunlight, or we didn't sleep at all. For weeks, I'd been climbing into bed before dark — those early days were endless, those first evenings everlasting; I fell asleep most nights before the stars came out. But this night was different, the gap wider than ever. This was the first of the white nights. We would later learn to shield ourselves, to carve out small patches of darkness amid the light, but that first clock night was radiant, as if the sun had never shone so brilliantly or bright.

On my bedroom ceiling was a scattering of glow-in-the-dark star stickers that I had recently tried to remove. My mother had stopped me — 'There's asbestos in that ceiling, leave it alone.' But my ceiling stars were invisible on this night anyway, just like the real ones were, every one of them washed out by our nearest, dearest star.

'Try to sleep,' said my father. 'It's going to be hard to wake up for school in the dark.' He sat at the foot of my bed, staring at the window, at the blazing blue sky before pulling the blinds shut. 'These are amazing times,' he said. 'We're living in some amazing times.'

The sun finally set sometime after two.

11

The next day our school returned to its clock time start of nine o'clock. That meant we stood in darkness at the bus stop, our faces lit yellow by a distant streetlight, which, like all the streetlights in our region, had been specially designed for dimness — bright lights spoiled the view for the enormous thirty-year-old university telescope that sat on a hill out east. *Light pollution*, they called it. But what were those astronomers staring at anymore, now that the real action was happening down here?

My mother waited in the car at the curb until the bus arrived, convinced that danger, like potatoes, breeds in the dark. To me, the bus stop seemed just as hazardous as in daylight, and no more so in the dark.

I'd been staying away from Daryl, but he ignored me and acted as if he hadn't done anything wrong. Somewhere in that dark dirt, I thought, my gold-nugget necklace probably still lay. Seth continued to keep to himself, like a lonesome survivor, blowing on his hands in an attractive, self-sufficient way, one foot on his skateboard, the other on the curb.

All around us that morning, the noise of the crickets was astounding, the squeak and whine of so many new bodies in the dark — they'd been multiplying since the slowing. All the bugs had. More and more birds were dying, and with so few of them left, everything smaller was thriving. More and more spiders were crawling on our ceilings too. Beetles emerged from bathroom drains. Worms slithered over the cement of our patios. One soccer practice was canceled when a million ladybugs descended on the field at once. Even beauty, in abundance, turns creepy.

Hanna's house was just visible in the distance down the street, and I thought I saw a small light glowing near the front door that morning. I felt a flash of hope that she'd come home. But it was only the porch light, probably left on by accident when they fled, the light unnoticed in the daylight.

We were all quieter than usual on that dark morning. We were sleepy and slouchy and dazed. Even Michaela seemed subdued, having slept too late to wash her hair or do her eyes. No one teased or talked. No one said anything. We stood together in the dark, the hoods of our sweatshirts high on our heads, our fingers curled inside our sleeves.

It was cold, maybe the coldest part of the night, but my watch read 8:40 A.M. The moon was a sliver, glowing low on the horizon. The stars were sparklingly clear.

It's hard to believe that there was a time in this country — not so long ago — when thick almanacs were printed every year and listed, among other facts, the precise clock time of every single sunrise and every single sunset a year in advance. I think we lost something else when we lost that crisp rhythm, some general

109

shared belief that we could count on certain things.

★　★　★

When the bus pulled up at school, we discovered that workmen were installing stadium lights all over campus. Under the floodlights, the faded green walls — painted, rumor had it, with surplus paint from the marine base up the coast — looked like those of a prison. That's one lesson I learned from clock time: So much that seems harmless in daylight turns imposing in the dark. What else, you had to wonder, was only a trick of light?

It was lunchtime when the sun finally appeared, the darkness lifting like fog. Sunrise: 12:34 P.M. We were all outside when it happened. This was California — we ate outside in every season. As the eastern sky turned a pale and promising pink, Michaela went right on teasing the boys around us while I performed the opposite maneuver: keeping quiet and trying not to stand out.

Slowly, the soccer fields began to glitter in the distance. I squinted toward the sunrise. That was when I noticed, on the far edge of the quad, the outline of a girl who looked remarkably like Hanna, except she couldn't be her, because I would have known if Hanna had come back to town. This girl was sitting alone at a table near the science labs, her head resting on one skinny arm, sulking in the pale light.

When I got close to the girl, I could see that it

110

was true. It was Hanna, all right. She was sitting at a lunch table, all alone, with no lunch.

'You're back,' I said.

'Hey,' she said in a casual way. She looked stylish and cute in dark jeans and a pink tank top. Silver hoops hung in her ears. Her hair was pulled back in a loose French braid. 'We had to come home for my dad's job.'

I waited for her to say something more. She didn't. A girl's giddy scream rang out from the lunch lines behind us.

'I'm so glad you're back,' I said finally. I dropped my backpack on the ground and sat down at the table. 'I was starting to hate coming to school.'

'In Utah we didn't have to go to school,' she said. Her blue eyes were watching something behind me. 'Everyone was kind of waiting around for, you know, the end. But my dad got tired of waiting.'

We'd been friends for years, but a new shyness had flowered between us. I felt as if she were some second cousin, the two of us stranded at a family reunion, connected in some loose way but with no idea what to say to one another. She'd only been gone for three weeks.

All around us, the roar of kids ebbed and flowed like an invisible tide. Hanna looked down at the table. She began to pick at a bit of peeling paint.

I caved: 'Why didn't you tell me you were back?'

'We only just got back yesterday,' she said. She bit down on the flimsy tip of her thumbnail. 'Or maybe the day before.'

A few stars persisted on the horizon, but the day was turning brighter by the minute. I had to squint to see Hanna's eyes.

'Why weren't you at the bus stop this morning?' I asked.

'I slept over at Tracey's.'

'Who's Tracey?'

'Tracey Blair.'

She pointed to another Mormon girl I vaguely recognized from classes but did not know. This girl was walking toward us now, her figure hazy in the dawn light. She carried two burritos wrapped in plastic and two bottles of water. As she got closer, it became clear that she was wearing the same outfit as Hanna, same pink tank top and same silver hoops, same French braid dangling down her back.

I felt suddenly tense.

'You're twins,' I said.

'We didn't even plan it,' said Hanna. 'Isn't that funny?'

'Hi,' said Tracey, turning to me. She had giant brown eyes that seemed never to blink. I guessed from her careful stride and the calluses on her hands that she was some kind of gymnast.

'Tracey was in Utah for a while, too,' said Hanna.

'Hi,' I said.

Tracey spit out her gum and sat down. She slid one burrito across the table to Hanna.

'See?' said Hanna, pointing at the crowd of kids across the quad. 'Now do you see what I mean?'

'Totally,' said Tracey. She leaned her head back in extreme agreement. 'Totally.'

'What?' I said.

'Nothing,' said Hanna.

As the sun made its way up into the sky, Hanna told me a little bit about Utah. Her life there was not nearly as bleak as I had pictured. She told a complicated story involving a Mormon boy who lived next door to her aunt. One night this boy had popped the screen on Hanna's window and climbed into her bedroom. They'd kissed while her sisters slept.

'Wow,' I said. I could think of nothing else to say.

'I still cannot believe that,' said Tracey. 'How did nobody wake up?'

'I know,' said Hanna, her cheeks a sudden red. She was smiling but trying not to smile. 'And we were on the top bunk.'

At last she asked how I had been.

There was a lot to tell. Nothing was going well. But on that day, Hanna didn't feel like Hanna to me, and Tracey kept cracking her knuckles.

'Oh, I don't know,' I said. 'I've been okay.'

Tracey's fat shiny eyes were watching me closely. Every few seconds came the sound of her small joints popping.

'I'm double-jointed,' she said as she started on her left hand.

'Actually,' I said, 'things have been great here. Really great.'

Tracey and Hanna exchanged a quick glance.

The bell rang, and Hanna groaned. 'Man, I

wish I was still in Utah, don't you?'

'Totally,' said Tracey. 'Totally.'

We stood and heaved our backpacks onto our shoulders. The two of them began to drift away from the table.

'See you later,' I said, but they didn't hear me, or they didn't seem to. They were already walking toward the science labs together, their strides in sync. I was walking in that direction, too, but I took the long way and walked alone.

★　★　★

At soccer practice that afternoon, Hanna showed up late and barely spoke to me. This was the same field where once we had gossiped nonstop between drills, but on this day, she spoke my name just once, and only as a forward addressing a midfielder during the scrimmage: 'Julia,' she called out as the ball spun at my feet. 'Over here. I'm open.'

Afterward, while we waited, sweaty and red-faced, to be picked up by our mothers, Hanna played with her phone.

'Want to come over this weekend?' I asked.

'I can't,' she said.

I didn't like the way she didn't look up from her phone while she talked. I was sure she was sending messages to Tracey, who, no doubt, was sending similar communiqués right back.

'Why are you being like this?' I said.

'What do you mean?' she said. She smiled a little and bit her lower lip. Her long blond braid dangled on her shoulder. She wouldn't look me

114

in the eye. 'I'm not doing anything.'

Something about the coyness in her face felt familiar. In that moment I recalled a pale redhead named Alison who had been Hanna's best friend before me. This was years earlier, fourth grade, but I remembered the way Alison used to float toward us on the playground sometimes, how Hanna would ignore her while we practiced our tricks on the bars where there was room for only two. 'I'm so sick of her,' Hanna would say to me whenever she saw Alison approaching, and then she would look at Alison with the same fake smile that she was now using on me.

That night I was too upset to fall asleep. I remember getting up at some late hour and cutting apart the bracelet I'd been making for Hanna. Then I dropped the scraps along with the charm bracelet she'd given me into a shoe box and shoved it into the back of my closet. Afterward, I felt no better at all.

★ ★ ★

The days passed. Clock mornings, clock nights. Darkness and light drifted overhead like passing storms, no longer tethered to our days or our nights. Dusk sometimes descended at noon; the sun sometimes didn't rise until evening and then reached its highest point in the middle of the clock night. Sleeping was difficult. Waking was harder. Insomniacs walked the streets. And still the earth turned, slower and slower by the day. While my mother stockpiled candles and survivalist handbooks, I developed survival skills of a different sort: I was learning to spend time alone.

'Why don't you go over to Hanna's?' my mother would say in the afternoons. 'I'm sure she'd love to see you.'

But Hanna was always with Tracey these days.

'Clock time won't last,' said Sylvia at my weekly piano lesson. Her living room glowed against the dark. It was three in the afternoon and pitch-black outside. Seth didn't show up for his lesson that day. I didn't know why, and Sylvia didn't say.

'You'll see,' said Sylvia. 'We'll go back to real time eventually. Trust me.'

But I was not convinced that we *would* go back. Instead, I sensed that someday, if we survived, we'd be telling stories of how it once was on Earth.

★   ★   ★

One thing that strikes me when I recall that period of time is just how rapidly we adjusted. What had been familiar once became less and less so. How extraordinary it would seem to us eventually that our sun once set as predictably as clockwork. And how miraculous it would soon seem that I was once a happier girl, less lonely and less shy.

But I guess every bygone era takes on a shade of myth.

With a little persuasion, any familiar thing can turn abnormal in the mind. Here's a thought experiment. Consider this brutal bit of magic: A human grows a second human in a space inside her belly; she grows a second heart and a second brain, second eyes and second limbs, a complete set of second body parts as if for use as spares, and then, after almost a year, she expels that second screaming being out of her belly and into the world, alive.

Bizarre, isn't it?

This is just to say that as strange as the new days seemed to us at first, the old days would come to feel very quickly the stranger.

12

Certain people had been sounding alarms for decades, since the earliest drops of acid rain fell, since the subtlest thinning of the ozone layer, since Chernobyl and Three Mile Island and the oil crisis of the 1970s. The glaciers were melting and the rain forests were burning. Cancer rates were on the rise. Immense flotillas of trash had been roaming our oceans for years. Antidepressants were swimming in the rivers, and our bloodstreams were just as polluted as the waterways. That the slowing could not yet be explained was beside the point. Enough was enough. They were taking a stand.

These were the individuals who were refusing to abide by clock time.

They were naturalists and herbalists and holistic-health enthusiasts. They were healers and hippies and vegans, Wiccans and gurus and New Age philosophers. They were libertarians and anarchists and radical environmentalists. Or else they were fundamentalists, or survivalists, or back-to-the-landers already living in the wilderness off the grid. They were hostile to corporations. They were skeptical of the government. They were contrarians by nature or by creed.

★　★　★

You didn't always know who they were, not at first, anyway. Some kept it quiet for as long as they could. Others announced it.

At the end of my piano lesson one week, Sylvia handed me a slim white envelope.

'Give this to your mother,' she said.

Seth Moreno was in the room with us, waiting for his lesson to start. He'd been staring out the window, but I could feel him glance in our direction when Sylvia mentioned the envelope.

'What is it?' I asked.

Both her finches were dead. The birdcage stood empty. The only sounds were the wind chimes clattering on her front porch.

'I can't do this,' she said. 'It feels like a lie.'

In the letter, Sylvia explained that she was giving up clock time.

'We'll find you a new teacher,' said my mother when she saw the note.

'I don't want a new teacher,' I said.

'Why can't she keep going to Sylvia?' said my father, who was sorting mail beside us, dropping most of it straight into the trash.

In the letter, Sylvia had explained that she would do her best to accommodate the schedules of her clock time students.

'I've never liked her lifestyle,' said my mother.

She was pouring tomato sauce on a prebaked pizza crust. This was one of those rare clock nights that really was dark. I could see our reflections in the French doors.

'What lifestyle?' said my father.

He was wearing his work clothes, a white dress shirt and a loosened yellow tie, but he'd rolled up his sleeves to his elbows. I could smell the hospital soap on his hands.

'You know what I mean,' said my mother. 'All that New Age crap.'

'What do you think, Julia?' said my father. His medical badge clung to his front pocket: An out-of-date photo dangled behind the plastic; a young man with thick hair stared down at me, right below the older man, who was staring down, too. 'Don't you like Sylvia?'

'I don't want a new teacher,' I said.

'Wait a minute, Joel,' said my mother. 'Hold on. You're the one who said this whole clock thing was the best of bad options and we would adapt to it and blah blah blah.'

'It's not our business how she chooses to live her life,' said my father.

'I'm getting you another teacher,' said my mother. 'End of discussion.'

Not everyone quit taking lessons from Sylvia. Seth, for example, continued going each week for a while. I never knew exactly when he'd arrive, but I could sometimes detect from my bedroom the sound of his skateboard grinding the pavement as he rode up to her house. On those days, I'd make sure I was walking out to our mailbox as he was leaving, or I'd casually water the lawn in a pair of sunglasses, my hair freshly braided. Sometimes Seth nodded at me as he passed. Sometimes he didn't.

★ ★ ★

Tom and Carlotta, our neighbors down the street, went public as real-timers right away. I guess it was no surprise that they would resist clock time — their roof sparkled with a dozen solar panels, and they drove two worn-out trucks, freckled with peeling peace signs and ancient, sun-bleached bumper stickers that proclaimed, among other optimistic dreams, MAKE LOVE NOT WAR. Tom was a retired art teacher who wore a hemp necklace and ragged jeans stained with stray paint. Carlotta's long gray hair swung near her waist, a ghost, I suspected, of its younger and sexier self.

A few days after the return of clock time, a new sign appeared in the corner of their front lawn. The sign was small and white and similar in style to the one in Mr. Valencia's yard, which alerted passersby to the fact that the Valencia home was protected by a Safelux security system. Tom and Carlotta's new sign carried a different message: THIS HOUSEHOLD LIVES ON REAL TIME.

'My mom thinks they're drug dealers,' said Gabby, whose house was right next door to theirs. Her mother, a lawyer, clicked around in high heels and navy blue suits. 'She thinks they're growing shitloads of pot in their house.'

'You think?' I said. We were sitting around in her bedroom.

'It's total bullshit, of course,' said Gabby. 'My mom thinks that anyone who's different is some kind of criminal.'

Two scabs had formed on the inside of Gabby's right wrist in the shape of a sun and a perfect crescent moon. Her parents, when they saw the scabs, had sent her to a psychiatrist whom she now met with every week.

'Guess what,' she continued. 'I met this guy online, and he thinks there's going to be some kind of revolution.'

'What do you mean?'

'He thinks millions of people are going to fight the government over clock time.'

While the rest of us purchased sunlamps and installed blackout curtains for sleeping through the white nights, several thousand Americans attempted to remain in tune with daylight. The human body could adapt, they claimed, right alongside the earth. Already their circadian rhythms were adjusting, they reported, gradually stretching like elastic. They simply slept longer, stayed awake for more hours, ate a fourth meal in the late afternoon.

I used to hear Tom and Carlotta outside sometimes in the middle of our night. On sunny evenings, they would work in their yard while the rest of the street tried to sleep. I recall the metallic ring of gardening shears, the shuffle of sandals on the sidewalk, the voices moving through the quiet air. It was like a haunting: two dimensions of time occupying a single space.

★ ★ ★

In science that week, our butterflies wiggled out of their cocoons. It happened in fifth period, the last class of the day, but the sun was just beginning to rise. We had learned that butterflies

122

almost always emerge in the morning.

'See?' said Mr. Jensen, a mug of coffee in his hand. 'You can't fool them. They know it's morning.'

We all watched the butterflies hop and flutter, then flicker off into the sky. We knew, of course, what those butterflies did not: how short and hard their lives would be.

I remember that Mr. Jensen's eyes looked red and watery that day. He seemed exhausted, his ponytail shaggier than usual, his beard a little wilder.

On the following Monday, we arrived in science to find sitting behind Mr. Jensen's metal desk a young woman in a gray pantsuit. She'd written her name on the board: Miss Mosely. A substitute. 'For a while,' she said. 'Probably for the rest of the year.'

That's the way it happened sometimes — people just disappeared.

Some of Mr. Jensen's things stayed in the lab with us for the rest of the year: his silver thermos, a mud-splattered pair of hiking boots, a blue windbreaker wadded up on a shelf. Some of our sundials would sit in the windowsill until June, forever reporting fantastical times. One butterfly cocoon remained smoothly sealed in the terrarium, its inhabitant never to emerge and, instead, weeks later, to be scraped off the ceiling by Miss Mosely's scalpel and tossed into the trash with the shards of a broken beaker.

We were not told the reason for Mr. Jensen's departure, but a rumor spread that he had gone off the clock, and unlike the earlier reports, which had contended that Mr. Jensen spent his nights in a sleeping bag under his desk, I sensed that this new rumor was true.

* ★ *

We never saw Mr. Jensen again, but I continued to see Sylvia sometimes on our street.

She soon lost most of her students, and I worried for her. She looked cheerful enough from a distance, though, always waving to me from her driveway as she unloaded her car of canvas bags from the health food store or set out for a run, her red hair flying in the breeze behind her.

But I knew that her life during that time must have been complicated. After all, most everything ran on the clock. It wasn't just the schools but the doctors and the dentists and the mechanics, the grocery stores and the gyms, the restaurants and the movie theaters and the malls. Inevitably, Sylvia and the other real-timers must have arranged certain aspects of their lives around ours, or else they simply went without.

It must have grown harder for her with each passing week as the earth continued to slow and the days continued to expand.

13

In the first few weeks on clock time, sales of prescription sleeping pills spiked. The manufacturers of blackout curtains could not keep up with demand. Sleep masks went on backorder for months. There were runs on valerian root and other herbal sleep remedies. Some grocery stores sold out of chamomile tea.

Sales of alcohol and cigarettes also increased, and there is some evidence that clock time spelled big business for the harder drugs, too. Urban police departments reported steep rises in the price per ounce of anything capable of knocking a person out.

In some parts of the country, people took to sleeping in basements on the brightest of the white nights, but most houses in California were built without roots, leaving us trapped aboveground with the light.

Certain clock nights still coincided with the dark, but perfect alignment was rare. Whenever a lightless night did roll around, we slept as much as we could. But it was never enough. We were like wanderers in a desert, blessed with a rare downpour but unable to store the rain.

★　★　★

Sleep had never come easily to my mother. Insomnia ran in her blood. On clock time, she could rest only when it was truly dark. I used to hear her in the kitchen, late on luminous nights, the teakettle whistling, the muffled music of the television on low. Sometimes she scrubbed the bathrooms all night, and the smell of pine and bleach would seep under the door of my bedroom. I lay awake, too, on some of those evenings. A thin square of light glowed around the edges of the quilts we'd tacked over my bedroom windows. You could always tell when it was daylight outside. You just knew.

My father, on the other hand, slept fine. He bought my mother all kinds of gadgets for her troubles. A special device, part sunlamp, part alarm clock, was supposed to mimic the effect of sunset with the slow fade of its bulb. A brand-new sound machine on her bedside table emitted the soothing sounds of ocean waves and waterfalls, breezes rustling through trees.

Nothing worked for my mother.

I don't know how she stayed awake to teach her classes or lead the rehearsals of her students' production of *Macbeth*.

The skin beneath her eyes turned a shadowy gray. She cried over the tiniest things. 'I don't know why I'm crying,' she'd say as she mopped up a broken wineglass or nursed a stubbed toe. She would wipe her eyes with the backs of her wrists. 'I'm not really this upset.'

I caught her sobbing once in her bathroom, crouched over a bottle of liquid makeup that had cracked open on the white tile, its contents slowly bleeding across the floor. Her spine arched and shook as she wept. It was the twentieth hour of light.

★ ★ ★

Meanwhile, the birds continued to suffer. I never thought about how many had lived among us until they started dropping from the sky. Once, an entire flock of starlings lay down together to die in the street near our school. Traffic was rerouted while a special crew cleared the bodies away. The flies lingered for hours.

As we stepped off the school bus one dusky afternoon, we found a tiny sparrow, half dead, in the middle of the sidewalk. A few of us crouched around it as the bus pulled away. The bird was breathing but otherwise motionless.

I reached down and touched it on its back. I gave it the gentlest stroke. I could feel the shadows of the other kids standing near me, watching.

'Maybe it needs water,' said someone behind me. I was surprised to hear Seth Moreno's voice. He usually rode away on his skateboard as soon as he got off the bus. 'Does anyone have any water?' he asked.

'I do,' I said. I pulled from my bag a half-empty bottle. I was glad that I could supply in that moment the one thing that Seth wanted. Our fingers brushed as I handed him the bottle. He didn't seem to notice.

Trevor sacrificed his retainer case, and then Seth filled it with water for the bird.

We stared at the sparrow. We waited. It

continued to breathe, a rapid irregular shudder, but it made no move for the water. It made no move at all. The sun was setting behind us, and the orange light shone brightly on its feathers.

I watched Seth watching the bird. He was only a few feet away from me, but I sensed an enormous space between us. I could not guess what he was thinking.

Then Daryl suddenly rushed into the circle, the Ritalin in his veins perhaps unable to override his desires. He grabbed the little bird with his bare hands and spun away with it and ran.

'Daryl,' we all shouted. 'Leave it alone!'

Seth took off after him, sprinting toward the edge of the canyon.

The next thing happened quickly: Before Seth could catch up to him, Daryl snapped his arm back like a pitcher and threw the bird up into the sky and over the lip of the canyon.

This was a time in my life when things were happening every day that would have seemed impossible only the day before, and here was one more. I still remember the bird's long arc through the sky. I kept waiting for its wings to flap open and catch the wind. But it dropped to the floor of the canyon like a rock.

'Fuck you, Daryl,' shouted Seth.

'It was dying anyway,' said Daryl.

That's when Seth pulled Daryl's backpack right off of his shoulders and hurled it into the canyon in the same direction as the bird. We watched the backpack soar and then fall through the air, the straps flailing as it fell, just as we had watched the bird.

Daryl stood at the rim of the canyon, staring down.

I felt a swell of gratitude for Seth. I wanted to say something, but he jumped on his skateboard right away and zoomed off, leaning hard into the turn that took him out of my sight.

Soon the rest of us scattered, too. We were growing more accustomed every day to the small terrors of life. There was nothing to do but go home.

★　★　★

Around that same time, we heard that the cancer had spread to Seth's mother's bones, and Seth stopped coming to school. I heard she died at home in the middle of a long white night.

I composed a letter of sympathy on the inside of one of my mother's notecards, the front of which shimmered with van Gogh's *Starry Night*. I wanted to communicate something important and right. But I quickly crossed out everything I'd written and pulled a fresh card from the stationery box. This time I wrote a single sentence, just two words: *I'm sorry*. I signed my name and dropped it in the mail.

14

By the end of November, our days had stretched to forty hours.

Those were days of extremes. The sun blazed longer each time it came around, baking our street until it was too hot to cross barefoot. Earthworms sizzled on patios. Daisies wilted in their beds.

The periods of darkness, when they came, were just as sluggish as the daylight. The air turned cold during twenty hours of night, like the water at the bottom of a lake. All over California, grapes froze on the vine, orange groves withered in the dark, the flesh of avocados turned black from the frosts.

Dozens of experimental biospheres were commissioned for the cultivation of essential crops, and the seeds of a thousand fragile species were rushed to a seed bank in Norway.

Certain scientists struggled to predict the future rate of the slowing and to map its multiplying effects, while others argued that the rotation might still correct itself. But some were inclined not to forecast at all, likening this new science to the prediction of earthquakes or brain tumors.

'Will we end up like the birds?' posed one ancient climatologist, interviewed on the nightly news. His dark eyes were nested in thick folds of sun-spotted skin. 'Maybe we will,' he said. 'I just don't know.'

But adrenaline, like any other drug, wears off. Panic, like any other flood, must crest. Six or seven weeks after the slowing started, a certain boredom developed. The daily count of new minutes dropped off the front pages of the newspapers. And television reports on the subject became hardly distinguishable from the more ordinary bad news that streamed each night into our living rooms and went largely ignored.

*　*　*

The few people who had rejected clock time carried on, living like bean sprouts, reacting to sunlight when it appeared and going dormant whenever our patch of earth slipped into the dark. Already, these real-timers seemed very different from us, their customs incompatible with ours. They were widely regarded as freaks. We did not mix.

The handful who lived on our street were left off the guest list of that year's fall block party, held every year in the bulge of our cul-de-sac on the night before Thanksgiving. Orange flyers were left on every doorstep on the street but theirs.

Later that same week, one sunrise revealed a hundred strands of toilet paper tangled in the branches of Sylvia's olive tree. Tom and Carlotta's house had received the same treatment. I watched Sylvia from my bedroom as she carefully tore the paper from her rosebushes. She

131

rested for a moment, hands on hips, looking around from beneath the wide brim of a straw hat, as if the culprits might be lurking nearby. She retrieved a stepladder from her garage. But she could not reach every piece. For weeks, bits of shredded toilet paper remained lodged in the highest branches.

The Kaplan family was eventually outed. Off the clock for the sake of their Sabbath, which ran from sundown to sundown on every seventh day, they'd been keeping it secret from the neighborhood. Once the news was out, Beth, the oldest daughter, was never again asked to babysit the Swansons' toddler. We mingled with them even less than we had before.

I spent a lot of time watching Sylvia through my telescope during that time.

On white nights, I might see her watering her roses at midnight or dropping pasta into a pot at three A.M. Sometimes she went walking by herself in the silent middle of the night.

She seemed more isolated than the other real-timers did. She was always alone. Sometimes when I couldn't sleep, I'd watch her play piano through my telescope. I was sure I could detect in the slight slump of her shoulders as she played, and in the heavy way she held her head, a certain persistent sadness. She looked lonely through the lens of my telescope, like one of those faraway stars, still visible to our eyes but no longer really there. She looked lonelier even than I was.

★ ★ ★

Certain disasters evolved into attractions. My father and I sometimes drove down to the coast to look at what the ocean had done to the beachfront houses, evacuated since the slowing had mysteriously swelled the tides. At high tide, waves rolled across rooftops, the rooflines forming a geometric shoreline, while divers secretly scoured the insides for treasures. At low tide, those mansions dripped and creaked like sunken ships, exposed. They were magnificent houses, the homes of movie stars and millionaires. But the ocean had aged them at high speed. All the windows had blown out and would someday wash up in pieces on the sand, bits of smooth sea glass mixing with the shells.

The beaches had been closed since the start of the slowing. But my father liked to explore at low tide.

'Come on,' he said one Sunday when I hesitated in the driveway of an abandoned Cape Cod. Dozens of yards of police tape flapped in the wind. No one else was around. Even the seagulls were gone, the sickness having swept them all away.

The house was enormous. Its shingles were warped from the water, and the front door was missing. Most of the contents had been flushed out by the waves. Everything inside was gray. One whole wall was missing; the living room faced out to the sea like an open garage.

'Look at these,' said my father. He had crouched down on the soggy carpet to watch sand crabs burrow into the mud that had collected there. 'Want to hold one?'

He looked like a clamdigger, his pants rolled up to his knees.

'No, thanks,' I said.

An extreme low tide had pulled the water hundreds of feet out from the beach that morning, but I could tell it was on its way back. Small waves were beginning to lap at what was left of the back porch.

'The tide's coming in,' I said.

'We have time,' said my father. 'Come on.'

There was plenty of life left in that house. Starfish clung to the granite countertops, and sea anemones lived in the sinks.

'Watch your step,' said my father as we headed down a hall.

The floors were littered with driftwood and seaweed and glass.

'I was in this house once, years ago,' said my father. He was squinting in the sunlight. I had noticed only recently how many wrinkles formed around his eyes when he smiled. 'I came to a Christmas party here once with an old girlfriend. This was her parents' house.'

A foamy surge of water rushed into the room. We were instantly ankle-deep. My sandals felt heavy under the weight of the cold water.

'Dad, please,' I said, looking back down the hall. A layer of white water swirled over the hardwood floor. Two teenagers had recently drowned in just this way in one of the old houses farther up the coast. 'Can we go now?'

'There was a huge Christmas tree right here,' said my father, motioning with two hands to indicate the width. He was almost yelling to be heard above the sound of the water. 'And a grand piano over there. We almost got married, that girl and I. This was before I met your mother, of course.'

The water was getting higher with each new surge. A small plastic bottle was adrift in the room.

'Dad,' I said. 'Seriously.'

'You'll see when you're older,' he said. 'You won't believe how quickly the years will pass. I feel like I was just here, but it's been twenty years.'

The tide had risen to my calves. I felt the strong pull of the water against my skin, and it scared me.

'Can we please go now?' I said.

'Okay,' he said. 'All right. Let's go.'

We waded together back through the house and out to the driveway. My father spotted a seagull as we climbed back up to the road.

'Look,' he said, squinting. I hadn't seen a live one in weeks. It did seem amazing, in that moment, that there had ever existed a creature with the power to fly.

My jeans were sticking to my thighs. The whole car stank of salt water.

'You used to be much braver, you know,' said my father as he started the engine. 'You really did. You're getting to be as bad as your mother.'

And he was right: I had grown into a worrier, a girl on constant guard for catastrophes large and small, for the disappointments I now sensed were hidden all around us right in plain sight.

135

15

It happened in the dark: the sweep of the headlights, the quick closing of car doors, the red lights flashing noiselessly at the end of the street.

From my window, I watched three police cars park in a crooked row outside Tom and Carlotta's house. My first worry, for some reason, was murder. Through my telescope, I spotted Gabby's mother in a pantsuit, arms crossed and face lit red by the lights, as she stood at the end of her driveway and peered at the house next door. I knelt on the carpet and waited. Minutes passed. It was four in the afternoon clock time, but it was the middle of the natural night. The sky was black and clear, the moon its slimmest, most delicate self. The crickets buzzed, a dog barked, a breeze rustled the eucalyptus trees.

Finally, a woman in white emerged from the house, ghostlike: Carlotta in a nightgown, her long gray hair hanging loose on her shoulders. I could see one of the officers walking beside her, his arm resting on hers. Tom shuffled behind them, his white hair disheveled from sleep.

Both husband and wife had been handcuffed.

Only later were the details of the crime revealed to the neighborhood. A police team spent three hours the next day carting dozens of potted plants out of Tom and Carlotta's ranch-style and into a giant white truck. The

136

plants were leafy and green, supernaturally healthy. They'd lived their whole lives inside, nurtured by sunlamps, which, we later learned, were powered by the solar panels that glittered on the slopes of the roof. Police officers trudged back and forth across the lawn, packing up whatever they could, even scooping the compost pile into three fat black sacks. When the work was done, I noticed that the small sign in the front yard had been uprooted and was now directing its message to the sky: THIS HOUSE LIVES ON REAL TIME.

According to a rumor that circulated after the arrests, Tom and Carlotta had been growing marijuana undetected for years, but the police had only recently received an anonymous tip from a neighbor. You had to wonder about the timing and whether the caller was motivated, at least in part, by a certain other life choice that Tom and Carlotta had made. There was no way around it: The real-timers made the rest of us uncomfortable. They too often slept while the rest of us worked. They went out when everyone else was asleep. They were a threat to the social order, some said, the first small crumbles of a coming disintegration.

I worried more and more about Sylvia.

Meanwhile, a trickle of real-timers had begun to leave the cities and the suburbs. They were turning up en masse in makeshift communities in the deserts and woodlands of this country. In those early days, they were a tiny, loosely organized minority, a scattering of shadow societies, the earliest advocates of a movement.

16

By early December, three weeks before Christmas, the days had swelled to forty-two hours. Changes had been detected in the currents of the oceans. Glaciers were melting even faster than before. Certain long-dormant volcanoes had begun to bubble and steam. There were reports that migratory whales were failing to migrate, remaining instead in chilly northern waters. A few fringe experts gave us only a few months to live, but they were roundly dismissed as extremists — as if nothing so extreme could possibly be true.

Meanwhile, colored Christmas lights blinked as usual from the rooflines in our neighborhood, and Mr. Valencia installed on his front lawn the same life-size animatronic manger scene he set up every year. Forests of Christmas trees bloomed at the fairgrounds and in the grocery store parking lots. All the usual carols wafted through the aisles of the drugstores and the malls amid concerns about the health of the holiday shopping season.

My mother and I spent one whole afternoon baking sugar cookies in Christmas shapes.

'It feels good to do something normal,' she said as she flattened the dough with a thick rolling pin. A strand of dark hair kept swimming out from behind her ear. I was glad that her hair was its usual shade again. She'd finally dyed away all the gray.

The Christmas season had turned my mother cheerful. But I felt there was something excessive about her interest that year in the choosing of the ideal noble fir, in the draping of tinsel and the wrapping of presents, the daily marking of the advent calendar. There hummed beneath her good cheer an undercurrent of dread, as if we were conducting each of our annual rituals for the very last time. I sensed it in her constant smoothing of the dining table's holiday runner, in her glue-gun repair job of a porcelain Santa Claus cookie jar that had lain broken in the closet for years. It was in the way she crouched low on the FoodPlus linoleum as she searched a bottom shelf for the silver sprinkles we used every year but which FoodPlus no longer carried.

'Things change,' she said. 'But not everything has to.'

When the last batch of cookies came out of the oven, we filled one whole tin for my grandfather and then divided up the rest for teachers and friends.

'Let's bring some to Sylvia, too,' I said, leaning on the counter while a buttery scrap of dough dissolved in my mouth. The last batch of stars lay cooling on a rack.

'I don't think so,' said my mother. She was wrapping each bundle of cookies in green and red cellophane, her fingers working gingerly to preserve the frosting.

'Why not?' I asked.

'It's not a good idea.'

Both cats appeared at the kitchen door and began to scratch furiously on the glass. They had a taste for sweet things, so they were not allowed inside until the mixing bowls had been washed, the cookie cutters cleaned, the pastry bag emptied and put away.

'But why?' I asked again.

'We didn't make enough cookies to give them out to everyone we've ever met.'

My mother had never forbidden me to talk to Sylvia or the other real-timers. It was never explicitly said. But it didn't need to be said. I understood well that I was supposed to keep my distance from them, from Sylvia especially. And mostly, that's exactly what I did.

But I felt sorry for Sylvia, so later that day, when the oven was off and the kitchen cleaned and my mother asleep on the couch, I collected a handful of cookies from our pantry, tied them with red ribbon, and left the house.

I waited a long time on Sylvia's doorstep before the knob turned and the door swung open, revealing a sleepy Sylvia in a purple silk robe, looking ballerina-thin as she leaned against the doorframe, her hair pulled back in a loose red bun. It was nearly my dinnertime, but the sun was high in the sky — late morning in the natural day.

'Merry Christmas,' I said, and handed her the cookies.

'That's very kind, Julia,' she said in a voice I wasn't used to, a heavy, low-pitched scratch. 'Excuse me,' she said, and then she spent a long time clearing her throat. 'Sorry. I haven't talked to anyone yet today.'

To me, this was more proof of how alone she was, as if, when too long isolated from other human beings, a person risked losing not only the need to speak but also the ability.

It seemed to me that even her movements, like her days, had turned slow, the unhurried raising of a wrist to brush away a wisp of hair, or the measured turn of her head when she nodded. I realized I was living almost two days for every one of hers. Eventually, if she went on like this, Sylvia would fall months behind us, then years.

I glanced over Sylvia's shoulder and into her house. 'Don't you have a Christmas tree?' I asked.

'Oh,' she said. 'I didn't feel like dealing with all that this year.'

Her wind chimes, made of seashells, rattled softly above my head.

'Thanks again,' she said, closing the door. 'Take care, Julia.'

★   ★   ★

A few days later, a delivery truck pulled up to Sylvia's house. Two young men in thick green gloves threw open the back door to reveal a Christmas tree, which they gingerly rolled down the ramp. It was the living kind. It came in a terracotta pot and was meant to be planted in the yard after Christmas. Sylvia lugged the tree into her house by herself. She set it up in her living room window and left it there, unlit and undecorated. But it seemed better than nothing.

Her house looked a little less sad.

That same day Tom and Carlotta returned home, released on bail. They were awaiting trial.

'How long do you think they'll be in jail?' I asked my parents that night. My grandfather had come over for dinner.

'It depends,' said my mother. 'Probably a long time.'

'What did they do?' asked my grandfather. He took a shaky sip of milk.

'They should have left those poor people alone,' said my father. It was his day off from work, but he was dressed nicely: clean-shaven, with a collared shirt.

'I still don't know what they did,' said my grandfather, talking louder than before. He took a big bite of salmon and looked at me for an answer as he chewed. 'Julia, do you know?'

'Drugs, Gene,' said my mother. 'They were growing drugs.'

My grandfather coughed and spit something into his napkin. Then he held a tiny bone, slim as filament, up to the light.

'Who were they harming?' asked my father.

'You didn't see how much pot they pulled out of that house,' said my mother. She was looking at me. 'It *is* illegal.'

My father shoveled the rest of his salmon into his mouth without looking up. My mother poured herself a glass of red wine. Our Christmas tree twinkled nearby, and in the silence that followed, I could hear the inner workings of those lights, a tiny, metallic clicking.

After he drove my grandfather home, my

father was called unexpectedly into work. There was a tricky delivery and the hospital was short-staffed.

My mother and I sat on the couch for a while watching a television show about one of the last uncontacted tribes of the Amazon. They had recently surrendered themselves to Brazilian authorities at the edge of the rain forest, convinced that the Brazilians held not only the power of flight — for decades, airplanes had cut across the tribe's sky — but now also held dominion over the sun and the moon as well.

My mother shifted under her blankets. It was a dark night. The house was cold.

'I think you and I should talk more,' she said.

I stiffened in my seat.

'What do you mean?' I said.

She pointed the remote at the television, and the volume slipped away.

'What about boys?' she said.

'What?' I said.

She looked over at me, and I looked away. A cinnamon Christmas candle flickered on the coffee table, and I kept my eye on the flame.

'I never hear you talk about the boys at school.'

'Why would I talk about them?' I said.

I hadn't seen Seth Moreno in a while, and I worried he might be gone for good. Michaela had heard that he and his father had moved to a real-time colony after his mother died.

'Do you ever talk to boys?'

'Mom,' I said. 'You're being weird.'

'Are you interested in any of them?' she pressed.

People were doing crazy things all over the world. Everyone was taking new chances, big risks. But not me. I kept quiet. I held my secrets tight.

'I'm really tired,' I said. 'I'm going to bed.'

'Wait,' said my mother. 'Stay down here with me a little while longer. We can talk about something else.' She paused. 'Please?'

I could no longer remember the way my mother's eyes had looked before the slowing. Had they always been so red around the edges? Surely, those pockets of gray beneath her lower lashes were new. She still wasn't sleeping well, but perhaps what I was seeing was just age, a gradual shift that I'd failed to register. I sometimes felt the urge to study recent photographs of her in order to locate the exact point in time when she had come to look so weary.

Some of the real-timers insisted that time had begun to affect them differently than it did the rest of us, that bodies aged less rapidly on real time than on the clock. The idea was taking root in Hollywood, an anti-aging measure known in that world as the Slow Time Cure. It had something to do with metabolism. I sometimes wondered back then if it would work for my mother.

Later, when I finally did go upstairs to my bedroom and looked out my window, I was glad to discover that Sylvia had decorated her Christmas tree. Dozens of tiny white lights were

144

shimmering from its branches.

Sylvia's curtains were closed except for a sliver. With my telescope, I could see through the crack that she was in there. She was a swishing skirt, an open mouth, a streak of strawberry hair gliding past the window. For once she was not alone: A man's arm swung quickly into view, his sleeve rolled up to the elbow. I watched as he lowered a glittery silver star onto the top of the tree.

The man curled his arm around Sylvia's slim waist. They kissed a quick kiss. I was relieved to see her smile.

Outside, Sylvia's car sat alone in the driveway, as if this man had come from nowhere, simply appeared in her living room by some magical means.

I watched for a moment longer.

And then it happened: I realized as he turned that I knew that man's mouth. I knew the sharp slope of his jaw, the long angle of his hairline. I recognized that blue shirt — I remembered exactly how it had looked when it was brand-new, on Father's Day at the steak house, the shirt starched flat and folded in a silver department-store box, topped with a purple card, handmade by me.

17

Five thousand years of art and superstition would suggest that it's the darkness that haunts us most, that the night is when the human mind is most apt to be disturbed. But dozens of experiments conducted in the aftermath of the slowing revealed that it was not the darkness that tampered most with our moods — it was the light.

As the days stretched further, we faced a new phenomenon: Certain clock days began and ended before the sun ever rose — or else began and ended before the sun ever set.

Scientists had long been aware of the negative effects of prolonged daylight on human brain chemistry. Rates of suicide, for example, had always been highest above the Arctic Circle, where self-inflicted gunshot wounds surged every summer, the continuous daylight driving some people mad.

As our days neared forty-eight hours, those of us living in the lower latitudes began to suffer similarly from the relentlessness of light.

Studies soon documented an increase in impulsiveness during the long daylight periods. It had something to do with serotonin; we were all a little crazed. Online gambling increased steadily throughout every stretch of daylight, and there is some evidence that major stock trades were made more often on light days than on dark

146

ones. Rates of murder and other violent crimes also spiked while the sun was in our hemisphere — we discovered very quickly the dangers of the white nights.

We took more risks. Desires were less checked. Temptation was harder to resist. Some of us made decisions we might not otherwise have made.

I like to think that this is how it started between my father and Sylvia. I picture my father arriving home from the hospital after midnight, as he often did, on some long white night, and finding Sylvia pruning her garden in a sun hat or reading a book in the grass while the rest of us tried to sleep. Maybe she waved to my father as he stepped from his car. Maybe they talked for a while. Maybe there were dozens of nights like this, the two of them squinting in the sun while all the curtains on the street were closed for the night. Maybe, in that excessive daylight, they both felt more reckless than usual, a little less likely to think before they acted.

But here's where my mother would interrupt me. 'You can't blame everything on the slowing,' she'd say. 'People are responsible for their own actions.'

*　★　★*

The next morning my father walked in through our front door as if he were the same man I had always known. I was sitting at the table, a bowl of yogurt in front of me. My mother was pouring coffee. I had not told her what I knew. I didn't tell anyone at first.

'Morning,' he said. It was dark outside. The cold rushed in behind him. He wiped his feet on the mat. He hung his keys on the hook in the kitchen. He kissed my mother on the cheek, and he touched me on the back of the head. 'Ready for your math test?'

'That was yesterday,' I said.

I swirled my yogurt back and forth around the bowl. I couldn't eat.

'That's right,' he said. 'Sorry. I lost track.'

I hated him right then, sweeping into our house in his white lab coat as if he hadn't thrown it on only moments before opening the door.

'How was work?' asked my mother. She looked old, sitting at the table in her bathrobe, no makeup. I felt bad for her.

'Fine,' he said. He leaned against the wall. He peeled an orange with his thumb. That was the worst part: He seemed relaxed.

'I'm exhausted,' he said. 'I need to get some sleep.'

He walked slowly up the stairs, eating the orange as he went, spitting seeds in the cupped palm of one hand. I heard the bedroom door close behind him, leaving me alone again with my mother.

For days afterward, a series of magical thoughts flew through my mind. For instance, it seemed somehow surprising that the hours continued to pass in spite of what I knew. It was almost shocking that time did not, in fact, stop. Instead, our lives carried on. My father came and went. Our hearts kept beating. I went to school as usual, hoping every day that Seth Moreno would return. We celebrated Christmas, and the world continued spinning.

⋆ ⋆ ⋆

Six days passed: New Year's Eve.

I've never understood why the slowing didn't affect the orbit of the earth right away, or why, on the last day of that first year, we found ourselves at roughly the same position in the solar system as we had the previous year on that day. The earth made its usual swing around the sun, its 400 billionth loop, one of the very few things that year to actually remain on course.

On New Year's Eve, the sun rose at three A.M. in California, and we were still squinting seventeen hours later at eight o'clock that night when my mother turned the key in the ignition and backed the car out of the driveway. We were headed for my grandfather's house, where I would spend the night so that my parents could attend a New Year's Eve party worry-free.

'I could've stayed home alone,' I said. A purple duffel bag slouched and settled on my lap.

'We already talked about this,' said my mother. 'It would have been different if you had somewhere to go.'

'I could have gone to Michaela's,' I said.

'You know you can't go to houses where the parents aren't going to be home.'

Michaela hadn't exactly invited me, anyway. 'You can come if you want,' she'd said the day

149

before at soccer practice.

We drove east from the coast on the old two-lane road beneath a wide and blazing sky. My father was at work — or so he said — but he planned to meet my mother at the party. We were driving a silver station wagon, although the police report would later describe it as blue.

'What's your New Year's resolution?' my mother asked me as we passed the racetrack. We had clinked glasses in the kitchen before we left: sparkling apple cider in mine, champagne in hers.

'No one keeps their New Year's resolutions,' I said.

Outside, the lagoon zoomed by.

'You sound like your father.'

She was chatty and flushed in a black strapless dress. She'd been losing weight since the slowing, and she had squeezed herself into one of the dresses she'd been keeping unworn for years.

'Why are you so grumpy?' she said.

I'd been avoiding my father all week. It felt hazardous to say his name, as if just the crispness of the two *D*'s in *Dad* might somehow transmit to my mother my anger, or somehow reveal what I had seen.

'One of my resolutions is to worry less,' she said. She glanced at her reflection in the rearview mirror. She smoothed one brow with the tip of a finger. 'And to live more in the moment.'

We passed a large white house on a hill where someone else's party guests were sliding out of clean, expensive cars. Two men in tuxedos strode through the front door as we idled at a stoplight, and a young blonde in a gold cocktail dress glittered as she smoked in the yard, stilettos sinking in the lawn.

A car honked behind us. The light had turned green. My mother hadn't slept since sunrise the night before, and as has been well documented, long stretches of daylight can dull a person's reflexes. Some studies have shown the impairment to be roughly equivalent to the effect of two drinks.

'But here's my main resolution,' she said as she pressed the gas pedal. 'Are you listening?'

I nodded.

'I'm going to start acting again.'

At the bend in the road, we flew past the reservoir, which for weeks had been clogged with dead birds. The water level was lower than usual, too. Some people were blaming the slowing for the lack of rain and for the way the banks of the reservoir lay exposed, the layers of black mud revealed — and somehow unseemly — and also the tangled roots of the nearby trees, unaccustomed to life out of water.

'I'm serious,' she said. Her crystal earrings swayed through the air as she turned to me. 'I called my old agent and everything.'

Her bare shoulders shimmered slightly in the light from a new bronzing powder she'd dusted on her skin. A speck of mauve lipstick flashed from one of her front teeth as she smiled.

That was when it occurred to me: Maybe she already knew about Sylvia.

We drove for a few minutes more. My mother

quieted. The road narrowed. The sun shone in our eyes. I remember the trees whipping past us outside, the branches black against a bright blue sky.

She would later describe the feeling as a kind of wooziness, a narrowing of her field of vision, but she said very little as it happened. She rubbed her forehead. She blinked a hard blink.

'I don't feel so well,' she said.

It was just a moment later that I lost her. I'd never seen anyone faint before. I remember the sudden slackening of her body, the rolling of her head, the way her hands fell from the steering wheel. It was later estimated that we were traveling at forty-five miles per hour.

★   ★   ★

Eyewitnesses reported seeing a bearded man, dressed in robes, howling Scripture on the side of the road. According to their accounts, a station wagon approached from the west at approximately 8:25 P.M. Opinions varied about the speed of the vehicle at the time of impact, but all agreed about the way the man lunged into the path of the car, bent on suicide or miracle. At least six other cars had swerved successfully around him. Ours was the seventh.

I saw him only briefly, and I was at the same time reaching for the steering wheel, which was suddenly free of my mother's grip, so I can't be sure I'm remembering properly, but they do say that time slows in times of danger — you see more. Anyway, this is what I remember: the look in the man's eyes at the moment when his expression shifted from a kind of certainty to fear, and then the animal flinch. He turned and curled his arms around his head at the last moment.

I remember the hollow thud on the hood and then the screeching of tires as my mother came to and hit the brakes — she was out for less than ten seconds — and the life rushed back into her face. My seat belt jerked. The car heaved. We stopped. I felt a breeze hit my cheeks and the accompanying stink of fertilizer from the nearby polo fields. The windshield had been rendered open air. A spindly curtain of safety glass hung shattered from the frame. But none of the blood that spilled elsewhere had left its mark on the glass.

My mother was breathing hard. Someone was moaning. Sequins of glass flickered on my jeans.

'You okay?' said my mother. She grabbed my shoulders with both hands. A narrow stream of blood was running along her hairline and pooling in her ear.

'Are you okay?' I said.

'What happened?' she asked.

Two surfers hopped out of a nearby VW van, sandals slapping the pavement, wet suits peeled down to their waists. They sprinted past our car to a spot of road just ahead of us, where they crouched low and conferred. Behind them, a jogger began directing traffic.

Sirens screamed in the distance.

My mother leaned out her window toward where the surfers were squatting and to where

153

the jogger kept glancing back. 'Oh God,' she said. She cupped one hand over her mouth but kept talking. 'Oh God,' she said through her fingers. 'Oh God.'

The surfers were partly blocking my view of the man's face, but I could see his lower half, his legs splayed, his hands, palms up, his whole body absolutely still. And I remember this, too: One knee was folded the wrong way.

I made a resolution right then, or something simpler, a prayer — *If this man lives, I will never complain about anything ever again.*

A scattering of orange flyers wafted up from the ground beside him, fluttering away like dandelion seeds. One flew into our car through the open windshield and landed on my lap. It was a Xerox of a Xerox of a handwritten note: *Attention all sinners. The trumpets are sounding, and the end is here. Repent or face the wrath of God.*

Two police cars and a fire truck swung around the corner and stopped on the side of the road. Two ambulances appeared, lights blinking. A rush of tears blurred my view. Here were strangers speeding to a stranger's aid.

According to the police report, the man was taken to St. Anthony's Hospital, two miles from the scene of the crash. Later that night, fourteen members of a suicide cult would pass through those same emergency room doors on fourteen separate stretchers, unconscious and breathing shallowly, their fingernails already turning blue from the arsenic swimming in their veins. Convinced the world was ending, they'd poisoned their wineglasses at the stroke of midnight. While others kissed and drank champagne, these fourteen would die to the chords of 'Auld Lang Syne.'

In the back of a parked ambulance, a young paramedic cleaned my mother's cut, then read her pupils for signs of concussion. A police-woman with a spiral notepad asked questions.

'How fast would you estimate you were going?'

'Is he dead?' my mother asked. She kept looking around. Orange cones had sprouted from the asphalt. A string of yellow caution tape flapped in the breeze. Our car remained frozen in its lane, its mirrors glinting in the sunshine.

'They're working on him,' said the police-woman. 'Forty miles an hour? Thirty?'

'But is he going to die?' My mother's dress kept slipping lower on her chest. A dark bruise was forming on her forehead near the cut. She had hit her head on the steering wheel. 'Was he conscious?' she asked.

'They're doing everything they can, ma'am.'

Years later, I heard the following statistic: Before the slowing, a pedestrian struck by a vehicle at a speed of forty miles per hour had a one-in-ten chance of surviving the impact. After the slowing, the survival rate dropped by half. It wasn't only baseballs that fell faster and harder after the slowing. Every body in motion was pulled more forcefully to the ground.

Eventually, my mother was taken to the hospital for tests. The paramedics suspected a concussion. I, unharmed, waited in the back of a police car for my father.

Meanwhile, our skid marks were measured. A tow truck arrived. Someone swept up the glass. The breeze became a wind, and the eucalyptus trees that fringed the road on either side began to whip around in the air, revealing, as they swayed, a crisp sliver of white moon hanging low on the bright horizon.

The sky was still blue and the sun still high when my father opened the police car door. 'You didn't hit your head, did you?' he asked.

'No,' I said. I imagined he'd come from Sylvia's. I sensed the rushed goodbye on her porch, a quick kiss in the entry hall, Sylvia pulling her hair into a bun as she waved. That was how I imagined these things went. In fact, I knew nothing about it. Perhaps he really had come from work.

'No dizziness?' he said.

I shook my head.

He studied one of my eyes and then the other, and I studied him, too: for evidence. But his collar was straight and his gray tie tied tight. His hospital badge clung neatly to his front pocket.

'Let's go,' he said, taking my hand in his.

⋆　⋆　⋆

My grandfather was in the midst of some kind of project when we arrived. Every cupboard was open, the insides bare. The shelves had been cleared of heirlooms, the mantels stripped of knickknacks. The pantry had been hollowed out, and the kitchen drawers hung open, drooping

156

toward the linoleum.

'That was quick,' said my grandfather when he saw me. The screen door bounced on the frame behind me. He turned the bolt hard in its lock. I'd never seen him lock that door before. 'You okay?'

'I guess so,' I said.

Outside, my father's tires ground the gravel of the driveway. He was headed to the hospital to be with my mother.

'Not a scratch on you,' said my grandfather. His hair, milky white, was sticking up like tufts of weeds, and he was wearing what he called his work clothes: faded denim overalls and a green flannel shirt. 'If you're hungry, I'll make you some tuna fish.'

It was still bright outside, but my grandfather's house was dark. The curtains were closed, the interior dimly lit by a few yellow lamps.

My grandfather shuffled through the gloom and into the dining room, where the contents of the whole house had been spread out on every flat surface. The dark top of the dining table was arrayed with treasures laid out in rows, as if for sale. A line of cardboard packing boxes waited on the floor, half full.

'Are you going somewhere?' I asked.

He'd taken a seat at the table and was leafing through a stack of antique postcards.

'Am I going somewhere?' he said. He looked at me, his eyes faint and watery, a disappearing blue. 'Where would I go?'

On the table stood his collections of ancient Coke bottles, sea glass, and sand dollars. My grandmother's silver tea service, dull from lack of polish, was ringed by a team of dusty porcelain figurines, beside which lay a decorative knife from Alaska, its handle carved from the ivory tusk of a whale. At the far end of the table, towers of limited-edition coins shimmered in their cases, each one packed in plastic, never circulated.

'Then what are you doing?' I asked.

He pressed a magnifying glass hard on the bottom of a faded postcard. His eyes had been clouding over for years, leaving him with a patchwork kind of vision.

'Do me a favor,' he said, tapping the card with a thick index finger. 'Tell me what that says.'

The photograph had been artificially colorized, the hillsides painted green, the rooftops an unrealistic red.

' 'Childer, Alaska,' ' I read out. ' 'Nineteen fifty-six.' '

'See this hill here?' he said, tracing a bulge of earth that loomed above a cluster of houses and steeples. 'A year later, this whole ridge came sliding down in a storm.'

In some distant corner of the neighborhood, firecrackers began to whistle and pop — it was New Year's Eve, after all. Daylight was radiating beneath the hems of the curtains. In here, the air smelled like dust and Listerine.

'I was at a wedding when it happened,' he continued. 'Twenty-three people were buried alive.'

Of my grandfather's eighty-six years on the planet, he had lived two of them in Alaska,

158

working in gold mines and, later, on various fishing boats. But those two years had expanded, spongelike, in his memory, overtaking much of the rest. Whole decades had passed in California without producing a single worthy anecdote.

'I was lucky,' he said. 'I was in the very back of the church. But the bride and the groom and their parents, the bride's brothers and sisters, and the minister: all swallowed up.'

He shook his head. A slight whistling sound passed from his lips.

'Boy,' he said.

He brushed the card with the tip of a finger. 'And see this house here?' he said. 'The groom's brother worked on a salmon boat, and it was salmon season, so he missed the wedding. He was the only one left in his family. Afterward, he hanged himself in that house right there.'

My chair creaked beneath me. I could hear the ticking of his clocks; he had a whole collection, all antique, including two as tall as he was, which clanged every hour and always out of sync.

'It seems like a lot of bad things happened while you were in Alaska,' I said.

He laughed and rubbed the pink creases of his forehead. 'I wouldn't say that,' he said. 'Not any more than anywhere else.'

He turned the card over in his hand. The back was blank, except for a bright red smudge in one corner.

'Are you bleeding?' I asked. It scared me how easily he bled.

He studied his fingers. 'Dammit,' he said. He stood slowly and trudged to the kitchen.

His skin had grown thin in recent years, his blood slow to clot. A paper cut could flow for many minutes. While he ran his finger under cold water, I explored the boxes that littered the dining room floor. Inside were albums of black-and-white photographs of my grandparents in stylish hats and fur-lined coats, of my father as a toddler and then in a baseball uniform leaning on a bicycle near an enormous rounded fender. There was a whole album of me, his only grandchild, from the day I was born up to my most recent school picture, in which my eyes were half closed, on the verge of a blink, rendering moot all the time I had spent selecting the cream-colored mohair sweater I wore on picture day.

Then there was this: In a dusty shoe box, I found four thick sticks of solid gold, packed together like chocolate bars.

'Hey,' said my grandfather. A crooked Band-Aid crowned his thumb. 'You shouldn't have gotten into those.'

I had pried one bar from the box. It was cold and heavy in my hand. He took it from me and laid it with the others.

'But since you did, I'll tell you something you should remember.' He dropped the lid on the box and slid it into a corner. 'Gold is the safest thing there is. It's better than dollars, better than banks.'

I sensed the sun was finally setting behind the curtains. A pinkish sunset glow was leaking in through the cracks. The darkness would last until at least the following evening.

'This thing is real, you know,' said my grandfather. 'I didn't believe it at first. But this thing is really happening.'

In other houses, I imagined, corks were popping, glasses fizzing, party hats landing on heads. I'd heard that Hanna had gone to Palm Springs with Tracey's family. I wondered what Seth Moreno was doing right at that moment.

'And no one's paying attention,' my grandfather went on. 'They put us back on the clock, and they think that solves the problem, but no one's doing a goddamn thing to prepare for what's coming.'

He sighed heavily and stood up from his chair.

'Think of the birds,' he said. 'Birds have always been messengers. After the flood, it was a dove holding an olive branch that told Noah the flood was over. That's how he knew he could leave the ark. Think about that. Our birds aren't carrying any olive branches. Our birds are dying.'

He had turned his attention to the old hunting rifle he kept in the hall closet. It was coated in dust, which he brushed away with the back of his hand. He hadn't used it in years.

'Next time you're over here, remind me to show you how to shoot a gun.'

'A gun, Grandpa?' I said.

'I'm serious,' he said. 'This is serious. I'm worried for all of us.'

Later, on his bulky television, I watched recordings of the earlier fireworks in Tokyo, Nairobi, and London, as the New Year drifted westward across the planet.

There had been some debate about the

timing. Technically, we were running a day behind, thanks to the weeks we had spent living off the clocks. But a quick solution had been crafted and agreed to by most of the world's governments: We had simply skipped December 30, an extra onetime leap, to make up for lost time.

Between firework shows, the television news reported that certain religious leaders had gathered their flocks inside churches, fearing or hoping that the last day of the year of the slowing might also mark the passing away of this world.

I fell asleep in an armchair before midnight. I dreamed of blood and broken glass, a car lurching to a stop. Hours later, I woke up, awash in the blue light of the television, my teeth clenched, my neck stiff from the armrest. The sun had sunk at last, and my grandfather had gone to bed. The year had turned while I slept. A new one had begun in the dark. Anything seemed possible in those days. Any prediction could turn out to be true. It bothered me in a fresh way: not knowing what the next year would bring.

* * *

In the morning my parents picked me up on the way home from the hospital. There was no news of the pedestrian.

My mother was still wearing her black party dress, now wrinkled. She held her crystal earrings in her palm. A hospital ID bracelet dangled from one wrist. My father gently guided her into our house as if she were blindfolded, flipping light switches with one hand and cupping the small of her back with the other.

The bruise would fade. The cut would heal. Every bone in her body was intact. With the help of an MRI, the doctors had searched her brain for hidden damage and found none. But that machine could not, of course, search her mind. And at that time, almost nothing was known about the syndrome.

18

We called it gravity sickness at first, the slowing syndrome later, and there would come a time eventually when you need only mention *the syndrome* and everyone understood what you meant. The symptoms were wide-ranging but related: dizziness, nausea, insomnia, fatigue, and sometimes, as was the case with my mother, fainting.

Only certain people were affected. A man might stumble in the street. A woman might collapse in a mall. In some small children, the effects included the excessive bleeding of gums. Some victims were too weak to leave their beds for days. The exact cause was unknown.

My mother stayed home from work that first week after the accident. She spent her days hunting for news of the pedestrian while the cut on her forehead scabbed over and began to scar. Her dizziness came and went. She moved slowly through the house, always bracing herself on a banister or a wall. Whenever the feeling cleared, she focused her attention on the pedestrian. She called the hospital but was given no information. She sent flowers: *To the man who was hit by a car on Samson Road on New Year's Eve.* She begged my father to find out if the man had lived or died, but he was reluctant for us to get involved. 'We'll find out eventually,' he said.

She slept even less than before, wakeful just as

often on the dark nights as the light ones. I would wake some nights in the pitch black and find her searching obscure local websites and police blogs, her eyes red and watery, the white light of the screen throwing her features into unflattering relief. On one of these nights, she fainted again. She fell right off her chair, bit her tongue, and made it bleed.

She stopped driving. She ate less and less.

I wondered what the symptoms were that had preceded Seth Moreno's mother's death. The illnesses were different, I knew, but I sometimes worried that the outcome could be the same. No one knew where the slowing syndrome might lead.

★　★　★

It was a bright clear morning the day Seth Moreno came back to school.

His dark hair had grown a little longer, and he'd developed a new habit of flicking his bangs away from his eyes with one thumb, but he looked otherwise the same, same tired look on his face, same slow gait, same skateboard tucked under one arm. I hadn't seen him since his mother died.

I felt my face flush when he showed up at the bus stop that morning. I wondered what he thought about my card.

Various rumors of Seth's whereabouts since his mother died had trickled down to me: He was staying with a relative in Arizona, or he'd moved to a real-timers' settlement in Oregon or

165

to a boarding school in France.

But here he was at the bus stop. He didn't speak to anyone that morning. He just stood by himself, like always. I wanted to talk to him, but I didn't. I wanted to be near him, but I stayed away.

In math, I went back to staring silently at the back of Seth Moreno's head.

★　★　★

Meanwhile, the oceans were shifting, the Gulf Stream was slowing, and Gabby shaved her head.

She called me over to her house one afternoon. The sun had set. The sky had turned black and clear. On the way to her house, I passed a group of younger kids playing Ghosts in the Graveyard on the street, some crouching behind parked cars or tree trunks while others searched in pairs, clinging to each other's sleeves and whispering as they moved through the shadows.

'Watch this,' said Gabby.

We were in her bedroom. She held a thick section of her dyed black hair out from her head and raised a pair of scissors to the root.

'You're cutting it yourself?' I said.

Downstairs, a construction crew pounded on a wall. They were remodeling the kitchen. Gabby's parents were at work.

'First I'm cutting it all off,' she said, and snapped the scissors shut. 'And then I'm shaving it.'

The hair fell from the blade and landed soundlessly on the carpet.

'But why?' I said. She cut another section. 'It's going to take forever to grow back.'

On the dresser, Gabby's cell phone rattled with a message. She looked at the screen and grinned. Then she dropped the scissors on the desk and locked the bedroom door.

'I have a secret to tell you,' she said. 'You have to promise not to tell anyone.'

I promised.

'You know that guy I met online?'

I nodded. The headlights of a passing car washed over the room and vanished.

'We've been talking every day,' she added.

I felt a stab of jealousy.

The boy was older: sixteen. He lived a hundred miles away in one of the new colonies that had sprouted from the sand in the desert.

'It's called Circadia,' she said. I could tell she liked saying the word. 'They have a school and a restaurant and everything.'

I'd heard that similar settlements had been popping up in every state, built by eccentrics who had rejected the clock. In the homes and streets of these communities, the sun governed the day and the night, and I suppose the pace of life really was slower, the time only inching along, a gradually advancing tide.

'A lot of the girls there shave their heads,' she added.

She tapped a text message in response. The dark polish on her fingernails flashed in the light of her lamp. Then she picked up the scissors and went on with her cutting, the strands of her hair collecting on the cream carpet beside her crumpled school uniform.

She used her father's electric razor to do the rest, the motor buzzing as she ran it over her head. Little by little, the architecture of her skull began to surface, the ancient curves and hollows now revealed.

'Holy shit,' she said when she looked in the mirror. 'This is awesome.'

She turned her head from side to side, running her fingers over the stubble. She looked ravaged by sickness or treatment.

She sat down on the bed. A lacy black bra and panty set was spread out on the comforter. She saw me looking at it. 'Do you like it?' she said.

'I guess,' I said.

'I ordered it online.'

One of the candles on her dresser had melted down to a pool of wax. The flame sputtered and then went out, leaving a thin puff of white smoke in the air.

'Hey,' she said, changing the subject. 'Did your mom really kill some guy on New Year's?'

I looked at her. 'We don't know if he died,' I said.

Downstairs, the workers dropped something heavy on the tile.

'I heard she ran over someone.'

'She's sick,' I said.

Gabby turned toward me. 'Sick with what?'

'We don't know.'

'Can she die from it?'

'I'm not sure.'

'Shit,' she said. 'I'm sorry.'

Gabby had recently painted her walls a deep maroon, and you could smell the paint fumes in the air, mixing with the vanilla from the candles.

'I should go home,' I said.

'Here,' said Gabby. She handed me a plastic bag bulging with hair clips and bobby pins. 'Take these. I can't use them anymore.'

I shook my head. I didn't want her things.

Outside, a pair of headlights approached as I walked home, a slim black BMW that belonged to Gabby's mother. She waved to me as she drove, and I waved back. I watched her pull into the driveway and wait for the electric garage door to trundle open on its tracks. I knew that those were the last few minutes before certain consequences would come down on Gabby's shaved head. The BMW floated into the garage. The door dropped down behind the car. I heard the engine die, the first soft pings as it cooled.

I would later learn that Gabby immediately lost access to her computer and her cell phone, leaving her unable to communicate with the boy in Circadia who was writing her poems.

★　★　★

That night I spent hours gazing at Sylvia's house through my telescope, looking for a glimpse of my father, but I spotted only Sylvia. Her habits had turned increasingly bizarre as the days had grown. She would disappear inside her house during every stretch of darkness, and while the neighbors' windows glowed all day, she left hers unlit, as if she'd learned to sleep for twenty hours or more in a row. A stranger passing Sylvia's driveway on some dark afternoon might have guessed the house was vacant or the owner out of town. The newspaper often landed in the driveway twice before the sun came around again.

But on white nights, Sylvia came back to life. I could see her slender fingers gliding over the piano keys long after the neighbors had gone to bed. She pulled weeds at midnight. She went jogging while the rest of us dreamed our dreams. In the hush of one bright night, I watched her drag her Christmas tree out to the sidewalk in the sunshine, the scrape of the pot on the pavement the only sound on the sleeping street.

Certain countries in Europe had made it more or less illegal to live the way Sylvia did. On that continent, the realtimers were mostly immigrants from North Africa and the Middle East, off the clock for religious reasons. Curfews had been imposed in Paris. Riots followed. One member of our own city council had proposed a similar ban. A small town nearby had successfully passed a clock curfew, but it was soon struck down by the courts.

That same week, the power went off in certain houses on our street. Televisions shut down without warning. Washing machines whirred to a stop. Music ceased to flow from speakers, and the lights went out over dinner tables.

The damage, however, was limited to just three homes: the Kaplans', Tom and Carlotta's, and Sylvia's. It was no accident. The real-timers

170

had been targeted. Someone had cut through the lines.

A pair of policemen showed up to examine the marks on the wires. They interviewed the neighbors. No one had seen a thing. It took six hours for the power company to reconnect the real-timers to the grid. The perpetrators were never caught.

19

At school, we dissected frogs, we ran the mile, our spines were checked for scoliosis. Soccer season stretched into January because of all the games we'd canceled in the fall. But I'd lost interest in the sport. What was the point anymore? What did it matter?

'But you like soccer, don't you?' said my father as I sulked in the car on the way to practice one day. After my mother got sick, he had changed his schedule so that he could drive me.

'How do you know if I like it or not?' I said.

He turned toward me. I never talked to him that way, and he looked surprised. Outside, the sky was a fiery orange, a sunrise in the late afternoon.

'What's going on with you lately?' he asked.

He looked tired. His hair, a pale brown, was beginning to thin at the edges. A layer of stubble had grown on his chin since the morning. I wondered if he sensed that I knew what he'd been doing with Sylvia.

'Nothing,' I said. 'I just don't want to do this anymore.'

My father didn't answer. We continued driving toward the soccer field.

The main thing I remember about those afternoons at the field were the moments when the boys' team would come jogging past our practice. We could hear the boys panting as they

172

got close, the synchronized click of their cleats on the asphalt. We could smell the sweat of their jerseys as they passed. I'd always search the pack for Seth, who ran at the edge of the group near the front and never looked in our direction. The eyes of all the other boys usually fell on Michaela as they passed — and she received their attention with a wide-open smile. I never understood how she knew what they wanted. I avoided looking at the boys as they approached, until the sound of their footfalls faded and then went mute as they hit the dirt path at the edge of the field. That was when I'd take one last look at Seth before he and all the other boys disappeared into the eucalyptus trees dividing their field from ours.

We reached the parking lot, and my father pulled up to the curb.

'Listen to me,' he said. 'You're not quitting soccer.'

I stepped out of the car, my soccer bag swinging on my shoulder. I slammed the door.

The parking lot was a long way from the field, and I walked as slowly as possible. I could see Hanna's skinny outline in the distance on the field. I hated the way our old closeness hung over us like a stink, unacknowledged but forever wafting in the air.

An idea flickered in my mind: I didn't have to go to practice — I could just walk away.

My father had already driven off. No one else was nearby.

Maybe the slowing was affecting *my* emotions, too: I felt brave and impulsive that day. I began to move away from the field, first slowly and then faster, until soon I was rushing down the steep slope of a landscaped hill, ice plant crunching beneath my cleats.

I landed in the shopping-center parking lot that neighbored the field.

The first thing I saw was a health food store that catered to real-timers. It was late afternoon, but the store was just now opening its doors for the day, revealing its rows of vitamins, dried kale, and herbal sleep remedies.

Next door, people were pushing carts in and out of the giant drugstore I sometimes visited with my mother. They were running a special on survival gear: A giant stack of canned goods stood out front beneath a sign that read, IS YOUR FAMILY PREPARED?

I wandered inside, conscious of the sound of my cleats on the linoleum, as if they might give me away, but no one seemed to notice. I could hear the buzz of fluorescent lights, the watery classical music flowing from the speakers in the ceiling.

Whenever I came here with my mother, certain aisles felt a little illicit to me, and I was eager to explore them on my own. In the cosmetics aisle, fifty feet of shelving displayed in glittering packages all the powders and the polishes and the creams, the shimmer sticks and eyebrow pens, the tweezers and clippers and razors that, I had begun to suspect, if applied in the correct combinations, might begin to transform me into a girl more lovely and more loved.

At the far end of the cosmetics aisle, an older

girl with perfectly straight black hair and car keys jingling in her hand was twisting open nail polishes and testing the colors on her nails. I remember the satisfying clink of the bottles against one another. I envied the casual way that she dropped the ones she liked into her basket.

Behind her, hanging from a circular rack, was a small selection of bras.

I was too embarrassed to approach the rack while she was there, so I wandered up and down the aisle for a while, picking up lipsticks and then dropping them back into place. When she was gone, I drifted toward the rack of bras. They had only five or six styles, and one seemed much nicer than the rest. I remember the way it looked hanging on the rack, a crisp bright white with blue polka dots and straps made of blue satin ribbon and tiny bows where the straps met the cups. When I was certain that no one was around, I held the bra up to my chest.

The tag said $8.99. I had my grandfather's ten-dollar bill in my soccer bag.

* * *

When my father pulled up to the soccer field, I was sitting on the curb as usual, my soccer bag in my lap, the bra radiating from deep inside it. The other girls on my team were beginning to move toward the parking lot, small figures in the distance, pausing to stretch their legs or adjust their ponytails, sweaty from the drills I had missed.

I climbed quickly into the car.

175

'How was practice?' my father asked.

I was taking big gulps from my water bottle. Deception, like algebra, was a newly learned skill.

'Fine,' I said.

'What did you guys do?'

I worried that he knew. 'We always do the exact same thing, Dad,' I said. 'That's why it's so boring.'

Here was the most amazing thing about it: He believed me.

As soon as we were home, I closed myself in my bathroom. I had a fluttery feeling that something might be finally starting for me, that this might be a beginning. I felt all my worries — all the more important things — sliding swiftly away. I could already picture how the strap would look on my shoulder, poking out from under my shirt the way Michaela's always did at school.

But when I tried it on, after struggling for many minutes with the clasp, I discovered that a terrible transformation had taken place between the drugstore and home: I had brought home a cheap and girlish bra. The satin ribbons were too blue and too shiny. One of the seams was already coming loose. Even worse was the way the cups rippled unsexily across my chest, like two empty water balloons waiting to be filled.

I heard my mother's footsteps on the stairs.

'What are you doing in there?' she asked through the door.

Just her nearness in the hall made me nervous.

'Nothing,' I said.

'Are you sick?' she called. She had begun to worry that I would develop the syndrome, too. 'Your father says you've been in there for almost half an hour.'

I could feel her wanting to open the door. I could feel her hand reaching for the knob. I unhooked the bra and threw on my shirt.

'I'm fine,' I called. 'I'll be out in a second.'

Later, when she was asleep and my father was at work, I buried the bra deep inside one of the trash cans in our side yard, so that no one would ever discover how little I understood what seemed so obvious to the other girls I knew.

20

February: The dark hours seemed somehow darker than before and the light ones more radiant than ever. The heat was so extreme you could see it, rising from the asphalt in waves. As the days grew longer and longer, I found it harder than ever to sleep.

My mother's illness fluctuated wildly. Some days she was fine: She'd go to work, run errands, make dinner. Other times we'd lose her to the force of some new symptom. I came home from school one day to find her wrapped in three blankets but shivering, her teeth knocking. It was the eighteenth hour of daylight. It was eighty-five degrees outside.

'Don't worry,' she said, shaking as she spoke. 'It'll pass.'

But I did worry. I watched her whenever I could.

In those days, some suspected the syndrome was psychological in nature, that the effects might be caused not by a shift in gravity but by an even more powerful force: fear.

'Maybe it's just anxiety,' said my father when he got home from work that night.

My mother took a deep breath. 'You think I'm making this up?'

'That's not what I said, Helen.'

My father slid a frozen pizza into the microwave for dinner. When my mother was sick, he did whatever needed to be done. But I sensed that there was something hollow about him during that time, that his mind and soul were elsewhere even as his hands poured me a glass of milk, even as his mouth spoke the appropriate words: *How was school? Have you finished your homework?*

'I'm just saying,' he continued, 'you're under a lot of stress.'

My mother shook her head. 'No,' she said. 'This is real.'

'Yeah, Dad,' I said. 'It's real.'

I always took my mother's side these days, but secretly, his theory appealed to me. You can't die from worry.

The next night we heard the first shimmer of good news in months: We had gained just six minutes the day before, fewer than on any day since the start of the slowing.

'That's good,' I said. My parents said nothing. 'Right?'

'It might be too late,' said my mother. Her hair looked flat. I realized she hadn't washed it in a while.

'Helen, come on,' said my father. Then he looked at me. 'Of course it's good news.'

A cold breeze rattled the blinds behind us.

'Denial doesn't help,' said my mother.

I wasn't sure my father necessarily agreed. He had different ideas about truth.

'It's good news,' he repeated. He stood and squeezed my shoulder.

My mother turned off the television.

'You might as well know the truth, Julia,' she said. 'Everything is going to shit.'

179

A string of tense days followed. My parents spoke less and less. After hours of spying with my telescope, I finally caught my father with Sylvia again. It was in the morning this time, after he'd left for work and while my mother was dozing on the couch. He'd left in his car but came back down the street on foot. He kept turning his head toward our house, once, twice, and once again, before disappearing through the side gate to Sylvia's. I had little sense of how these dramas worked. I worried more and more that my father would one day leave us for good.

And then, one night my father told a lie. This was not the first lie I ever heard him tell, and it would not be the last. It was just the boldest and the best. Simple and succinct. An elegant, outlandish fiction. One untrue sentence.

It happened on a Saturday, a daylight day: The sun rose in the morning and shone all afternoon. A salty breeze rustled the eucalyptus trees while the twins splashed in the neighbors' pool. My mother, feeling better than usual, was reading a magazine out back, a glass of iced tea sweating beside her, as a fleet of hot air balloons drifted across the open sky. The passengers were waving from the balloon baskets as they floated over our roof. It was seventy-six degrees. You might never have guessed from that scene that six astronauts remained stranded on the space station, their food supplies dwindling, ten thousand miles higher than the silk of those balloons. It did not feel at that particular moment in time as though we were stranded, either.

I was in the kitchen when the phone rang. My father was upstairs. My mother turned her head toward the house at the sound of the ringing but let it go. I happened to pick up the receiver in the kitchen just after my father had answered it upstairs.

'Joel?' said the voice on the phone. 'It's Ben Harvey at St. Anthony's.'

I curled my hand over the mouthpiece and listened.

'So?' said my father.

I held my breath and stood still, barefoot on the tile.

'It's not what you want to hear,' said the other man.

He paused. I took a quick breath.

'The guy was dead on arrival,' said the man.

My father sighed heavily.

'Skull fracture, crushed vertebrae, subdural hematoma,' he said. 'Apparently, he was some kind of transient. There's no next of kin.'

I can't explain how it was that we believed the pedestrian might have survived. My mother and I had seen him out on the asphalt, after all, looking lifeless, death suggested even by the way he was lying; the living don't lie that way. And yet we *did* still hope.

I didn't hear what else was said on the phone. I leaned on the kitchen counter, feeling faint. When the conversation ended, I hung up as softly as I could, and then I heard my father moving toward the stairs.

Out on the deck, my mother turned the page

of her magazine and sipped her iced tea. I didn't want to be there when he told her.

★　★　★

I walked down to Gabby's house, but no one was home, so I sat alone on our porch for a while, watching the fat white clouds glide eastward overhead. It was about the time when Seth sometimes had his piano lesson with Sylvia, and I thought he might be in her house. I listened for the sound of her piano but heard nothing.

At the end of the street, I saw a giant moving van blocking the Kaplans' driveway. A mattress stood up on one end against the front door, and the family cat was howling from his carrier on the porch.

The for-sale sign had appeared in front of the Kaplans' house three days after their electricity was cut. The two youngest Kaplans were playing with the boxes in the yard as two movers and Mr. Kaplan fed a long brown couch into the mouth of the truck. I could hear their voices in the distance, the arguments of men carried down to me on the breeze.

They were moving to one of the colonies, one where everyone was Jewish and everyone agreed on the Sabbath: sundown to sundown on every seventh day. Their days were completely out of sync with ours, their Saturdays no longer falling when ours did. I'd done the calculations one white night when I couldn't sleep: The real-timers were dozens of days behind us by

182

then — and those days would eventually pool into years.

From across the street came the click and creak of a door swinging open. I looked up, hoping it might be Seth, but it was only Sylvia, in sun hat and clogs, a trowel dangling from one hand.

She waved. 'Lovely day,' she called to me from her garden. She asked me how I was.

'Fine,' I said.

I no longer felt sorry for her. Now she made me nervous, as if I were the one with something to hide.

She knelt near her roses, which had begun to wither in recent weeks. Sylvia, on the other hand, seemed to be thriving. Most of us walked around with sleepy eyes and slow minds — my mother claimed she hadn't dreamed in months — but Sylvia looked rested and peaceful and alert. It was hard not to see that she was beautiful, so much more so in those days than my mother. I began to hope that Sylvia would move away, like the Kaplans, and like so many of the other real-timers were doing at that time.

Or maybe I wished that *we* would move far away. I wondered about the colonies that were forming in the desert. I liked thinking that time really did pass less quickly there than it did where we lived. And if so, if every event took a little longer to transpire, then were the consequences of those events also less swift?

★   ★   ★

When I went back inside, I found my parents together out on the back deck. Through the kitchen window, they did not look the way I had expected. My mother was laughing and shaking her head. My father pressed one hand on her knee. My mother spotted me through the window and waved me out to join them. I could tell even before I opened the French door that my father had not delivered the news.

'Guess what,' said my mother as I closed the door behind me, the cold brass handle locking into place.

'What?' I said.

She was shielding her eyes from the sun with her hand. She turned to my father.

'Tell Julia,' she said. She was sitting up in her chair, her knees pressed to her chin like a teenager. 'Tell her.'

My father looked me right in the eye. 'You know the man from the accident?'

Behind him, a faint breeze shook the honeysuckle, now desiccated.

'Yeah?' I said.

And here came the lie, crisp and smooth and clear: 'I found out today that he survived.'

'They released him from the hospital,' my mother said. She kept rearranging herself in her chair. 'He just had a few broken bones,' she went on. 'That's all. Can you believe it?'

I felt a flash of anger at my father. She deserved to know the truth.

But my mother looked better than she had in months. Her posture relaxed. Her laugh lines resurfaced. Her whole face looked different

— eyes half squinting, cheeks bulging, lips spread apart to show teeth: a smile.

All I wanted to do in that moment was smile right back at her.

It didn't feel right at first. I felt guilty. And I hope my father did, too. But the shift in mood was impossible to resist.

The lie improved everything.

My mother took down the nice crystal glasses and uncorked one of the special bottles of red wine they saved in a rack above the liquor cabinet. She cooked linguini with the sun-dried tomatoes my parents had brought back from Italy a few years earlier, cut from the vine and packed in olive oil long before the slowing started. For dessert we ate canned pineapples. They were the last pineapples we'd ever eat in our lives. We sat on the deck in the sunshine, food filling our bellies. I wish I recalled more nights like that one. The sun was high. The air was warm. The earth continued turning. But for once, it was not our concern. My mother was happy, her conscience clear and I knew I'd never tell.

My father was pleased, too. I watched him watching my mother. Maybe he loved her. Maybe he really did. He must have saved hundreds of lives at the hospital over the course of his career, but never before and never again did he bring a dead man back to life.

21

Cynodon dactylon, also known as Bermuda
grass, the main variety of which is Arizona
common: a hardy breed of grass, resistant to heat
and drought and thus popular at one time for
lawns and golf courses throughout the south-
western United States. But Cynodon dactylon
requires abundant sunshine. It cannot thrive in
shade or endure prolonged periods of darkness.
And thus, when the days grew beyond fifty
hours, thousands of yards, including ours and
seven others on the street, began to suffer. The
grass thinned, browned, and then died.

Mr. Valencia replaced his lawn with lava rocks.
I woke one morning to a great clattering of
stones as two workers poured them into the
shallow bed where the grass once lived. Blankets
of artificial turf soon landed in front of some
houses. Giant sunlamps sprouted in the yards of
others.

While my parents debated what to do about
our yard, the whole lawn went bald. The dirt
turned to mud. Earthworms wiggled to the
surface, some lighting out for better territory
only to crisp on the cement of our driveway,
baked by the sun, then flattened by the tires of
our cars.

Our honeysuckle withered, too. The bougain-
villca quit producing flowers.

All across America, giant greenhouses were

swallowing up the open-air fields of our farms. Acres and acres were put under glass. Thousands of sodium lamps were giving light to our tomato plants and our orange trees, our strawberries and our potatoes and our corn.

'The developing countries are going to be the hardest hit,' said the head of the Red Cross on one of the morning shows. Famines were predicted for Africa and parts of Asia. 'These countries simply lack the financial resources to adapt.'

Even for us, the solutions were temporary. Industrial farms were guzzling up electricity at an impossible rate. The twenty thousand lights that hung from the ceiling of just one greenhouse could eat up in half an hour as much power as most families used in a whole year. Grazing pastures quickly became too expensive to maintain — beef would soon become a delicacy.

'We need to be moving in the exact opposite direction,' said the head of a large environmental group interviewed on the nightly news. 'We need to be reducing, not prolonging, our dependence on crops that require so much light.'

Bananas and other tropical fruits had already vanished from the grocery stores. Bananas! How strange a word can sound when you haven't heard it said aloud in ages.

Scientists raced for a cure. There was hope in genetic engineering. There was talk of a miracle rice. Some researchers turned their attention to the mossy floors of rain forests and the sunless depths of the oceans, where certain plants had long survived on very little light; scientists hoped to splice the genes of these hardy species with those of the world's food supply.

We were nervous sometimes, other times not. Anxiety rolled over us in waves. The national mood was contagious and quick to change. Weeks sometimes passed in relative calm. But any bit of bad news provoked runs on canned goods and bottled water. My mother's collection of emergency supplies continued to grow. I'd find candles stuffed in the coat closet, boxes of canned tuna in the garage. Fifty jars of peanut butter stood in rows beneath my parents' bed.

Still the slowing went on and on. The days stretched. One by one, the minutes poured in — and even a trickle, as we have come to understand, can eventually add up to a flood.

22

But no force on earth could slow the forward march of sixth grade. And so, in spite of everything, that year was also the year of the dance party.

Whenever the birthday of one of my classmates rolled around, invitations were mailed to a select list of boys as well as girls. Gone were the days of single-sex parties. Now D.J.s were hired and dance floors rented. Strobe lights and disco balls were strung from the ceilings of basements or from backyard fences or, in the case of Amanda Cohen, from the eaves of a cavernous hotel ballroom. Michaela used to describe these festivities to me while we waited for the school bus on certain mornings. But sometimes I didn't need to be told: On one particular Monday, all the prettiest girls showed up at school zipped snugly into matching pink sweatshirts with Justine Valero's name and birth date spelled out in rhinestones on the back, favors from the previous Saturday's party.

I know that it was considered good fortune for a birthday to land on a dark night, the romance upped considerably by the moonlight and the stars. But as for the precise goings-on of these events, I couldn't say. I was never invited.

'I'm sure Justine just forgot to invite you,' said Michaela. A brand-new set of feathery red bangs

189

dangled above Michaela's eyelids. 'She probably just forgot.'

Hanna was leaning against the fence nearby in a mint-green sweater set and a blond French braid. She laughed into her cell phone. We hadn't spoken in weeks.

'Besides,' Michaela added, 'you wouldn't have fun anyway. You're too shy. I bet you'd just stand in the corner.'

'That's not true,' I said. 'I would dance.'

My own birthday was only a few weeks away. There would be no party. There would be no dancing.

'You'd dance?' said Michaela. 'Really?'

It was dark that morning, the air wet with fog, which glowed around the streetlights as it rolled up over the lip of the canyon, where, like everywhere else, dozens of native plant species were slowly dying from insufficient light.

'I danced with Seth Moreno on Saturday for like an hour,' Michaela continued.

Seth's name flared in my head.

'He was there?' I asked.

'He's super-hot up close,' she said. She shivered in her miniskirt. 'I could feel his thing.'

Right then Seth pulled up to the bus stop on his skateboard, and Michaela stopped talking.

★ ★ ★

Our school had shed a quarter of its population since the slowing began, but five hundred and forty-two of us remained. Every morning before the first bell rang, five hundred and forty-two

190

voices called out to one another from five hundred and forty-two throats. Five hundred and forty-two mouths battled to be heard, the roar mounting as buses dumped load after load of kids on the quad. Rumors surged from group to group — there were cliques inside cliques inside cliques. Loud rounds of laughter exploded constantly into the air. Five hundred and forty-two voices bounced and echoed off the stucco exterior of the walls, accompanied by the ringing of five hundred and forty-two cell phones. Someone was always shocked by a thing they'd just heard. Someone was always screaming. From where I stood lately, at the far edge of the crowd, the sounds seemed as meaningless as if all those tongues were speaking different tongues, a great, incomprehensible chatter.

In that environment, silence was deadly. Talk ruled. It did not pay to be the quiet kind.

Every school day I looked forward to the soft landing of afternoon, to the click of my key in the lock of our door, the hush of the empty house. My mother tried to keep going to work, so she was gone most afternoons, or else upstairs asleep.

I was reading on one of these days when I heard a hard knock at the door.

We were reading Ray Bradbury in English class. That day's assignment was a short story about a group of human schoolchildren who live on Venus, where, according to the story, the sun breaks through the rainy cloud cover only once every seven years, and then for only one hour.

The doorbell rang twice before I got to the

door. On the other side stood Gabby, still in her St. Mary's uniform: green plaid skirt and white polo, navy sweater tied around her waist.

I opened the door.

'Your parents aren't home, are they?' she said. She was rubbing her hands together and kept glancing back at the street. Her hair had grown out some but not much. A layer of brown fuzz covered her scalp.

'They're still at work,' I said.

She came into the house and motioned for me to shut the door.

'I need to check my email on your computer,' she said softly, as if the house might be bugged.

For several weeks, she said, she'd been cut off from the Internet, and her cell phone had remained locked inside a drawer in her mother's desk. During these two weeks, she'd had sparse contact with the boy in Circadia, but of course, those were the exact conditions under which love grew best.

Once at the computer, she worked quickly. A rattle of fingernails on keys, a few clicks of the mouse. Then she stood up.

'I probably won't see you for a while,' she said.

'Why not?'

'I'm getting the fuck out of here,' she said. 'Tomorrow Keith is picking me up from school, and I'm going to go live with him in Circadia.'

This was not the first time she'd threatened to run away. Gabby was always scheming and dreaming, but she never followed through.

'What about your parents?' I said.

'You better not tell them.'

'They're going to freak out,' I said.

She was pacing our entry hall. Her loafers, school-issued, squeaked with every step.

'Everything here is bullshit, anyway,' she said. She waved her hand in a broad way.

Beside her, our ficus was withering away in its pot. House-plants were faring even worse than the outdoor varieties.

'Are you really serious?' I asked.

'I guess I shouldn't have told you,' she said. 'You're too much of a goody-goody to understand.'

Gabby opened the front door and stepped out onto the porch.

'Wait,' I said.

'Keith's right,' she said. 'Everyone is half asleep here. Clock time is just another way for society to keep us numb.'

The sun had dropped behind the hill. The sky was pink. Sunsets had always been beautiful where we lived, but they seemed even more dramatic these days, made more so for being twice as rare.

'Please don't tell anyone,' she said.

Anyone who knew Gabby the way I did would have assumed that she wasn't actually going anywhere. The plan, if there was one, would likely fall apart. Something would change: Her mind shifted quickly, her mood even faster. I was pretty sure that Gabby would return home from school as usual the next day. She would sleep in her own bed and go right on plotting another improbable way to flee.

She gave me a quick hug and said goodbye. I

went back to my homework.

I still remember how that Bradbury short story ended: On the day the sun finally shines on Venus, after seven years away, one boy convinces the other children to lock one little girl in a closet. When the sun emerges, the other children rush outside to feel the sunshine on their faces for the first time in their lives. It shines for only one hour. The girl remains trapped in the closet. By the time someone remembers she's there, the sun has moved back behind the clouds not to return for another seven years.

★   ★   ★

It was dark when I got home from school the next day. Sunrise was several hours away. I walked straight to Gabby's house, shivering as I passed Tom and Carlotta's driveway. They still lived there, but the house was unlit; it was the middle of their night. Within months, they were both convicted and sentenced, the house sold to pay the legal bills.

When I reached Gabby's driveway, I saw that her house was dark, too. The porch light glowed alone.

I rang the doorbell. No one answered. I rang it again.

Through the kitchen window, a row of brand-new stainless-steel appliances gleamed in the moonlight.

I'd grown up hearing stories about the special hazards that girls faced. I knew where the bodies were found: naked on beaches or cut into pieces,

194

parts frozen in freezers or buried in cement. These stories were never kept from us girls. Instead thcy were spread around like ghost stories, our parents hoping that fear would do the job that our judgment might not.

Now I saw Gabby's situation in this same light: A twelve-year-old girl had run away from home with a man she'd met on the Internet. He claimed to be sixteen, but who knew? Supposedly, he lived in one of the daylight colonies, but I did not even know his last name. Narratives like that one didn't usually end well, and since the start of the slowing, these stories had become only more frequent. The rates of every kind of violent crime were going up.

The worry began in my stomach, a tightening that spread up to my chest and out to my shoulders until it reached the back of my neck. The worry smoldered all afternoon, and I was surprised my parents couldn't see it on my face.

That night my mother brought up my birthday. 'We have to do something,' she said. 'Why don't we have a party?'

I didn't want a party. Who would I invite? My mother had no way of knowing that I'd been spending all my lunch periods pretending to be on the phone. The change had happened so quickly, a shifting of sands. Now Gabby was gone, too.

'In times like these,' said my mother, 'it's even more important to celebrate the good things.'

I finally agreed to a dinner. 'But just us and Grandpa,' I said.

'Let's invite Hanna, at least,' said my mother.

'I haven't seen her in months.'

'No,' I said. 'Not Hanna.'

By dinnertime, my whole body was hot with guilt about Gabby. It seemed to be radiating off my skin, like pheromones or smoke or some other chemical signal with the power to attract Gabby's mother to our porch, where she arrived just after eight o'clock to ask if we had seen her daughter.

My mother looked apologetic in the doorway. 'We haven't,' she said. 'Have you tried her other friends?'

Gabby's mother looked right at me. She wore a skirt suit and heels. Lip liner ringed her lips from the workday, but the lipstick had faded away.

'Please don't tell her I told you,' I said.

'You know where she is?' said my mother.

'I think she went to Circadia,' I said. I paused. 'With a boy.'

'What the hell is Circadia?' said Gabby's mother.

She wore contacts, but they dried out her eyes. She was always blinking, and she blinked even more at that moment as tears flooded her dark eyes.

'You know,' I said. 'It's one of the daylight colonies.'

*   *   *

Gabby's mother called the police and she and Gabby's father drove out to the desert right away, knocking on doors all night as the sun

196

blazed in the sky — it was daytime in Circadia. Everyone there was awake.

By morning Gabby had been found drinking wine at a barbecue with a teenage runaway from a different part of the state: Keith. She spent only one night in Circadia.

She was never the same after that. Back on our street, she lay around, dazed and disappointed, a traveler forced to return from an exotic and enlightening land.

'Did you tell my mom I was there?' she said.

'No,' I said.

She rolled her head in my direction, skeptical. 'Really?'

'I swear,' I said.

'I'm going back there someday,' she said. A new knowingness had seeped into her voice. 'It's hard to explain, but Circadia is like one of those places, you know, what do you call it? A utopia? Everyone's totally mellow. And they treat you like an adult. No one cares what you look like or what you wear.'

The history of Circadia was brief, and I learned it only later. A hundred miles from anything, those cement foundations were poured a year before the slowing started by a developer who dreamed that the wild sprawl of California's coastal cities would soon penetrate that particular stretch of desert. But the developer went bankrupt six months before the slowing started. The work stopped. For months the houses stood empty and half built — until a group of committed real-timers bought the land and everything on it and named it after their own internal clocks.

Gabby described for me a golden land, a reverse negative of where we lived. Time really did flow differently, she insisted. Every hour had felt to her like a day. Hearts beat fewer beats per minute. People breathed deeper breaths. Anger took ages to bloom. They would live longer, she swore. And everything lasted: a good meal, a crackle of laughter, the look in Keith's eyes after they kissed for the first time.

'Living like that changes people,' she said. 'They're so much better than the people out here.'

In the Circadia of Gabby's telling, the inhabitants were a new wave of gentle pioneers, hardworking but well rested — sleeping for twenty-four hours straight and then staying awake for just as long or even longer without tiring. It did not sound possible to those of us on the outside, but already the science was bearing it out: Human circadian rhythms were turning out to be vastly more malleable than anyone had previously thought.

Gabby's memories of Circadia stayed with me. I liked the idea of going somewhere far away. Sometimes on white nights, as the sunlight crept in beneath my curtains, I tried to recall what it felt like to sleep in sync with the sun. How strange and peaceful it sounded to dream every night in the dark. And how quiet that thick desert darkness must have been with only the stars to light the land. No freeways rumbled there. No power lines buzzed. Maybe I'd never heard such a silence as that one before. Not even the ticking of clocks could wake you — because no one kept clocks in Circadia.

As soon as Gabby's hair grew out enough to be mistaken for a cute pixie cut, she was sent to a boarding school a hundred miles away. She was the last friend I had left, and just like that, she was gone.

23

In the great reshuffling of fortunes and fates that followed the start of the slowing, most of us had lost. We were worse off, most of us, than we had been before. Some grew sick, some depressed. A great many marriages dissolved under the stress. Billions of dollars had drained from the markets. And we were missing certain other valuables, too: our way of life, our peace of mind, our faith.

But not everyone was suffering. A lucky few had gained. Michaela and her mother were among them.

Michaela had begun the school year, six months earlier, in a rented apartment that overlooked a parking lot at the far edge of the district line. A rusted black staircase clung to the exterior of the complex, and a knock on 2B would produce a rattling of the security chain as Michaela unhooked it from the inside.

By February, though, a visitor could reach Michaela's front door only by showing a driver's license at a guardhouse out front. The guard was required to call Michaela's house for authorization before opening the electric gate. Her mother had a rich new boyfriend, and Michaela and her mother had moved into his house.

I was shocked to be invited. No one had asked me anywhere in months.

'And bring a swimsuit,' Michaela had said on the phone. 'There's a pool and a Jacuzzi in the back.'

Once inside the gate, my father and I drove in silence past a dozen large houses, each one set off from the road and fronted by fountains or ponds. Stables and tennis courts fanned out in all directions.

'Look at this place,' said my father. 'Who's this guy she married?'

My mother was at home, having one of her spells. There was no predicting when a fog might descend upon her.

'They're not married,' I said. 'But I think he started some kind of company.'

The sky glowed an extraordinary orange as we drove. Wildfires were burning in the open country out east, and the smoke had drifted to the coast. It wasn't the right season for brushfires, but they were feeding on the remains of dead and dying plants. You could smell the burning in the air. You could see it in the dimming of the light. Everything white looked faintly amber.

At the address Michaela had given me, a circular driveway surrounded a giant artificial lawn. It looked almost real, that grass, no two blades exactly alike. It was made of something soft, an engineered texture designed to fool feet. It smelled real, too. Some of the priciest brands came scented that way, a fad that fell away, I guess, as we less and less clearly remembered the smell of real grass.

The house was a vast ranch-style spread out

across the property like a sunbather stretched beside a pool. A thick iron knocker hung on the front door. Michaela appeared in the doorway before I could ring the bell. She was already in a swimsuit, her pink bikini showing through her white tank top. Pink strings dangled down her neck.

'Come on,' she said.

Inside, a small Mexican woman was zipping her purse near the door. The air smelled sweet. Something was baking.

'Alma made cookies,' said Michaela.

'Thanks, Alma,' called a voice from another room. I recognized it as Michaela's mother's. 'See you tomorrow.'

A nearly endless road of terra-cotta tile led us eventually to the kitchen, just visible in the distance.

'You can leave your stuff here,' said Michaela. My backpack and my sleeping bag formed a neat stack against the wall.

In the kitchen, every surface was stainless, barely used, brand-new. In my memory, Michaela's mother looked that way, too, as she leaned on the counter in a silk peach robe. Her face was heavily made-up. A silvery charcoal shimmered on her eyelids and at the corners of her eyes. Her blond hair had been straightened to form a smooth shiny sheet.

'You girls want me to read your horoscopes before I go?' she said. An astrology chart was spread out across the marble counter.

'Do Julia's,' said Michaela.

On the countertop shone a deep glass bowl

full of green grapes. I hadn't seen grapes since before Christmas.

'These cost like a hundred dollars a pound,' said Michaela, tossing one into her mouth. 'Isn't that weird?'

It was the last time I ever tasted a grape.

A series of small explosions boomed in the adjoining living room. On a white leather couch sat a boy a little older than we were, a video-game controller in his hands.

'That's Josh,' whispered Michaela. 'He's Harry's son.'

Harry was her mother's boyfriend. This was Harry's house.

'Julia, honey, do you know your sign?' asked Michaela's mother.

I didn't.

'When's your birthday?'

'March seventh,' I said.

'So soon,' she said. 'Are you having a party?'

'I don't think so,' I said.

The doorbell rang, and Michaela skipped down the hall.

'You should have a party,' said Michaela's mother. Then she turned her attention to the chart. 'If you're a Pisces, and you were born the same year as Michaela — '

She ran two fingers over the chart until the two red tips of her fingernails met in one corner.

'Hmm,' she said. She frowned.

I could hear Michaela's distant laugh at the front of the house.

'Is it bad?' I asked.

'The important thing isn't so much your

horoscope as what you do with it,' said her mother. 'Anyway, the slowing totally changed the charts. Everything's a little unstable right now, so we can't necessarily trust it.'

Michaela was coming closer. I heard a boy's voice.

'But be careful, okay?' said her mother to me. Her eyelids shimmered as she blinked. 'If I were you, I'd just be a little more careful than usual for a while.'

Michaela returned to the kitchen with a boy I recognized from school. Kai was a year older and half Hawaiian, and he made me shy, the way he stood there in the kitchen, no smile, waiting to be entertained. His skin was a creamy tan, his teeth a crisp white. He kept his two thumbs hooked on the pockets of his blue board shorts and glanced at Michaela's mother in her robe.

'Is it seven already?' said Michaela's mother. 'Shit, I better get dressed.'

She left the three of us alone in the kitchen. A silence opened up behind her. The only sound was the running of water from the pair of swan-shaped fountains that streamed into the swimming pool outside. Then the music of the video game surged behind us.

'Is that Street Avenger?' asked Kai.

These were the first words he'd spoken. He shuffled toward the living room, his flip-flops brushing the tile.

'Isn't he hot?' Michaela whispered to me as we followed him. 'He's not really my boyfriend, but he kind of is.'

'Is anyone else coming?' I asked.

'No,' she said. 'Why?'

Josh and Kai played three rounds of Street Avenger while Michaela and I watched. I tried to look casual, constantly crossing and uncrossing my legs. I often had the feeling in those days that I was being watched, but I think the sensation was a product of the exact opposite conditions.

Michaela's mother reemerged in a glittery dress and heels, with Harry at her side in a brown sport coat. He was trim and athletic, but he must have been twenty years older than she was. They'd known each other for three months.

'Have fun, kids,' said Michaela's mother. 'We'll be back late.'

My mother would not have let me come over if she knew we would be here alone.

'Josh,' said Harry to his son as they left the room, 'you're in charge.'

The clicking of Michaela's mother's heels moved quickly down the hall, and soon we heard the rattle of the garage door opening and closing, the hum and fade of the car driving away.

'I'm sick of video games,' said Michaela. 'Let's go in the Jacuzzi.'

'First,' said Josh, 'we need some beers.'

'You guys have beer?' said Kai.

I tried to affect the appearance of a girl who could not be surprised by beer.

'They'll notice if we take it,' said Michaela.

'Not if we take it from the safe room,' said Josh.

'What's the safe room?' I asked.

Josh hopped up from the couch and hurried down the hall. We followed. He was older — 13

— a tall skinny kid, all limbs. He stopped at a full-length mirror that hung on one wall, bordered by a heavy mahogany frame. He ran his fingers along the edge, then after a moment, he pulled. The mirror was secretly hinged; it swung open like a door. In the wall behind it was embedded a second door, this one made of metal.

'That's steel,' said Josh as he entered a code in a nearby keypad. We could hear the sound of the locks releasing. 'And it's six inches thick.'

At that time, I'd never seen anything like it.

It was dark on the other side of the door. A flip of the light switch revealed a huge room lined with wooden shelves, each one overflowing with supplies: dozens of boxes of candles, hundreds of packs of batteries, crates of canned fruit and canned tuna, canned vegetables, canned juice, condensed milk, and powdered milk, and twenty-five jars of peanut butter. A cluster of clear plastic bins held oats, grains, and rice. A pile of slim silver packages glittered under the lights.

'Freeze-dried meals,' said Josh.

Hundreds of gallons of bottled water stood three deep on one shelf. There was a pyramid of toilet paper. A large green tub was labeled in thick letters: SURVIVAL SEED VAULT. Several rolled sleeping bags were piled near a hand-crank radio and a camping stove. Towering above us were boxes of bandages, gauze, soap, and bottles of pills organized in rows: antibiotics, vitamins, iodine.

'Holy shit,' said Kai. He was staring at a glass

case on the far wall, inside of which hung two rifles and seven sheathed knives. Six boxes of bullets sat stacked beneath the guns.

'What is all this?' I asked.

'What does it look like?' said Josh.

He was handing out beers. I held mine with two fingers by the neck. I didn't even know how to handle the bottle.

'His dad thinks that the end of the world is coming,' said Michaela, 'so he put all this stuff in here.'

'We have enough food to live for a year,' said Josh. 'And this room is architecturally invisible, so you can't tell it's here. That way, when everyone else runs out of food, no one will break in and take ours.'

Compared to this, the supplies my mother had gathered were nothing.

The safe room was not the only special feature in the house. The whole place had been retrofitted. The lights in all six bedrooms were equipped with sophisticated dimmers, set to the clock and meant to mimic the effects of sunrise and sunset. State-of-the-art blackout shutters could block 100 percent of the natural light on white nights, and the master bathroom's tanning bed — which Michaela called a sunbed — could deliver in twenty minutes a full day's worth of sunshine on days when the sun never bobbed above the horizon. A fully functioning greenhouse, where carrots and spinach grew, was hidden in the pool house out back. A solar-powered generator stood ready for service.

'You'll see,' said Josh. 'One day you're going to

go to the grocery store, and all the shelves will be empty.'

★ ★ ★

The Jacuzzi was so hot that it hurt. We sat on the rim for a while, legs dangling, adapting, before finally dropping in, one by one. Michaela landed in Kai's lap. He twisted a strand of her hair while we talked. Josh sat right beside me in the water. I drank a little beer. It tasted awful. But I began to feel bold, sitting there with those kids in my new two-piece, steam rising between us.

Meanwhile, the sun shone — dusky and smoke-dimmed — and the wind blew bits of ash around until it settled on the patio like snow. Those distant fires only added to our enjoyment. They meant we were living in important times.

'Did we show you the cult house?' said Michaela.

She turned and pointed to one of the nearby mansions. There were no fences out there, for some reason, so you could see the back of one house from the back of another. This one looked like any other house out there — a two-story Spanish-style with a three-car garage. But it was between those walls that fourteen people had killed themselves with poisoned wine on New Year's Eve.

'One guy wasn't home when they did it,' said Michaela. 'So now he lives there all by himself.'

Josh's foot brushed mine under the water. I decided he looked a little like Seth Moreno. I took a tiny sip of beer. A cluster of eucalyptus

208

trees swayed above the pool. They looked remarkably healthy, those trees, kept that way — I later learned — by sunlamps hidden among the branches.

★　★　★

We ordered pizza, extra cheese. We ate in our swimsuits, soaking the couch through our towels. We tracked wet ash right into the house and left the door wide open behind us. We watched whatever we could find on television, lingering on a long German sex scene. We ate cookies and ice cream and opened more beers. It came back to me quickly: the old feeling that I belonged.

Josh suggested a game I'd never heard of.

'But that's only fun in the dark,' said Michaela. It was ten o'clock on a white night; sunset was at least six hours away.

'We can make it dark with the shutters,' said Josh. 'Watch this.'

He entered a code into another keypad in the kitchen. A sequence of short beeps was followed by a soft mechanical whir that radiated from every direction. Gray metal sheets descended slowly over the windows behind us.

'What the hell?' said Kai.

The sunlight faded fast as the shutters slid toward the ground. Michaela flipped a light switch before the house went dark.

'Those shutters are made of steel, too,' said Josh. We stood around the one lamp as if it were a campfire, a yellow glow on our faces. 'They're not just for the light. They can keep people out, too.'

They were preparing for a time of monsters, it seemed to me, but the monsters were only the neighbors, maybe even their friends.

Michaela explained the rules of the new game while running her fingers through Kai's black hair. It was like hide-and-seek, she said, except when you found the person, you joined whoever it was in the hiding place. The last to find the others lost.

We rolled dice to see who would hide first, and the dice chose me. The others closed themselves in Michaela's bedroom to give me time to hide. At the count of twenty, they would turn out the last light and start searching in the dark.

I hid in the safe room, which we'd left open. I crouched low, near the toilet paper at the back of the room. After a while, I saw the light go out. I heard the sound of distant laughter.

I waited for my eyes to adjust to the darkness, but they didn't. Not a trace of daylight made its way through those shutters. Only blackness remained, a kind of blindness. It was, as we used to say, *dark as night*.

After a few minutes, I heard footsteps outside the safe room, the creak of the door swinging open, the sound of breathing. Someone was in the room with me.

Several cans toppled to the floor.

'Shit,' said a boy's voice. I could tell it was Josh, but I couldn't see him, not even an outline, not a shadow, nothing.

He felt around the room until his hands

bumped my shoulder.

'Found you,' he whispered.

I was glad. He sat down next to me on the floor. He touched my shoulder again, as if by accident. We had a miraculous new power: invisibility.

'You looked pretty in your swimsuit,' he said.

'Thanks,' I said. I smiled an unseeable smile. It might have been the first time a boy had said he liked the way I looked. We sat without speaking for a long time.

'I've never kissed a girl,' he whispered.

There are creatures at the bottom of the ocean that can live without light. They've evolved to thrive where other animals would die, and the darkness endowed us, too, with certain special abilities. What was possible in the dark never would have worked in the light. I kept quiet and waited for something to happen.

I felt his breath on my cheek and held still. Seconds passed. And then: His lips pressed my chin. He'd misjudged in the dark.

'That's okay,' I said.

He didn't answer. He cleared his throat. 'Can we try again?' he asked.

But I'd lost my nerve. 'We're in the middle of the game,' I said.

When I felt him lean toward me again, I leaned back.

'Come on,' he whispered. 'We're all going to be dead in a year or two, anyway.'

'No one knows what's going to happen,' I said.

I listened for Kai and Michaela but heard nothing.

'When we run out of food, there's going to be wars,' he said. 'Major wars.'

He tried to kiss me one more time, but I jumped up, bumping one of the shelves behind us. Something crashed to the floor. In case of catastrophe, they'd have one less jar of jam.

'Fine,' he said. 'I should have known you'd be totally lame.'

I heard him stand and shuffle toward the door in the dark. The smell of strawberries began to waft through the air.

'Anyway,' he said, 'Michaela only invited you because her mom made her. She wouldn't let her have her boyfriend over here unless someone *responsible* was here, too.'

I knew it was true as soon as he said it — the whole night, an optical illusion, now made clear. Michaela hadn't invited me anywhere all year.

The door creaked open and clicked closed. I was alone again in the dark.

I huddled there awhile longer. The only option seemed to be to continue the game. But no one else came, and soon a crack of light appeared beneath the safe room door. They'd turned on the lights in the house — or raised the shutters.

In the hall, I had to squint to see. My eyes were slow to adjust to the light. They were watching television again: Michaela and Kai, legs intertwined on the couch. Michaela was eating bonbons from a carton. Josh was not with them.

'There you are,' said Michaela. She was in her bikini and nothing else. Her hair was still ropy from the Jacuzzi. 'We couldn't find you anywhere.'

The blue light of the television flickered on her face. Kai kept his eyes on the screen.

'You stopped looking?' I said.

'We couldn't find you,' she said. She turned back to the television. 'Josh said he checked the safe room and you weren't in there.'

★　★　★

Later, I fell asleep in my jeans on the couch. I woke up twice: once when Michaela's mother and Harry breezed into the house — the tapping of her heels on the tile, the two of them laughing — and later, to the sound of one of the boys — Josh, I think — throwing up in the bathroom.

I was the first one awake in the morning. A pizza box lay open on the counter, and a full carton of melted ice cream sat slumped beside it. Someone had cleared away the beer bottles.

The sun had set overnight. It was dark and cold, and it would be dark all day.

I called home, and my mother sent my father to pick me up. I left without saying goodbye. Someone must have answered the phone when the guard called because my father's car soon appeared in the circular driveway, headlights blazing.

'Why so early?' he said as I climbed into the car. 'Is something wrong?'

The air smelled heavily of smoke. The firefighting planes could not fly without the light, so the fires would burn free for hours. The car radio carried news of one more strange story: An earthquake had struck rural Kansas. It was the first of its size ever recorded there.

'I just felt like coming home,' I said.

24

Two days before my twelfth birthday, a group of whales washed up on our coastline. Nearby residents awoke one morning to find the whales slumped in the sand, twisting weakly as the tide receded without them. Ten sea creatures: stranded on earth.

Mass beachings were growing common all over the world. In Australia two thousand pilot whales and twelve hundred dolphins were laid out together on one beach. In South Africa, it was killer whales. Eighty-nine humpbacks had run aground on Cape Cod.

Theories abounded. But proof was scarce. The ocean was changing, that much we knew. The currents were shifting. The tides were coming loose. Every high tide crept higher. Every low tide swept lower. The food chain was withering, and new dead zones had formed in certain waters. Starving whales might venture into the shallows in search of food.

But there were some who took a more conservative view.

'These events have occurred throughout history,' said Miss Mosely, our new science teacher, as we shifted on our lab stools.

Under Miss Mosely's direction, we had stopped updating Mr. Jensen's solar-system wall. The black butcher paper had begun to fade. The paper planets were curling at the edges, and the moon had fallen from the sky. Under Earth, the label still read *28 hours and six minutes*, though the natural days had more than doubled in length since then.

Miss Mosely bent over a laptop at the front of the lab, in gray pencil skirt and white collared shirt, to show us photographs online of hundreds of whales scattered on a nineteenth-century beach.

'See?' she said. 'These new beachings might have nothing to do with the slowing.'

But we didn't buy it. We knew what was coming.

★ ★ ★

I had begun spending my lunches in the library, land of the friendless, where Trevor Watkins sat hunched at a computer, powering a spaceship with the fuel of correctly answered algebra problems, and Diane Kofsky read romance novels, sneaking cheese puffs from her backpack. There was no eating in the library, and no talking, either.

The only good excuse for choosing to be in the library at lunch was if you had to do homework for the next period. But my homework was done. I tried instead to read, but I couldn't concentrate on the words. Mrs. Marshall read the newspaper at her desk, looking up now and then to watch the movements of Jesse Schwartz. Maybe we were all in the library against our will, but Jesse was here as punishment for some unknown but easily imagined infraction. He sat alone at a distant table, fidgeting and gazing out onto the quad where he belonged, his natural habitat, the sounds of which reached us here as a faint underwater murmur.

On the first day of honors pre-algebra that year, Mrs. Pinsky had drawn a funnel chart on the whiteboard to illustrate that a sifting process had begun. 'You've all been placed in the honors class for now,' she said. 'But the number of kids who can understand the math is going to shrink every year from now on.' It was that time of life: Talents were rising to the surface, weaknesses were beginning to show through, we were finding out what kind of people we would be. Some would turn out beautiful, some funny, some shy. Some would be smart, others smarter. The chubby ones would likely always be chubby. The beloved, I sensed, would be beloved for life. And I worried that loneliness might work that way, too. Maybe loneliness was imprinted in my genes, lying dormant for years but now coming into full bloom.

About halfway through the period, the glass door of the library swung open. The noise from outside surged in but was quickly sliced away again as the door banged closed.

When I looked up, I was shocked at who was walking down the ramp. He was different from the rest of us in the library — better-looking, better liked. Seth Moreno: I had never seen him in the library at lunch.

He sat down two chairs away from me. I wondered for many minutes whether this nearness was accident or will.

He rested his skateboard against the chair. Diane looked up from her book. You didn't see many skateboards in the library.

From his backpack, he pulled out a spiral notebook and a mechanical pencil. He turned to a fresh page and smoothed it with his palm.

He began to draw. I could see the shape of a small bird in flight emerging slowly from the tip of his pencil, its wings tucked at its sides. He drew a second bird a few inches higher in the sky. He began to outline a third, erased it, began again.

The sounds of the library were these: the squeaking of our chairs as we breathed, the tapping of Trevor's computer keys, the muted crunch of cheese puffs beneath the force of Diane's teeth — and the soft, pleasing scratch of Seth's pencil on paper.

Outside, someone banged on the window.

'Man,' Seth whispered to me. 'I can't handle it out there, you know?'

He looked over at me and then down at his drawing. His eyelashes formed a thick fringe as he blinked.

'I know,' I finally said.

The bell rang. We began to pack our bags. Diane struggled with the zipper of her backpack. Trevor remained hunched at the computer.

'Trevor,' said Mrs. Marshall from her desk, 'the bell has rung.'

And then, suddenly, someone was standing next me: It was Seth, and he was saying something. Seth was saying something to me.

'Hey,' he said.

There's a certain kind of shock that's possible only when you're young. I had the idea that he might be talking to someone else.

'Thanks for the card,' he said.

'Oh,' I said. 'You're welcome.'

'Did you hear about the whales?' he asked.

I had to look up to see his eyes. I worried I would say something wrong, so I said nothing for a moment.

'Yeah,' I said.

He waited for me to say something more. I could feel my face turning red. The flags of every country in the world fluttered from the ceiling tiles above the library.

'Maybe someone can help them get back into the water,' I said.

Seth shook his head.

'They would probably just beach themselves again,' he said. 'My dad's a scientist. He says that when whales beach themselves, there's a reason.'

Other kids began to trickle into the library. These were the ones with doctors' notes excusing them from PE.

'I'm going down to the beach after school to see them,' said Seth. The wheels of his skateboard spun slowly as he shifted it from one hand to the other. 'Want to come?'

'What?' I said.

Of all the strange phenomena that befell us that year, maybe nothing surprised me more than the sound of that small question rolling out of Seth's Moreno's mouth: 'Want to come?'

I can still remember the red diamond pattern

of the library carpet, the way the opening and closing of the library doors caused the overhead flags to swing back and forth above our heads.

'Okay,' I said.

'Okay, then,' he said.

And that was it. He turned and walked away.

★　★　★

On the way home, we sat separately on the bus. We both stepped off with the usual kids at our stop. It was hot and hazy in the neighborhood. Dust blew across the empty lot. The other kids scattered. I drifted in Seth's direction. I thought he might throw his skateboard on the asphalt and fly down the hill without me. Perhaps I'd misunderstood. Maybe this was some kind of joke.

Instead, he turned, squinting, and said, 'We can drop our backpacks at my house on the way.'

We were quiet as we walked. We communicated with our feet, mine following his down the sparkling sidewalk to his house.

I did not tell my parents where I was going. They wouldn't be home from work for hours anyway.

Seth lived two streets away from us in a beige ranch-style with a rusted basketball hoop overhanging the garage. The front yard had turned to dirt. A row of terra-cotta pots stood empty of flowers.

The front door was unlocked, and we walked right in, leaving our backpacks in the hall, which was cluttered with newspapers and laundry.

Thick quilts served as makeshift blackout curtains. An oxygen tank and its accompanying tubing lay tangled like wreckage in one corner. Seth's mother had died in this house.

'Want a Coke?' he said.

'Okay.'

We drank them at the kitchen table.

His father was at work, he said, he was there most of the time. He was a bioengineer, Seth explained, at work on a new type of corn.

'If it works,' he said, 'it'll be able to grow without light.'

* * *

Seth knew a shortcut through the canyon to the beach. It was a steep and sandy trail littered with pinecones and shaded by limestone bluffs. The smell of the canyon was the same as ever, like soil and sage, but the colors of California were turning starker. All the greens were fading away. Most everything was dying. Still, the canyon buzzed with beetles and mosquitoes and flies — whatever the birds had once eaten was flourishing, unhunted.

'Watch out for snakes,' said Seth.

I liked the way he walked: loose and unhurried, a boy who knew his way. I was the girl walking with him, so I walked that way, too.

The trail swung around a corner, and the beach came into view. It was low tide — lower than I'd ever seen it. The slowing was throwing off all the tides. Hundreds of feet of sea floor lay exposed, the sand ribboned black with bits of iron. These were the ocean's insides, revealed.

We stopped on the trail for a moment watching the ocean, side by side, our hands so close, they almost touched.

We crossed the coast road, ducked beneath the caution tape, and cut through the space between two ruined mansions, wet from the last high tide. One house had collapsed like a cake. Its walls were lined with barnacles. Sea anemones carpeted the front steps.

I bent to take off my shoes.

'Look,' said Seth.

There they were: the whales, dark and still, prehistoric in size.

A small crowd of people had gathered on the beach. Good Samaritans were dumping salt water on the whales. Other volunteers were returning from the distant tide, swaying with buckets full of fresh seawater.

We could hear the whales breathing, a slow rising and falling. We listened. We watched. They were social creatures, the whole group distressed by the stress of any one individual. It was obvious they were dying. But we couldn't help it. We were mesmerized.

Seth picked up two empty plastic cups from the sand. They were bits of ancient litter. He handed one to me.

'We have to do something,' he said. 'Come on.'

We ran barefoot down to the water, cups in hand. It was a long run. The mud sucked our feet. Creatures slithered unseen beneath my toes. Dead fish sparkled in the sun as my hair whipped in the wind. When we reached the lapping water and looked back, the humans on the beach were barely visible. Their hairline arms and hairline legs fluttered soundlessly around the whales. The only noise was the churning of the ocean.

We rushed to fill our cups with water and then ran back across the thick band of mud. We looked for the driest whale, the one most in need. We found it at the edge of the group, and we imagined that it was older than the others. Its skin was striped white with scars. I shooed flies from its eyes, one eye at a time. Seth poured our meager water supply over its head and into its mouth. He petted its side. I felt an urgency like love.

'Hey, kids,' someone called from behind us. It was a man in a beach hat, an empty white bucket swinging from one hand. A gust of wind drowned out what he said, so he shouted it again: 'That one's already dead.'

⋆   ⋆   ⋆

We were solemn as we climbed back up through the canyon. We were hot and exhausted. It was the twenty-third hour of daylight. The sun showed no signs of sinking.

'It's the magnetic field that's doing it,' said Seth.

'What is?'

A strong wind blew through the canyon, kicking up dust and dried leaves.

'That's why the whales are beaching them-selves. They use the magnetic field for

223

navigation, and now it's decaying because of the slowing.'

I glanced at the sky, a smooth, unblemished blue.

'You can't see it,' Seth said. 'It's invisible.'

Those were only the first of the whales. Hundreds more would soon wash ashore on the California coastline. Then thousands. Tens of thousands. More. Eventually, people stopped trying to save them.

'It's not just the whales who need the magnetic field,' said Seth as we arrived at the edge of the canyon and took our first steps on paved ground. 'We need it, too. My dad says that all the humans would die without it.'

But that day I could hardly hear him. My mind was elsewhere. I was a little bit in love. I'd spent an entire afternoon with Seth Moreno.

25

The eucalyptus first arrived in California in the 1850s. Imported from Australia, the seeds crossed five thousand miles of open ocean before reaching the soil of our state. The trunks were supposed to be a miracle wood, perfect for a hundred different purposes, railroad ties especially. But the wood turned out to be useless. It curled as it dried and split when nailed. The state's eucalyptus industry went bust before it ever boomed.

But the trees remained — and they spread. They were everywhere in my youth, and in my grandfather's youth, too. Their slender silhouettes once swayed along the coastal canyons, the beach bluffs, the soccer fields. Their long leaves floated in the swimming pools and the gutters. They drifted along the banks of saltwater lagoons. For over one hundred and fifty years, the eucalyptus thrived in California, surviving every calamity: earthquake, drought, the invention of the automobile. But now the trees were suffering en masse. The leaves were losing their color. Orange sap oozed from openings in the trunks. Little by little, they were dying.

★   ★   ★

On the morning of my twelfth birthday, I was lying awake in the dark, recalling in detail all the moments of the previous day's events: the way Seth squinted in the sun as we walked through the canyon, the tenderness in his hand as he petted the backs of the whales, the sound of his voice at the end of the day, and those words — *see you later* — as he turned and jumped on his skateboard, pushing off hard with one foot and then sailing sideways down the hill, his white T-shirt rippling in the wind behind him. I had to remind myself again and again that it had really happened: *He* had invited *me*.

My room was dark. The house was quiet.

In a few hours, I'd see Seth at the bus stop, and I wanted to say the exact right thing when I did, to divine whatever the words were that would lead to a second afternoon at his side.

That was when I heard it: a loud crash from outside. I remember the breaking of glass and the screeching of car alarms on the street. I rushed to my window and looked out: The tallest eucalyptus on the street had sliced through Sylvia's roof and crushed one corner of her house.

Over time, I have come to believe in omens. But I wonder if I might have developed a more strictly rational mind had I lived in a time before the slowing. Perhaps in some other era, science instead of superstition might have sufficed.

My parents rushed outside, my mother in her bathrobe, my father without a shirt. It was a dark night, cloudy, no stars. The tree lay diagonally across the yard, blocking Sylvia's front door. The roots were exposed, hanging in the air, like a molar wrenched from a gum. One section of

Sylvia's roof had collapsed.

All along the street, lamps flashed on in bedrooms, doors swung open, the voices of neighbors rose from front yards. Sylvia's house stood dark and silent. Some of the men jogged toward it in pajamas, but my father was first, dashing through the side gate, out of sight. My mother stood with her arms crossed in the middle of the street. I stood beside her, shivering in my nightgown.

'She should have had that tree cut down,' said my mother.

Two of ours had been removed already. There were stumps all over the neighborhood, and crews of men in reflective suits worked constantly along the roads, felling trees one by one and then carting the pieces away.

'We should cut the rest of ours down, too,' said my mother.

She took a few steps closer to Sylvia's house, stood on tiptoes, angling for a better view.

'Where *is* he?' she asked.

I used to think my mother knew at least as much as I did about Sylvia and my father and that every question she asked was code for something else. But maybe she only sensed it.

She kept her own secrets too. She was hiding a massive new store of emergency supplies in the closet of the guest room. She was hoarding hundreds of cans of food and hiding them from my father. And she had placed an order for a greenhouse without telling him.

Finally, my father emerged through the side gate. Sylvia was with him, draped over his shoulder but walking, barefoot in a short white nightgown.

My father guided her to our porch, where she sat with her head in her hands.

'She's okay,' he said. 'She's just shaken up.'

My mother brought her a glass of water, though she kept her distance as she handed Sylvia the glass.

Sylvia's nightgown left her whole back exposed. In the front, the shape of her small breasts was apparent through the thin cotton. She sat for a long time, hunched on our steps like a girl. You see only a few adults cry the way she did on that night, open, abiding, unashamed.

'It hit the piano,' my father said softly.

'This was not an accident,' said Sylvia, wiping her nose with the back of her hand.

The other neighbors had trickled back into their houses. The lights were switching off. It was five in the morning on a dark night.

'The tree was sick,' said my father.

'No,' said Sylvia. She shook her head. She had the thinnest, most swanlike neck. The knobs of her spine surfaced as she turned her neck. 'Someone did this.'

Sylvia was the last real-timer left on our street. The Kaplans were gone. Tom and Carlotta were gone; a young family had moved into their house and begun remodeling.

'I'm telling you, Joel,' said Sylvia. The way she said my father's name was not the way one neighbor speaks another neighbor's name. My mother heard it, too. She glanced at my father and pulled her bathrobe closed at the neck.

Sylvia continued: 'They're trying to drive me out.'

Later, I tried but mostly failed to sleep the last hour before my alarm clock sounded. Meanwhile, my parents argued through their bedroom door. I could hear not what was said but what was expressed, the anger radiating through the door.

★　★　★

It was tradition among the girls at my school to bring each other a balloon on the day of each girl's birth. It was always the same variety of balloon, the shiny Mylar kind you buy at the party store. You carried it around with you all day or fastened it to your backpack, letting it float behind you, fat and lovely, through math, English, life sciences, PE. Weighted by a tiny beanbag, each balloon bobbed above the sea of heads in the halls, a buoy marking the precise location of a happy and well-liked girl. This tradition had not been interrupted by the slowing.

The year before, Hanna had brought my balloon — but that was a past life, or someone else's, an earlier, uncomplicated spring.

I tried not to look at Hanna that morning at the bus stop, the way she was sitting against the fence, her phone pressed hard to her ear. She didn't even say hello.

This year I knew my birthday would go unmarked at school.

I stood at the edge of the crowd at the bus

stop, waiting in the darkness for Seth to arrive. I had spent a long time choosing what to wear, settling finally on the cream mohair sweater I'd worn for picture day and a knee-length jean skirt.

The stars glowed. Headlights flashed. Kids trundled in on foot from various directions. Some emerged from the passenger sides of running cars, backpacks swinging from their arms. Seth was not among them.

Minutes passed. I began to shiver.

I shifted my weight from one foot to the other and then discovered, to my horror, that the hairs on my legs were glittering under the streetlights. I was suddenly embarrassed standing there, just a few feet away from Michaela's smoothly shaved calves, which were right at that moment standing attractively in a pair of heeled black sandals as she laughed into the ear of one of the eighth-grade boys.

Finally, there came the sound of plastic wheels grinding asphalt in the distance, the rattle of a board scraping the curb. My heart began to race. There he was: Seth Moreno.

He stepped off his board. He tucked it under one arm.

I wanted to tell him that I'd heard about another group of whales beached a few miles farther up the coast. But I wasn't sure how to start. This was new to me, the special communications that tethered boys to girls.

The bus heaved up to the curb, and kids began to climb the stairs, but I lingered on the pavement, waiting for Seth to show me how things would be. Our eyes met. Seth nodded slightly.

I'd been rehearsing this moment for hours, and I had outlined a hundred different scenarios. Mr. Jensen once tried to tell us that there existed somewhere a set of parallel universes, unreachable but real, where every possibility came true; whatever didn't happen here happened somewhere else, each option unfolding in a separate universe. But in this one world, at least, the outcome that morning was reduced finally to just this one version.

Seth stood on the sidewalk for a moment, averting his eyes from me. He didn't smile. He didn't speak. Then he walked right past me and kept going, as if the two of us were strangers. He stepped onto the bus and didn't look back.

I don't know how much time passed after that — thirty seconds, maybe longer — but I became aware eventually of the bus driver yelling down at me from his seat.

'Hey you,' he called over the hum of the engine. 'Are you coming?' All the other kids were on the bus by then. A few were staring down at me through smudged windows, snickers forming on their faces. I was a girl standing alone in the dirt in a cream mohair sweater and a stupid jean skirt. It was hard to breathe.

It occurred to me too late, after I'd stepped onto the bus and sat down in the front, fifteen rows from Seth, that I could have disappeared into the canyon and no one would have noticed.

*　*　*

I spent the break between classes in the bathroom. I spent another lunch period in the library. Diane was there, as usual, the gold cross around her neck glittering beneath the fluorescent lights. Trevor clacked the computer keys, busy with the game he always played; he held all the high scores. Mrs. Marshall was returning books to the shelves — we could hear the whine of her cart as she wheeled it over the carpet, the crinkle of the cellophane book jackets as she slid each one into place. Every time the door squeaked open, I hoped it would be Seth Moreno — come to apologize or explain.

A bleak thought had begun to bubble in my mind: Maybe he didn't want to be seen with me at school.

Through the windows simmered the muffled squeals of the other kids, running loose on the quad. Those kids never traveled anywhere alone.

Christy Casteneda swanned past the library window — it was her birthday, too, and not one but two balloons swayed from her delicate wrist, each one signed on the blank silver side in loopy, loving cursive.

I pretended to read. The clock ticked. Seth did not appear.

On dark days like that one, the library windows looked lit up like an aquarium, the inhabitants on display for all the other kids to see: here the most exotic fish, the lonely, the unloved, the weird.

★ ★ ★

By evening Sylvia's eucalyptus had been cut into pieces, and the pieces lay stacked like cleaned boncs in the driveway. White plastic sheeting covered the hole in the roof, rustling whenever the wind blew. The sun had yet to rise.

My father spent a long time that night inspecting the last eucalyptus in our own yard. Half of it produced leaves, but the other half was dead, and the death seemed to be spreading. He called a tree removal service before we left for my birthday dinner.

My mother came home with a present for me: a pair of gold ballet flats with a crinkled finish. The other girls at school had been wearing them for months. I slipped them on. They squeaked on the tile.

My father gave me a book.

'This was my favorite book when I was about your age,' he said. On the cover was a series of mountains, a valley, a moon. The pages smelled like dust and mildew. 'It's about a kid who's all alone in the world. He's really lonely for a long time. But then, well, you'll see.'

I remembered that book passing through our classroom two or three years earlier. I hadn't read it, but I was too old for it now.

'Thanks,' I said, and pressed it to my lap.

He squeezed my shoulder. We left for dinner.

'It's lucky I'm not sick on your birthday,' said my mother as we drove east toward my grandfather's house. We were picking him up on our way to my favorite restaurant. I was looking forward to seeing him. His voice had a way of cutting through everything else.

'I still think we should've had a party,' said my mother. 'We should be celebrating the good things.'

'We are,' said my father. He glanced at me in the rearview. 'This is what she wanted.'

The landscape outside looked less alive each time we did this drive. It wasn't only the grass and the eucalyptus trees. There were subtler signs, too. I was certain the banks of the lagoon were browner than they used to be, the cattails and the reeds less abundant than before. We avoided saying it out loud — we had the greenhouses and the sunlamps to keep us fed for now — but it was hard to ignore the way the plants were quietly slipping away, a creeping devastation. God knows what was happening on the less fortunate continents. But the golf course, when we passed it, looked better than ever, more lush and more pristine than it had ever looked in life. All the old greens had been replaced with high-end artificial turf, and now golf carts trundled slowly over the hills: the golf course in afterlife.

'I don't know why we couldn't invite Hanna,' said my mother. She turned toward me in her seat, the seat belt cutting into her neck. 'You two used to be such good friends.'

'Well, we're not anymore,' I said.

My grandfather's property looked worse than usual. He had refused to cut down any of his eucalyptus trees. Some stood leafless and grim against the sky. Others had fallen to the ground. But the pines, at least, were persisting and still kept his house hidden from the road and the surrounding development.

We pulled into his driveway. I jumped out onto the gravel, ran up to the door. My parents waited in the car, engine running.

He didn't answer the door, so I rang the bell again. I knocked. A group of gnats was circling the porch light. Behind me, the black sky was fading, turning ever so slightly light. A slow sunrise was beginning. I tried the doorknob: It was locked.

I went back to the car, my ballet flats crunching hard on the gravel.

'He's not answering,' I said.

'Maybe he forgot to put in his hearing aid,' said my father.

He turned off the car and followed me back up the walk to the house. My mother cracked the car door for air.

My father had keys to the house. He unlocked the door, and we stepped inside.

'Dad?' said my father. The house was hot and quiet. The only sound was the ticking of clocks. The only light was the overhead in the kitchen. 'We're here.'

The windows were closed, and the shelves were as bare as they had been the last time I visited.

'Where is everything?' asked my father. He ran one finger along a vacant shelf. He peered through the glass front of a mahogany cabinet, empty of its guts of china and crystal.

'On New Year's,' I said, 'he was kind of sorting through his stuff.'

'What do you mean?' said my father.

235

We took my grandfather out to dinner most Sundays. He was usually waiting on the porch for us, ready to get in the car, insisting we were late.

'He was also putting some of his stuff in boxes,' I said.

'What?' A spark of concern flickered across my father's face. 'But I just talked to him last night.'

The boxes were gone. The table was clear. Everything of any value had vanished. We checked his bedroom and found the bed empty and unmade. We opened the closet: At least half of his clothes were missing, maybe a few pairs of shoes.

In the kitchen we discovered a stack of obscure newsletters and leaflets. A small newspaper was dominated by this headline: WHAT THEY DON'T WANT YOU TO KNOW: THE TRUTH ABOUT CLOCK TIME. To the refrigerator was clipped a political cartoon in which people wandered the street, eyes glazed. The caption read: THE CLOCK ZOMBIES.

My mother wandered in behind us.

'Where is he?' she said.

'I don't know,' said my father.

'Oh, God,' said my mother. 'This place looks like it's been robbed.'

'Julia says she saw him packing.'

Something was bubbling in my father, a fast current running beneath ice.

'Not exactly packing,' I said.

My mother turned to me, frantic.

'You need to stop keeping secrets, young lady.'

Outside, my father called my grandfather's

name, shouting into the dawn light: 'Dad, are you out here?' Through the window, I watched my father search the old stable, the backyard, the dying woods at the edge of the property.

My grandfather could no longer drive. He did not even own a car. He could not have left on his own. He relied on us and on Chip, the teenager who lived down the road, to help him with groceries and rides.

'He's too old to be living alone,' said my mother. 'We should have known.'

I felt tears coming to my eyes.

My father jogged down to Chip's house, which was one of the new ones in the regular development.

My mother began calling the phone numbers that were posted on my grandfather's refrigerator. They were mostly members of his church, the phone tree, the carpool. The house still smelled like my grandfather, like Listerine and old paper. An antique clock chimed seven times in the living room. My mother's voice cracked as she talked, leaving her cell phone number in case he turned up.

My father soon returned to us with news: Chip had dropped out of high school and moved away.

'Moved where?' said my mother.

My father rubbed his forehead and blinked a slow blink. A sliver of sun had peaked above the horizon and was shining through the windows, illuminating the dust that floated everywhere in that house. Back then a certain euphoria usually accompanied the arrival of sunshine after so many hours in the dark, but we barely noticed it that night. We all just squinted in the brightness.

'His mother says Chip went to that place in the desert,' said my father. 'Circadia. He left last night.'

26

Circadia did not exist on any map. In the section of the Thomas Guide where we had heard it would be, we found only a patch of blank space, a slight crease in the page, a wash of beige symbolizing desert. So it felt as if we were heading to a fictive place, some imagined land, dreamed up or invented. And in one sense, we were. Once in the desert, we would leave the two-lane highway for a hairline road that dead-ended on the map but would lead eventually to a second road, unpaved and too new for the maps to register. This was how we would reach Circadia.

'Do you think he's really there?' said my mother. Sunlight was streaming in through the windshield. She adjusted the overhead visor.

'Maybe,' said my father. His eyes were narrow against the rising sun. It was nine o'clock at night. 'Maybe not.'

We had called the police from my grandfather's house, but he was not a missing person. Old and eccentric but not senile, he had packed up his own things before leaving.

We drove toward the desert right away, skipping dinner. The highway curved through the hills, some of them blackened from the recent fires. The temperature rose with every mile. Out there, plant life had always struggled to survive, so the land looked less ravaged than the coastal regions did. A few scruffy bushes persisted on the rocky slopes, looking no more spindly than usual.

'It's just so hard to picture your father joining anything,' said my mother.

'He belongs to a church,' I said from the backseat.

Power lines were whipping by beside the road, undulating as they traveled from pole to pole.

'Don't you think it's hard to imagine?' said my mother.

'Helen,' said my father. He sat stiffly in his seat, both hands on the wheel, eyes straight ahead. 'I just don't know.'

The radio turned to static as the last of the suburbs fell away. Traffic thinned. The land flattened. The desert peeled open all around us, and the blue sky hung low to the ground. The sun hovered for hours on the horizon.

The surface of the road blurred in the heat, and I began to smell the leather of the seats in the car, the surfaces cooking in the sun. My mother turned up the air.

As the hours passed, we all began to yawn. My father rubbed the edge of his chin, where a layer of stubble had formed since the morning.

We passed the ruins of an ancient gas station where one pump remained, rusted red. Beside it stood a humble sun-bleached structure leaning heavily to one side, without its roof. There was a certain heartbreak in that scene. Someone had built those walls. Someone had once felt some kind of hope for the future of this place. Now you could see right through the cracks in the walls to the sky on the other side.

Eventually, I fell asleep, my head against the window. I dreamed that we moved to Circadia but that we brought our house with us — only the views and the neighbors changed.

★ ★ ★

I awoke sometime after ten P.M. to the bumping of the car over dirt.

'Go slower,' said my mother. She was holding tight to the handle in the ceiling. We were driving straight into the sun.

Through the haze, I could see the outline of rooftops in the distance, neat rows of white houses bordered by an ocean of sand dunes rippling across the desert.

The developer's original sign still stood at the entrance, a heavy slab of granite, fronted by a dry fountain and a patch of dead grass. Etched in thick cursive were the words: THE HOMES AT RANCHO DOMINGO DEL SOL. Above the sign, a makeshift banner flapped from two posts: WELCOME TO CIRCADIA. Beneath that, someone had written, *Land of the Free*.

I was secretly thrilled. I had the idea from Gabby that maybe this was a place where life was more fair.

The streets had names like Desert Rose Lane and Dune Way. Some were paved. Others weren't. Clear Sky Drive ran paved for a few hundred feet and then sputtered out into dirt, as if to record the precise moment in time when the developer had run out of cash.

'Can you imagine living out here?' said my mother.

The houses stood in varying stages of completion. Some lacked garages, others roofs. Some were just wooden frames naked of drywall and stucco, the studs beginning to weather in the hot, dry air. But you could see what the developer had been aiming for: twelve streets aspiring to a suburb. The nearest grocery store was an hour away.

Though it was ten-thirty at night, Circadia was just waking up. Twenty-five hours of daylight stretched out ahead of us. Hammers echoed in the distance. Somewhere, a saw buzzed.

A man in a faded blue T-shirt and a wide-brimmed hat was crouched in a gravel driveway, pouring white paint into a tray. Beside him, a ladder leaned against a house.

My father slowed the car, rolled down his window. It was hard to breathe the desert air.

'Excuse me,' my father called out from the car.

The man turned, squinted.

'I'm looking for my father. He's in his eighties, and his name is Gene. Have you seen him?'

The man walked over to our car. His face was badly sunburned, and the beginning of a black beard was growing on his cheeks and chin.

'Did he tell you he was coming here?' he said when he reached my father's window.

I had the idea that the people of Circadia had not only escaped the clocks but had also managed to slip loose of time itself. I searched the man's face for evidence that he was different from us, somehow changed. I imagined the transformation might be deep, molecular, as if every atom in his body were right then spinning at a slightly slower speed than the atoms in ours. Sweat dripped along his hairline. Sweat was showing through his T-shirt.

'He would have arrived last night,' said my father, who was still in his white collared shirt. His wristwatch flashed in the sun. The air conditioner struggled against the wafting heat.

The man glanced at me through the window. He chewed his lower lip. I was aware of the ticking of our dashboard clock as it registered in neon the passage of one more minute, our Volvo a separate universe in which time raced by at high speed.

'He might have come here with a seventeen-year-old kid,' said my mother, leaning toward the driver's side. 'Named Chip.'

The man rubbed his forehead with the back of his wrist. He touched the brim of his hat.

'If he didn't tell you he was coming here,' he said, 'maybe he didn't want you to know.'

We gave up and drove on, but the man stood in his driveway for a while, his hands on his hips, watching our car move down the street.

We came to a fork in the road and turned right, where we found a woman walking a yellow lab.

'Sorry,' she said. 'Haven't seen them.'

She kept walking.

'Not the friendliest bunch,' said my mother.

We passed a series of greenhouses. Everywhere we looked, sheets dangled from clotheslines.

At the end of one cul-de-sac, we arrived at

what was obviously meant to be the community swimming pool, no doubt touted in the original brochures for the project. But it was only a dry hole in the ground, deep at one end, shallow at the other, and not yet lined with cement.

Beside the pool was a small playground where a girl in a green sundress was sitting on one of the swings, her brown hair flying around in the wind. I recognized her from soccer: Molly Kopachek.

'Stop here,' I said. I rolled down my window. 'Molly?'

She looked up, pulled her hair from her face, and twisted a makeshift bun. We'd been fullbacks together one year, but she was not the competitive kind. She used to pick dandelions in the penalty box during games.

Now she hopped from the swing and walked to my window, her sandals grinding the dirt.

'Are you moving here, too?' she said.

Behind her stood a skeletal structure, a wooden frame, suggestive of a house.

'We're just looking for my grandpa,' I said.

She hadn't seen him, but when I said Chip's name, she pointed across the street.

'I think there might be a guy named Chip staying at that house over there,' she said.

My father pulled the parking brake.

The exterior of the house was coated in unfinished gray stucco. Paint cans lay scattered nearby.

A wisp of a girl in a white tank top stood smoking a cigarette out front. She was lanky and pale, her head was shaved, and she stared at us through a pair of oversize sunglasses as we approached the house. I could see the sky in her lenses. It was everywhere, that sky, somehow wider in the desert, more visible, than anywhere else on earth.

'Are you his parents?' she said when my father asked about Chip. From inside the house, guitar chords floated out to us in waves. Someone was singing. It was so hot I could barely breathe.

'We just want to talk to him,' said my mother.

The girl took a long slow breath and exhaled. She held her cigarette with two fingers near her hip. The smoke smelled different from other smoke: cloves.

'I think he's out back,' she said. She nodded toward the front door but didn't move. 'It's unlocked.'

Inside, we found a living room empty of furniture but lined with sleeping bags, at least one of which was occupied. A ceiling fan spun insufficiently, circulating hot air.

'Hello?' said my father. He looked around. He didn't seem to know where to stand. A recycling bin had overflowed in the hall. Empty wine bottles lay like bowling pins on the hardwood floor.

The music was coming from the kitchen, where two girls — each one as willowy as the one out front — sat in mismatched chairs while a boy without a shirt played guitar.

The boy was the first to see us. The music stopped.

'Yes?' he said.

The girls turned sluggishly toward us. Their eyes were watery and red. They laughed as soon as they saw us. My small family was in the kitchen of strangers.

'We're looking for Chip,' said my father. His words, crisp and quick, sliced embarrassingly through the air. I thought I could feel it then, the slowness of the house around us, the sluggish pace at which time unfolded in this place.

The girls glanced outside to the back of the house.

'Hey, Chip,' called the boy. 'Your dad's here.'

The girls laughed, and the boy began to play again.

They were college kids, or formerly so — I'd heard they were dropping out by the thousands, stealing clocks from classrooms and smashing them in the streets.

Outside, Chip looked the same as ever: black T-shirt and cutoff black shorts, black tennis shoes, dyed black hair. Under the shade of a frayed umbrella, he was reading a book in a faded beach chair.

He was startled to see us.

'What are you doing here?' he said.

'Did my father come here with you?' said my father.

By now the question sounded ridiculous. My grandfather was not in this house.

'No,' Chip said. He set the book flat on his lap. 'Why?'

A few feet away, a young couple lay intertwined on a lawn chair. They didn't notice

246

us, or they didn't care. They kissed for a long time, and my mother made a show of holding her hand up to the side of her face to block the view.

My father showed Chip one of the flyers we'd found at my grandfather's house.

'I know he agrees that clock time is total bullshit,' said Chip. 'But if he's not at home, I don't know where he is.'

The back patio was fenceless. There was no yard. It opened out to the desert, where a vast field of solar panels sparkled in the sun.

'That's where we get our power,' said Chip when he saw me staring.

The electrical grid did not extend this far into the desert. Water had to be trucked in as well.

'You should think about joining us out here,' said Chip. 'You know, tune out, drop in.'

'It's tune *in*, drop *out*,' said my mother. She was fanning herself theatrically with a magazine she'd pulled from her purse. 'Let's go.'

My father wrote his cell phone number on a scrap of paper and handed it to Chip.

'If you see him or hear from him,' he said, 'please call.'

Chip walked us back through the house and outside. The girls were still laughing as we passed. They couldn't seem to stop.

'You probably think we're a bunch of pipe dreamers out here,' said Chip. The girl beside him lit another cigarette. 'But it's just the opposite. We're not the ones in denial.'

The wind was picking up, blowing bits of dust and trash around in little circles in the street.

Soon we would leave this place, and I would listen to my heartbeat for a while, trying to catch it speeding up as we drove.

'We're the realists,' Chip added. 'You're the dreamers.'

27

My grandfather once had an uncle who disappeared in Alaska. It was 1970, early summer near the Arctic Circle, twenty-two hours of daylight per day. This uncle was a fisherman who had come to Alaska from Norway three decades earlier and had become a legend along a certain stretch of coastline, renowned for his ability to predict where the salmon ran thickest as they spawned. He lived alone on a tiny island a few miles off the coast. He was frugal. He slept in a one-room cabin with no electricity or running water, and he buried the money he made in a secret location on the island. My grandfather spent two salmon seasons working for him, and for decades afterward, my grandfather kept a small photograph of him, dressed in waders and a black knit cap, a tangled net draped over thick knuckles.

One day this uncle set out alone on his fishing boat. It was a short trip from the port to the island. The sky was clear. The sea was calm. He was never seen again.

'It was June,' my grandfather used to say, as if he'd been there on that day. By 1970 my grandfather was living in California again, but whenever he told this story, he made a sweeping gesture with the palm of his hand to indicate the flatness of the ocean on the day his uncle vanished.

'The weather was perfect,' he'd say. 'Not a shred of wind.'

His uncle was presumed lost at sea. But my grandfather never believed it. Several searches of his property failed to unearth his fortune.

'Rolf could handle anything on the water,' he would often say. 'There's no way that boat sank.'

Fifteen years passed. No one heard from the uncle.

And then my grandparents took a trip to Norway — this was years before I was born. They were riding a bus in the northern part of the country, where my grandfather's relatives lived. When the bus stopped in a small fishing village, an old man boarded the bus.

'I knew it was him as soon as I saw him,' my grandfather used to tell me.

At this moment in the story, he would shake his head slowly, close his eyes, and whistle slightly, satisfied by the proof in flesh of a truth long sensed.

'I always knew he was alive,' he would say. 'I always knew.'

My grandfather once lost his wedding ring — it flew off his finger and into an Alaskan snow bank — but he found it months later, in the spring. The snow had melted. The gold ring was lying in the dirt. Finger was reunited with band. My grandfather liked any story in which the unlikely turned out to be true.

'But why did Rolf disappear in the first place?' I always asked. For my grandfather, this was not a key part of the story. Or perhaps the reasons for a man to leave his life were too obvious for him to name.

'I know he recognized me on that bus,' my grandfather would say. 'But he didn't say anything. At the next stop, he just stood up and got off. Didn't even look back.'

His uncle disappeared into the woods on the side of the road. My grandfather never saw him again.

'That would be just like Rolf,' my grandfather used to say with a certain admiration crackling in his voice. 'Just like him.'

★　★　★

It was after midnight when we got home from Circadia. Our street was bright and quiet, almost everyone asleep. It was the lifeless middle of a bright white night. Our cul-de-sac looked evacuated. Not even Sylvia was out. The slamming of our car doors echoed against the stucco. A pair of clouds scudded westward on the breeze. The only sign of life was a skinny Siamese cat squinting in the sunshine as it traipsed across the Petersons' artificial lawn.

My parents stayed up all night, calling hospitals.

I pulled my curtains and tried to sleep. Cracks of sunlight streaked the carpet. My alarm clock ticked on my dresser, and I was newly aware of its swiftness: the ticking, ticking, ticking. Minutes zoomed. Hours flew. I slept little. I dreamed unsettling dreams. Days, months, years, whole lives — everything was rushing toward its end.

251

At the appointed hour, my alarm clock exploded; it was time to get up for school. I woke with a racing heart, out of breath and sweaty in my sheets.

Later that morning, the police called with a report of an elderly man who had been found wandering, disoriented, in a nearby grocery store. My father drove down to the police station to confirm what we already knew: It wasn't him.

28

Three days passed. There was no word from my grandfather.

And it felt as if Seth Moreno had gone missing from my life as well. He arrived later and later at the bus stop each morning. In math, he stared straight ahead, always rushing from the classroom as soon as the bell rang. We had not exchanged a single word since the day we saw the whales. I did not know what I'd done wrong.

Meanwhile, the days kept growing, the nights kept spreading. There was talk of tipping points, feedback loops, points of no return.

Later that week, NASA announced that the astronauts were coming back, in spite of the risk. No one knew exactly how the slowing would affect reentry, but they had run out of food in the space station. A thousand calculations were made, some necessary guesses. We'd been told that the *Orion* would streak across the southern California sky at three minutes past four o'clock on its way to Edwards Air Force Base.

I planned to watch it through my telescope, alone.

★　★　★

It was bright and hot outside as I stepped off the bus that afternoon. The sun had been shining for

253

twenty-something hours. The asphalt was glittering. A warm breeze was blowing leaves and litter through the neighborhood.

As I walked toward home, I was thinking of the astronauts. They'd been away for ten months, the last humans left who had not yet experienced a day longer than twenty-four hours.

As I cut across a vacant lot, I was surprised to see Seth on his skateboard. He had disappeared from the bus stop right away but had paused here and was using the curb to do jumps near a fire hydrant.

I resisted the urge to look in his direction as I walked. I could hear the clean clip of his board striking the curb again and again. I kept walking.

But when I turned in the direction of my street, the noise stopped. In its place, I heard the most unbelievable sound: the three syllables of my name shouted on the wind.

'Yeah?' I said.

A sudden lump formed in my throat.

The other kids had scattered. It was just the two of us and the dust from the dirt lot blowing across the street.

'Are you gonna watch the rocket?' he said. He shielded his eyes from the sun with one hand. Our shadows mingled on the sidewalk.

'Maybe,' I said. I was skittish and shy.

'I'm gonna watch it from my roof,' he said. A breeze blew. Seconds passed. 'Come on.'

Maybe I should have been angry about the

way he'd acted before, but all I remember is the wave of his hand as he motioned for me to follow him, the way he pronounced the exact words that my ears most wanted to hear.

From his cluttered garage, we dragged two rusty beach chairs into the house and then up the ladder through the attic and out. We arranged them side by side on a flat section of roof, lined with black tar paper and wiring, mounds of ancient bird poop. Seth brought us two Cokes and some pretzels, and then we leaned back and waited for the *Orion* to zoom over our heads. The sky was clear. The air was warm. The chairs smelled like sunscreen and salt. I could feel Seth sitting next to me. I could hear him breathing near me. We didn't talk for a long time.

Seth broke the quiet.

'Why were you being like that the other day?' he said.

I felt a rush of panic.

'Being like what?' I said.

He didn't look at me. He sipped his Coke and set it down on the tar paper. We could hear cars whooshing past on the freeway in the distance.

'I don't know,' he said. 'You were being kind of weird at the bus stop last week.'

I felt a tightening in my chest. I gripped the metal arm of my chair.

'I wasn't being weird,' I said. 'You were.'

He was careful not to look in my direction. I was aware of his nose in profile, the left line of his jaw, one ear, one eye, as he stared straight ahead toward the mountains that rose to our east. He looked better than ever.

He cleared his throat and added: 'It kind of seemed like you didn't want anyone to talk to you.'

'That's not true,' I said. 'That's not true at all.'

They say that humans can read each other in a hundred subtle ways, that we can detect messages in the subtlest movements of a body, in the briefest expressions of a face, but somehow, on that day, I had communicated with amazing efficiency the exact opposite of what I most wanted in the world.

'And you were all dressed up and stuff,' he went on. 'Why were you so dressed up?'

I could hardly breathe, but I felt a tiny thrill. Here was proof that he'd given me some thought.

'You were the one being weird,' I said. 'You didn't even say hi.'

He turned and looked at me for the first time in several minutes. He had dark brown eyes, a thick fringe of lashes, no freckles.

'You didn't say anything, either,' he said.

And then his mouth opened into a wide and sudden smile. I saw his front teeth were a little bit crooked.

'It was my birthday that day,' I said.

'Oh,' he said. 'Well, happy birthday.'

Who knew what would happen next, but we were together for now, sipping our Cokes and looking at the sky.

'Wait,' said Seth, sitting up in his beach chair. 'What time is it?'

He was the first to realize it: The *Orion* was overdue.

'Something's wrong,' he said.

His dark eyes, squinting, searched the open sky.

We waited a few more long minutes, but the sky remained a perfect blue, ominously empty of aircraft and contrails.

It was as if we knew even then what had happened.

We learned from Seth's television the details of the *Orion's* final fate. It disintegrated two hundred miles off the coast of California, cause unknown. All six astronauts on board were killed.

Seth and I sat stiffly on opposite sides of his couch, watching the stream of news reports flow into his living room.

Already, the networks were flashing photos of the astronauts from the day they'd left the earth ten months earlier, their faces fresh and happy, their white suits so crisp and bright in the sunshine, their gigantic helmets gleaming beneath their arms as they waved — so different from the way they looked in the recent video transmissions, after they'd grown so thin and frail in space that it seemed almost natural the way they floated, weightless, while they spoke to Houston via satellite link.

We said nothing for a while. I shifted in my seat. The couch squeaked beneath me. There were holes in the leather.

Seth was the first to speak.

'Would you rather die in an explosion?' he

asked. 'Or of a disease?'

I let the question hang. His mother had died here. I didn't want to say the wrong words.

'The thing about an explosion,' he said, 'is that it only takes a second.'

29

After that, Seth and I were often together.

Ours was a sudden bond, the kind possible only for the young or the imperiled. Time moved differently for us that spring: A string of long afternoons was as good as a year.

We quit spending lunches in the library and stretched out instead beneath a pair of dead pine trees at the far edge of the quad, where we watched the clouds drift across the sky. Seth started saving me a seat on the bus every morning and every afternoon.

At first I was aware of the other kids watching us. I sensed their chatter. But soon I ceased to notice. I stopped caring what they thought.

'He seems like a nice boy,' said my mother. 'Let's have him over for dinner.'

But I only wanted to be alone with Seth. I didn't want anyone else around.

★ ★ ★

I was with Seth on the day we passed the wheat point. Now it was official: Wheat could no longer grow on this planet without the aid of artificial light. We watched from a hillside as people pushed grocery carts across the supermarket parking lot, heaped full of canned food. Panic had returned. You could feel it in the air, an ending, a tingling, like a taste in the back of your throat.

'Would you rather starve?' said Seth. 'Or die of thirst?'

This had become a game of ours. We were serious kids made more so by the times.

'Starve,' I said. 'You?'

'Thirst,' he said. He kicked a rock down the slope. Dust sputtered behind it. The rock disappeared into a tangle of desiccated ice plant. Seth always chose the quickest death.

Seth was at my house when my mother's greenhouse was delivered. We watched the workers assemble it out back. The glass glittered as they mounted the sunlamps and poured the soil. We watched them unfurl an orange electrical cord and then insert the fat plug into an outdoor socket. We were one of the last families on our street to buy one. My mother had ordered it without consulting my father, and while she lowered a series of small plants into the soil, my father watched from the dining room table, his arms crossed. Then he went upstairs. By the end of the day, we had two rows of green beans and three rows of strawberries growing in the greenhouse.

'Strawberries are a waste,' said my father. 'If we're going to be growing anything, we should be growing mushrooms. They don't depend so much on light.'

A rash of white-night crimes also struck our city. The real-timers were blamed. Who else would be out at those late hours? The windows of Sylvia's car were smashed in her driveway. Her garage was soon spray-painted with thick, drippy words: *Get the fuck out.*

I wondered how my father felt about that, but I didn't ask, and he didn't say.

★ ★ ★

It seemed to me that time moved at high speed that spring. Seth's hair grew long again and began to fall into his eyes. I grew out my bangs, and Seth said he liked them. I started shaving my legs, and I bought a real bra — one that fit this time. One dark afternoon Seth taught me to ride his skateboard, and I still remember the way his hand felt on my back as he jogged beside me in the glow of the streetlights, me wobbling over the cracks in the sidewalk, content.

After school, we'd go searching in the canyons for the skeletons of birds — they were everywhere, a profusion of bone and feather, as abundant as seashells. We hunted for the last living eucalyptus, which we found, we were certain, withering on the edge of a sandstone bluff by the ocean. We collected the neighborhood's last blades of grass. We kept the final flowerings of daisies, of marigolds, of honeysuckle. We pressed petals between the pages of dictionaries. We lined our shelves with relics from our time. *Look here*, we pictured saying someday, *this one we called maple, this one magnolia, this aspen, this oak.* On dark days, Seth drew maps of the constellations as if those bodies, too, might soon fall away.

Seth's father was frequently at his lab. He left home early. He came home late. He was the coffee cup in the kitchen sink, the cigarettes in the ashtray out back, the lab coat slung over the banister. He was a name on the envelopes that piled, unopened, in a huge stack by the door, a voice on the phone instructing Seth to order pizza, eat without him. My parents never knew how little Seth's father was at home when I was there.

We were home alone at Seth's house on the day the power went out.

The television snapped off, the lights, too. I grabbed Seth's hand in the dark. It was four o'clock in the afternoon. A quiet flooded the house, as if silence were a condition of the dark. We had sixteen hours, maybe more, until the sun would rise again. We fumbled together to the front door, swung it open: It was dark out there, too, a prehistoric dark, the soundless glittering of stars.

My mother called my cell phone from work. 'Stay put,' she said. 'Just stay put. Lock the doors, and don't let anyone in.' We scoured the house for flashlights. We bumped each other in our blindness and ran into the walls. We broke a lamp and laughed for a long time. Seth lit candles with one of his father's lighters. We carried them around like torches, our faces shadowy in the flame light. We wondered if it might last forever, the age after electricity.

Finally, we sat down on the hardwood floor of the living room, our candles flickering around us. Seth produced a deck of cards.

'Watch this,' he said.

He began to build a tower, three cards at a time.

The house was so silent in the dark that I could hear the sound of the cards brushing one another as he worked. He looked older in candlelight. I watched him for a long time.

'Try it,' he said. He held out a pair of cards. His eyes were shining in the candlelight.

But my hand turned shaky. I worried I'd knock the whole thing down.

'That's okay,' he said. 'The second level is a lot harder than the first.'

I'd been wanting for weeks to tell Seth about my father and Sylvia — and it felt possible, in that low light, to say the words out loud.

I took a breath and swallowed hard.

'I'm going to tell you a secret,' I said.

Seth stopped what he was doing and looked at me.

'I've seen my dad at Sylvia's house.'

I felt aware of the quiet, of the refrigerator not humming, of the cable box not glowing, of the digital clocks failing to tick.

'What do you mean?' he said.

'I've seen them, you know.' I paused. 'Together.'

Now that I'd said it, the facts seemed more true than they ever had before.

Seth didn't say anything at first. I waited. Then he nodded as if he'd come to expect such things from life. He never talked about his mother — and I had learned never to ask — but I sometimes sensed her absence in his reactions to certain events, as if he knew even then that there existed under everything a universal grief.

'Does your mom know?' he said at last.

'I don't think so,' I said. 'I'm not sure.'

He slotted two new cards into the tower. The whole structure moved slightly in response, and then he held his hands in the air for several seconds, as if he commanded some invisible force that could keep the cards upright. It seemed to work: The house of cards continued standing.

'It's not fair to your mom,' he said. 'I hate things that aren't fair.'

I nodded. 'Me, too.'

We said nothing else, but the secret buzzed between us. It felt good to have told. It felt good to be known by this boy. Later, after the cards had collapsed to the floor and the candles had burned down to nothing, we put on our swimsuits and dropped into the pitch-black waters of Seth's Jacuzzi. We couldn't see a thing except the stars. Our legs grazed one another under the surface. Seth leaned over and kissed me. I kissed him back. I felt happier than I had in a long time.

Two hours later, the power was restored.

Officials blamed the outage on the sunlamps and the greenhouses — they were straining the electrical grid. That was when the energy rationing began.

No lights after ten P.M. No air-conditioning unless the temperature exceeded eighty-eight degrees. But the industrial greenhouses went on guzzling up light. The entire food supply was being nursed by sodium sunlamps. All the farms in the country were reliant by then on periods of artificial sun.

One day in the middle of that spring, thick pink envelopes showed up in our mailboxes, announcing in glitter the details of Michaela's twelfth birthday party at the Roosevelt Hotel. It was the first time I'd ever been invited to one of the big dance parties, and I wondered if it was because of Seth. If I had torn the seal of that envelope a few months earlier, I would have felt grateful and glad.

But Seth and I decided right away not to go.

'I hate these things,' he said. 'And Michaela gets on my nerves. Let's watch movies at my house instead.'

'You're not coming?' Michaela said to me at school the next day. 'Are you kidding me?'

She'd invited a hundred other kids. Plenty of people would show.

'It's just not my kind of thing,' I said.

Her mouth tightened.

'Does that mean Seth's not coming, either?'

I felt a burst of pride that she thought of us as linked.

'I don't think he is,' I said.

She bit her lip hard and put her hands on her hips.

'Fine,' she said. 'Whatever. I don't care if you two losers come or not.'

But I didn't care what she thought as she swished away in her sundress, her glittery flip-flops slapping the cement.

★ ★ ★

Meanwhile, the heat on certain days was becoming dangerous. It was only April, but we were warned to stay indoors whenever the duration of sunlight exceeded twenty-five hours. Record-high temperatures were often produced at these times.

But the weather could swing just as wildly the other way, too. I woke one dark morning to a miraculous sight.

'Holy shit,' said my mother in her green bathrobe.

I looked out the window: snow.

This was California, sea level, spring.

Five inches had fallen while we slept, and it was still snowing. Temperatures had been dropping further and further as each darkness stretched longer. Now the neighborhood shimmered, bluish in the moonlight: sugar-coated cars, fences frosted white, the terra-cotta roofs encrusted in snow. The sidewalks looked repaved. The artificial lawns had been swallowed whole overnight in one smooth sheet of clean, creamy white. Our street sparkled.

Seth showed up on my porch in a red ski parka I'd never seen before and a frayed knit cap, which sat crooked on his head. Snowflakes were melting on his shoulders.

'We have to go sledding,' he said. He held up the blue boogie board he'd carried down from his house.

I grabbed a coat and followed him out to the whitened street.

'Wait,' called my mother from the doorway. 'I

266

don't know if I want you going out there.'

'Helen,' said my father. 'It's just snow.'

We were beach kids, sunshine kids. We did not know the properties of snow. I had never seen it fall, never knew how soft it felt at first, how easily it collapsed beneath feet, or the particular sound of that crunch. I never knew until then that snow made everything quiet, somehow silencing all the world's noise.

Our garages did not contain snow shovels or snowblowers. Our cars lacked snow tires. The nearest snowplow was parked in the mountains a hundred miles away. And so that was that: We were snowed in. School was canceled, and my father had the day off. There was nothing to do but throw ourselves down and make snow angels, or build snowmen, or sled down the nearest hill on whatever we could find. All the kids in the neighborhood took to the streets. We caught snowflakes on our tongues and in our eyelashes, let them melt in the palms of our hands. We watched Tony, our Southern California cat, stepping on snow for the first time — he hated it, shook his paw and retreated inside.

My father laughed when he saw that, maybe the first time he had laughed since my grandfather disappeared. My father had been spending all his weekends driving out to various real-time colonies in search of his father. A visit to one colony often led to another, farther out in the desert or else somewhere up in the mountains. There were dozens of colonies scattered across the state. He handed out missing-person flyers wherever he went. Six weeks had passed with no word. It was hard to imagine that my grandfather would let so much time pass without calling. I began to worry that something had happened to him, but I kept these fears to myself.

'I hope he's seeing this,' said my father, bending to touch the snow. 'Wherever he is.'

He grabbed a handful and tossed a snowball in my direction. Later, he helped Seth and me build a snowman in our yard.

The snow would all melt away as soon as the sun returned two days later. But for now, on this day, beauty was momentarily restored to our world.

I was only dimly aware of my mother that morning, a peripheral shape of worry.

'This is not right,' she kept saying, her voice barely audible over the squeals of children at play. She wouldn't come near the snow. 'This is California,' she said. 'This isn't right.'

30

One day we heard a strange sound in the sky: a crinkling, a tearing, like cellophane rustling in the wind.

It came from every direction. The sound lasted for three minutes. It was heard — some say *felt* — from Mexico City to Seattle. Nothing was seen. Whatever swirled in the atmosphere that day was invisible to human eyes.

During the following darkness, a great stream of green was spotted undulating on the horizon. Thousands of cameras recorded its flamelike movements. At the same time, navigation systems failed. Certain satellites went dark. My mother suffered one of her worst episodes yet, sliding to the kitchen floor for balance, as if on the deck of a pitching ship. She was briefly unable to stand.

By the time the sun came around again, the news had spread: Something was happening to the earth's magnetic field.

★ ★ ★

At the time of the slowing, little was known about the dynamo effect. More theory than fact, it was just an elegant mathematical guess that hovered like string theory at the crossroads of science and faith. Untested and untestable, the dynamo theory was a dreamy speculation that the earth's magnetic field might somehow depend upon the steady rotation of the planet.

For millions of years, the magnetic field had been shielding the earth from the sun's radiation, but in the eighth month after the start of the slowing, the magnetic field began to wither. A massive breach, the North American anomaly, opened up over the western half of the continent.

It was not the first time I ever heard the word *radiation*, but if you'd asked me to define the word on any day before that one, I would have linked it to history, to the atomic bomb and the wars of a previous century.

Now, we were told, radiation was streaming into our upper atmosphere.

Aircraft and satellites were rerouted throughout the region. The government insisted that the threat to humans was minimal, but we were advised to avoid all exposure to the sun — just in case. It would take time to determine the true risk.

And so, as the days grew to sixty hours long, amusement parks and outdoor malls began to close during daylight hours. Some sporting events were canceled or moved to covered stadiums. The industrial greenhouses were tented; radiation could kill plant cells as easily as ours. After that, the crops lived entirely on artificial light.

At the time, of course, we hoped these measures might be temporary. All the officials were repeating the same neat phrase: *out of an abundance of caution*. It was only later that I would come to think of this shift as not just one more weird phenomenon but as something different, a final swing.

My parents took the warnings seriously. The schools did as well. Our travels during daylight were immediately limited to the route of the school bus, which itself had been outfitted with blackout shades. We kept our curtains perpetually closed. We saved our errands for the dark. Every time the sky began to lighten, we hurried home and shut our doors against the radiation of the sun.

We swallowed vitamin-D tablets to make up for what we were missing from the sunlight. We hunkered down and waited for the all-clear.

Those daylight days were dreary. Those daylight days felt slow. My mother would not allow me out of the house except for school, so I saw much less of Seth on those bright days. I spent my time alone in my bedroom, longing for the freedom of the dark.

Sunset took on new importance for me during those weeks, no matter when it struck. Whenever the sun slipped down behind the earth, there'd be a knock at my door a few minutes later, and there Seth would be, standing on our porch in the twilight.

'Hey,' he'd say.

'Hey,' I'd say, and then I'd wave him into the house.

On dark days, we spent almost all of our time together.

★ ★ ★

I hadn't seen Sylvia in weeks. Her curtains were perpetually closed these days. My telescope was of no use. I couldn't tell you what went on in her house. Her roses, like all the others, were dead, but she'd made no effort to clear away the remains. Instead, the bushes stood skeletal near her driveway. She'd done nothing about her lawn, either, as all the other neighbors had done by then. No artificial turf surrounded her house. A fine dirt blew perpetually across the driveway. She never seemed to come out. The graffiti had been covered hastily with a splash of brown paint that stood out against the white garage. The hole in her roof continued to gape, the white plastic sheeting slowly browning in the air.

Superstitions about Sylvia brewed among the younger kids, who now crossed the street to avoid passing her house or else dared one another to ring the bell, though none were brave enough to do it. I once watched a pair of Jehovah's Witnesses inspect Sylvia's house from the sidewalk. They moved on without knocking, kept their message to themselves. If my father ever crossed into that house again, I hadn't seen him do it. As far as I could tell, no one entered Sylvia's house. And no one, seemingly, left.

'Maybe she only goes out on white nights,' said Seth. 'When everyone else is asleep.'

We were sprawled out on separate couches in his living room, eating ice cream from metal bowls and enjoying the last few hours of darkness. Through the windows, we watched the sky flare — the Northern Lights had swooped down almost to the equator, one more result of

272

the changes to the magnetic field. There was a new name for this new effect: the aurora medius.

'Maybe,' I said.

'That's what I would do if I were her,' said Seth.

'Maybe she moved away,' I said.

Seth considered the possibility. His ice cream spoon clinked against his front teeth.

'Without her car?' he said.

We had noticed that Sylvia's newspapers never piled very high before they disappeared from the porch. The mailbox never overflowed.

'I think she's still in there,' he said.

The lights in Seth's living room flickered. It was happening more and more often. We were using more and more fuel.

'I know what we should do,' said Seth. He sat up quickly and set his empty bowl on the coffee table. A strip of tan stomach flashed as he moved. I liked the way his hip bone jutted out above his belt. 'We'll sneak out in the middle of a white night and see if she ever comes out.'

As soon as he said it, I knew we would do it that night. The idea was irresistible. Sylvia was one more rare specimen for the two of us to observe: the last real-timer in the neighborhood.

I called my mother and told her I was spending the night at Hanna's. It was getting easier to lie.

'Oh, good,' said my mother. She sounded sleepy on the phone. 'I knew you and Hanna would make up eventually.'

I could tell from the seconds beading up between her words that she was recovering from

273

another wave of dizziness. She never would have believed me if she were well. I hadn't been to Hanna's in months.

'But Julia,' she said, 'just please stay out of the sun.'

'I will,' I said. 'I promise.'

★   ★   ★

But that night we ignored the warnings.

Seth and I spent that evening alone by the pool, watching the sun climb over the hills. Weeks had passed since I'd seen the sun directly. The old sunrises never produced so much pleasure, but these new ones, more rare — and now forbidden — arrived like mercy and set off something chemical: a euphoria of daylight.

Seth's father came home around nine. 'Julia should probably go home now,' said his father as he headed up to bed.

'She's leaving right now,' said Seth.

I nodded. Seth's father rubbed his beard in the doorway. He looked exhausted.

'Good night, then,' he said, and disappeared into his bedroom.

But I didn't leave.

Instead, we lay out on lawn chairs, Seth and I, waiting in the dimness, waiting, waiting, waiting for the sun to touch our skin. When it finally did, we let it heat our bodies to the point of faintness, and then we stumbled, delirious, into the shade.

I learned later that the radiation was more hazardous to children than to adults. Our bodies were smaller, incomplete. We had more time ahead of us for cell damage to ripen into cancer. Our brains were still developing. Whole regions were not yet fully formed — most crucially, we understood later, the frontal cortex, realm of decision making and forethought, the weighing of costs and consequence.

In other houses, the sick were growing sicker. New cases of gravity sickness were sprouting throughout the region. Projections about the future were turning more and more dire. But Seth and I felt fine. We felt better than fine. Sometimes death is proof of life. Sometimes decay points out a certain verve. We were young and we were hungry. We were strong and growing stronger, so healthy we were bursting.

At midnight we left Seth's house. It was a radiant night. In my memory, that night was brighter than usual, but that can't be true — the radiation was invisible to human eyes.

Three hundred miles to our north, Yosemite was burning. Dead trees make good kindling. The smoke had drifted south to us, thinning to a whitish haze that produced in our skies an unfamiliar sunshine, still brilliant but diffuse.

The streets were silent. Nothing moved. All the windows in all the houses were blacked out against the sun. We were the only ones out at that late hour. We didn't bother with sidewalks that night; instead we walked right down the middle of the road. It was as if the time of cars had passed.

'We can do anything we want right now,' said Seth. He knelt in the middle of the street and then lay down flat on his back, face up to the midnight sun. I lay down beside him, my hair pooling around my head, the asphalt hot against my skin.

'Close your eyes,' he whispered, and I did.

We lay in the street for many minutes, blind and vulnerable. There was a certain romance to the acrid smell of the blacktop, a pleasant rush of danger. Finally, a noise made us jump. My eyes snapped open — it was only a cat running on the side walk.

We walked past the bus stop, dusty and deserted, and the shopping center, its stores shuttered for the night. We wandered across the parking lot, the quietest parking lot on earth — it was empty of cars — and we imagined we were visitors to this strange world: what purpose this vast open space, these rows of cross-hatched lines?

Then we ran down the hill to my street, our shadows long in the early light.

Soon we reached Sylvia's house. My father was at work for the night, but my mother was home sleeping — or not sleeping — right across the street. I was afraid of getting caught, so we crouched low behind a parked car.

Up close, I could read the graffiti beneath the paint on Sylvia's garage door, the sloppy letters still blaring: *Get the fuck out*. I wondered what the house now looked like inside and whether she'd had her piano removed or if it remained on the floor in broken pieces. I pictured everything in ruins — the floors sagging, shelves collapsed, the macramé long ago frayed to threads. The only sound was the faint buzzing of the electric lines that ran above the roof.

Sylvia's side gate, we noticed, was standing open, revealing a thorny tangle of dead bushes in her backyard.

'Let's go back there,' whispered Seth.

Before I could argue, he sprinted through the gate. I liked the way he looked in that bright light, rushing past the stucco and then squinting as he turned his head and motioned for me to follow, which, of course, I did. Leaning against the side of Sylvia's house, we laughed as softly as we could, shoulders shaking, unable to breathe. We were kids, and it was summer. We were trespassing and half in love.

We tried to look through a window, but the curtains were closed. We saw no sign of Sylvia.

The natural days had stretched to sixty hours: almost two days of darkness, then two days of light. If Sylvia was still living there, she couldn't possibly be sleeping through the length of every darkness or staying awake for the whole stretch of each daylight. But we didn't know for sure. And we wanted to — we wanted to know everything there was to know.

We could have waited in that yard for hours and never spotted Sylvia, but instead, suddenly, the side door swung open, and there she was in the side yard, as thin as ever in an orange linen dress, no shoes. We hid behind a row of trash cans and watched her walk toward the driveway. She looked up and down the street, then up and down again. She sneaked out like a thief. She carried two cardboard boxes, taped shut. She set them down in the driveway and then went back inside.

'You were right,' I whispered. 'Guess she's been here all along.'

Seth nodded. He raised one finger to his lips.

Sylvia returned with two more boxes and headed again for the driveway. She slipped out of sight, but we heard the rattle of keys out front, the trunk of her car opening and closing.

Seth coughed a soft cough. He put his hand over his mouth, trying to muffle another one, but the cough burst out just as Sylvia returned to the side yard. She looked in our direction.

'Jesus Christ,' she said, her hand on her chest. 'You scared me. What are you guys doing back here?'

We stood when she saw us, but we didn't say anything. We'd been caught.

Sylvia glanced at the side door. The usual sweep of her gestures, formerly so graceful, had been replaced by the tight crossing of her arms, the anxious biting of her lower lip.

'Well?' she said.

We didn't speak.

'I think you should both go home,' she said. 'Right now.'

I'd never heard her talk this way. As a teacher, she was endlessly patient and calm.

'You shouldn't be here,' she said, her voice rising.

We heard the side door creak open behind her. Sylvia closed her eyes.

And there he was: my father, carrying two brown suitcases, one on either side.

Maybe I should not have been surprised to see my father emerge from her house like that, but I was. He stopped when he saw us. I heard him take a sharp, quick breath. He set the suitcases down on the pavement.

'What are you doing here?' he said. He looked at Seth, then back at me. A pair of sunglasses dangled from his shirt.

I was too stunned to answer.

'I thought you were at Hanna's,' said my father. He was about to say something else, but Seth cut him off.

'She thought *you* were at work,' said Seth. He looked wound up, ready for a fight.

'Don't talk to me that way,' said my father. 'I'm talking to Julia.'

My father suddenly noticed the open gate and looked alarmed. If my mother were to wake up and look out, she could easily see us in the side yard.

'Shit,' he said.

This was the first time I noticed it, the inevitable space between father and man. A frustrated man was standing there on that pavement. A stranger would have recognized the signs from a distance as my father rushed to close the gate. These were the sharp movements of a furious human being.

'Where are you going?' I asked.

'Nowhere,' said my father. But the suitcases glowed like hard evidence against him.

'Tell me the truth,' I said.

Sylvia began to move away from the scene. She was floating almost imperceptibly back toward the side door.

'I want you to go home right now,' my father said to me. He indicated our house, just visible over the top of the gate, and it looked so sad and lovely sitting there across the street, its simple white stucco almost shining in the sun: our home.

'No,' I said.

Sylvia was back inside now. I heard the door shut behind her.

'Now,' said my father.

But I stayed put. Maybe it was the effect of Seth standing next to me, or maybe it was the sunshine — we know the daylight makes us more impulsive than the dark.

'I'm not going home,' I said.

Seth grabbed my hand.

'He can't make you,' said Seth. 'You could go tell your mom about this right now.'

Anger flashed on my father's face, anger and disbelief.

'Your mother and I have already talked about this,' he said.

'I don't believe you,' I said. I started to cry. I felt Seth's hand on my back.

'If you won't go home, then go back to Seth's house.' He was pleading. It was something I hadn't seen him do before. 'Please,' he said. 'It's not safe to be out so late, and you shouldn't be in the sun.'

After some argument, we agreed, but we refused to let him drive us. He followed us in his car, moving at the slow pace of our strides. Seth held my hand the whole way. I had the feeling as we walked that I was glimpsing in tableau the world of someone older, the odd dramas that took place only in the middle of the night.

When we reached Seth's driveway, my father called my name. 'I'm not going to tell your mother that you lied about going to Hanna's.' He paused. The engine fan began to whir. 'Okay?'

'You're the one who's lying,' I said.

'Julia,' he said again, but I didn't answer. I did not know when I would see my father again.

Seth and I walked hand in hand across the dirt where the lawn used to be. We climbed the steps to the front door and crept inside, so we wouldn't wake his father.

Inside, we sat for a while on the living room couches. The light was low from the blackout curtains. It was late, nearly two.

'You should tell your mom,' Seth said. He yawned and stretched out on the carpet.

I lay back on the couch and looked at the ceiling. A few minutes passed. Somewhere a faucet was dripping. The refrigerator hummed. Outside, the sun was beating down on the land.

'She's going to find out anyway,' I said.

When I turned to look at Seth, I found he was asleep. He was curled on the floor in his T-shirt and shorts. I listened for a while to the reassuring sound of that boy breathing near me. I watched the slight movement of his eyelids as he dreamed. It wasn't enough just to be near him. I wished I could see what he was dreaming right then. I would have traveled even there with him.

31

It was not until we woke the next morning that we discovered the burns. Sunburns, the worst of our lives.

We were feverish and thirsty, our whole bodies bright red. It hurt to bend our knees. It hurt to turn our heads. Seth ran to the bathroom and threw up. I still remember how he looked afterward, coughing as he lay down on the couch. In his eyes I saw the beginnings of tears and something else too: fear.

My mother was horrified when I got home. Bits of white skin were already peeling from my cheeks.

'Jesus,' she said. 'I told you not to go out in the sun.'

She came alive that day, as if my sunburn were her cure. She spent a long time smearing aloe on my face. The touch of her fingers — the therapeutic sting — made me feel like a younger girl.

'Was this your idea?' she said. 'Or Hanna's? And where the hell were her parents?'

I couldn't look her in the eye.

'I want your father to take a look at this the minute he gets home,' she said. Tiny flakes of skin were coming off in her hands. I could see the flurry in the lamplight. 'He'll be home from work in an hour.'

I hoped she was right, but I knew that

something had swerved in the night, some final shift that had led eventually to the packing of two suitcases and the loading of the trunk of Sylvia's car. My father and Sylvia could be in Nevada by now, or halfway up the coast of California. I didn't tell my mother that. I just waited for the truth to land.

My mother leaned toward me, inspected my cheeks. Up close, she looked older, the wrinkles around her eyes more profound, her whole face like the dried flower petals that Seth and I had collected that spring.

She turned me around, lifted the back of my shirt. I was wearing the plain white training bra I'd secretly bought. I closed my eyes and waited for her to say something about it. But she didn't mention it. Instead, I heard only the sound of her gasping at the sight of my skin.

'My God,' she said. 'Weren't you wearing a shirt?'

But the sun had developed an alarming new trick — it had burned us right through our clothes.

★ ★ ★

That same morning a moving van appeared in front of Sylvia's house. Through my curtains, I watched box after box bob across the dirt in the arms of two movers. They carried floor lamps, shag rugs, two baskets of yarn, yards and yards of macramé. Furniture followed: the rustic dining room table, the brown velvet couch, two overstuffed armchairs, a bed frame, the birdcage.

The packing of the van went on all morning, but Sylvia did not appear. Her car was already gone by then. A patch of oil was drying in the driveway.

After a while, the moving van drove away.

Twelve o'clock came and twelve o'clock passed, and there was no sign of my father.

My mother tried his cell phone. No answer.

'His shift should be over by now,' she said.

I kept quiet, but the knowledge gathered like a storm. I could see the future: My father wasn't coming back. And this one fact seemed to point to other facts and others still: Love frays and humans fail, time passes, eras end.

Around twelve-thirty, the lights flickered. A few minutes later, they went out.

'Shit,' said my mother. 'Not again.'

Every window in our house was draped with a blackout curtain, but a little sunlight was seeping through, so it was not quite pitch dark in our kitchen, where the two of us sat waiting and worrying like women of some earlier time, my mother lighting candles in the gloom.

I rubbed my face with the palms of my hands. Small flakes of sunburned skin fell to the floor.

'Don't do that,' said my mother. 'You'll only make it worse.'

It was not long after the power went out that the cats began to yowl. I'd never heard them make that sound. Chloe moaned into the empty air. A trail of fur stood straight up on her spine. Tony paced the kitchen, ears swiveling. He growled a low growl. When I reached for him, he hissed.

Soon the neighborhood dogs began to bark. They howled from all directions, their voices swelling like a tide. A Great Dane sprinted down our street, his leash whipping behind him. In the nearby rural areas, cattle charged; horses broke through fences.

We humans didn't feel a thing. The sky looked blue and simple to our eyes.

When we tried the radio, static poured from the speakers. No voice drifted on any frequency. Only later would we recognize what seems so obvious in retrospect: This was the first of the solar superstorms, triggered by the withering of the magnetic field.

My mother called my father again. Nothing.

Chloe's cry grew mournful, a relentless wavering chord. My mother shut her in the guest room and then went around closing the windows against the noise.

She called my father again. This time his phone went straight to voice mail.

'Where is he?' she said.

I think she knew that he was more than late. Something had changed, and she knew it.

'Maybe you should save the battery,' I said.

She looked about to cry.

An hour passed, then two. There was no word from my father. My mother called his hospital. He wasn't there.

She tried his cell phone once more. I remember the quick beeps of the numbers being dialed again and again, her fingers moving more urgently each time, the soft sounds of a lost cause.

Before the start of the slowing, no one would have predicted my father to be the kind of man who would abandon his wife and child. Here was a man who showed up, a man who did his work and went home every night. Here was a man who handled crises and paid his bills on time. Much study has been devoted to the physical effects of gravity sickness, but more lives than history will ever record were transformed by the subtler psychological shifts that also accompanied the slowing. For reasons we've never fully understood, the slowing — or its effects — altered the brain chemistry of certain people, disturbing most notably the fragile balance between impulse and control.

32

Thirty miles away, a different drama was unfolding. It began with a golden retriever — or you might say instead that the story starts earlier, much earlier, more than sixty years back, in the year 1961, when Americans first received instructions on how to build a backyard bomb shelter, a time when everyone knew how many inches of cement it took to shield a human being from nuclear fallout.

But the events of this day begin with the golden retriever. Like the animals in our neighborhood, this dog was spooked by the solar storm, this dog especially so. He leaped over his backyard fence and went running.

He sprinted for ten blocks, passed driveways, tree stumps, the plastic approximations of lawns. This was a planned community, still new at the time of the slowing, and bent on appearing as little changed as possible. The slopes were naked of trees, of course, but the houses now offered distant ocean views, unobstructed for miles. Finally, this golden retriever scuttled up a hill and burst onto a piece of property that lay just beyond the development, a slice of parched land on which my grandfather's house stood. By the time the dog's owners caught up to him, he was digging at a piece of metal that was half buried in the dirt behind the woodpile. It was a rusty trapdoor pressed flat into the earth.

The owners of the dog soon called the police.

* * *

Some say that love is the sweetest feeling, the purest form of joy, but that isn't right. It's not love — it's relief.

I remember the exact pitch of my mother's voice as she called up to me from downstairs. 'There he is,' she said. 'There he is.'

Our whole future was rewritten by the brief sound of my father's engine dying in the driveway.

'Sorry,' he said, shaking his phone in the air. 'I tried to call.'

Only later did we discover that the solar storm had wiped out the cell phone satellites. A million desperate calls flew into space that day but landed nowhere.

'Where have you been?' asked my mother.

But I didn't care anymore. He was home. He was here. I forgave him in an instant.

I didn't notice right away the look of trouble on my father's face. I should have known by then that it's never the disasters you see coming that finally come to pass; it's the ones you don't expect at all. There was a reason my father was late that day. He'd been to my grandfather's house.

* * *

Behind my grandfather's woodpile, where wildflowers once grew, there lay an ancient trapdoor, flat and rusted. This was the entrance to the underground shelter he had built six decades earlier in case of nuclear war.

I had not known about the shelter. My father remembered it from his youth but could barely recall its location in the yard. In fact, he would later say that he had assumed the shelter had collapsed years ago. But in the months before he disappeared, we now discovered, my grandfather had secretly repurposed the space for the fears of this new age.

It was ten feet by twelve, the walls lined with thirteen inches of cement. Inside were cases of bottled water, rows of canned food, two shotguns, and a hand-crank radio. There were four sleeping bags and four cots, one for each of us. There were several boxes of my favorite granola bars. Much of what was missing from his house was also found in the shelter. In one corner stood several boxes of photographs and valuables, shoe boxes full of the gold bars I'd seen him packing in his dining room. A two-year calendar hung on one wall. This was a cavity designed for waiting out the crumbling of society and whatever else came next. It was designed not only for him but for us, for my parents and for me. I guess he wasn't so eager after all to escape the confines of this life.

Spilled across the floor were the contents of my grandfather's final bundle: a deck of cards, an old edition of Monopoly, a checkerboard and checkers. All the pieces were scattered on the cement. On the floor of the shelter, a wooden ladder lay at an unnatural angle. According to the police report, it was here that my grandfather's body was found.

He was once a hardy man, but the first thing I thought when I heard the news was how delicate his skin had become, how easily and often it released his blood.

Later, I would spend a great deal of time obsessing about the rules of cause and effect, how the tipping of that ladder was one in a long chain of events. What if the floor of the shelter had been lined with carpet instead of cement? What if the ladder's manufacturer had coated the feet with rubber for better grip? Maybe such a ladder would not have slid so easily across the floor. If the Soviets had decided not to ship nuclear missiles to Cuba in 1962, my grandfather never would have built the shelter; had the earth's rotation remained in a steady state, he never would have reclaimed it. I used to lie awake at night tracing the thousand other things that might have prevented my grandfather's death, but from the moment the ladder wobbled, the possibilities narrowed: His head struck the cement, the blood of his veins poured into his brain, his heart quit beating, and he left this earth for good.

It was later estimated that he died on the same day he disappeared, two months earlier, my birthday. At the time of his fall, he was wearing his gray slacks, his leather shoes, and his corduroy sport coat. He was dressed for our dinner. The police surmised that he had climbed down into the shelter less than an hour before we arrived that night, and that he likely only intended to carry one last load of supplies — all the board games he knew I liked best — to the shelter before joining us for dinner. In his coat pocket, they found a pale blue envelope with my name written in my grandfather's shaky letters on the front. Inside was a birthday card and a twenty-dollar bill. There was a brief handwritten note: *Happy Birthday, Julia. God bless.*

33

It never used to rain where we lived, but it rained on the day we buried my grandfather. We held the service in the cool safety of the dark. My father was quieter at the cemetery than I had ever seen him. My mother cried softly behind me. The black casket gleamed beneath the floodlights as raindrops rolled down the sides. I could not believe he was in there, my grandfather, lying dead. I could still hear the sound of his voice in my ears. I could still see his face. I'd never been to a funeral before.

Soon the dirt turned to mud, and the rain turned to sleet. Somewhere on the other side of the planet, the sun was shining, and the people there were hiding from the light. I remember shivering in my parka and wondering about the difference between coincidence and fate.

★   ★   ★

I recovered quickly from my sunburns, but Seth was sick for weeks. The skin on his arms bubbled and sloughed. A succession of fevers washed over his body. The doctors couldn't say if it was from the sunburn or from something else. He stayed home from school for two weeks. I sat with him in the afternoons, but he spoke little and slept often. The old hours opened up again like scars — I went back to spending my lunches in the library, anxious and alone.

Seth eventually revived, but I worried even then that some damage had already been done. Some things that happen during youth, you carry with you into later life, and certain experts were already predicting an approaching tidal wave of cancers.

April dissolved quickly into May, and May was the month when the earthquakes began. They were mild back then but frequent, an almost daily rumbling. That same month, we built a second greenhouse in the backyard, and we sunproofed our windows. My mother bought padlocks for all the doors in the house. My father bought a gun.

Seven sunsets later, it was June.

★   ★   ★

The last day of school that year was the quietest last day in memory. We failed to summon the usual glee. It was partly the darkness that muted us, the slim sickle moon, but it was something else, too: a new sense of time, I guess, how swiftly it slides away. There was a feeling on that last day of school, as we zipped up our backpacks and stacked our books in the book room, that we might never return to those halls. September loomed just three months away, but we had stopped predicting the future. The signing of yearbooks was taken more seriously that year. Nostalgia flowed from every pen. I hadn't spoken to Hanna in months, but she insisted on signing the page in my book near her picture, snapped at a time when we were still friends. I never saw Hanna again. She and her family drove back to Utah that summer to wait for whatever would come.

The afternoon dwindled. The moon slipped out of sight. The English teachers handed out the summer reading lists: *Animal Farm, Tom Sawyer, The Diary of Anne Frank*. Never before were we so comforted by the screech of our chairs on linoleum, the squeak of a marker on a dry-erase board. But the clocks ticked at the usual speed, so the end of the day arrived on time. The school buses groaned at the curb, headlights blazing in the mist. The bell rang. Some hugged. Some cried. We all scattered. We were less eager for summertime than we'd ever been before.

★ ★ ★

The solar storms raged all summer. Seth and I kept close track of them. We never felt them when they struck, but they damaged wiring and sparked fires all over the world. More and more radiation was leaking into the atmosphere. We could trace its presence in the wild arcs of the auroras that shot through the sky whenever it turned dark. We never knew when the electricity might go out. A surge of magnetic particles could knock out the power grid at any time, and so we kept our flashlights close, candles ready.

We continued to stay away from the sun.

By then much of what came from the mouths of scientists was unintelligible to the rest of us.

But we understood certain stark facts. The same solar wind now pummeling our skies had once, long ago, lapped away the oceans and the atmosphere of Mars.

'We've seen effects like this in the magnetic field before,' said one scientist, 'but never on such a grand scale. It should take thousands of years for this kind of deterioration to take place.'

Their statements sometimes lapsed into poetry. Their imaginations began to run wild. Some speculated that a third force was involved, as yet unknown.

'We're seeing something here,' said one researcher, 'that undermines our entire understanding of physics.'

* * *

My mother's sickness ebbed and flowed, but she learned to predict her dizzy spells by the faint metallic taste in her mouth, one more symptom that her doctor could not explain.

I noticed that my father began to care for her in a newly tender way. I read their interactions from a distance, but I sensed a new closeness between them. Something had shifted, but the cause was mysterious to me. I studied them from afar that summer, the way, as we'd learned in school, astronomers could sometimes detect a distant planet — not by seeing it but by measuring how its mass bent the path of starlight. The clues were in the curve of my father's arm around my mother's shoulder, the softening tone of her voice. Sometimes my mother would emerge from her nausea in a state almost cheerful, and we'd play Monopoly or Chinese checkers for a while, my parents sipping beers. Once she felt well for a whole week straight, and they stayed up late together every night, talking softly, laughing now and then. 'See?' I remember my father's voice insisting. 'You'll be fine.' The more time that passed, the less I understood the bond between them, but I began to suspect that the tipping of that ladder in my grandfather's bomb shelter had changed the course of my parents' marriage. I'll never know the exact order of events or which decisions were made when. I'll never know if my father really had been planning to leave with Sylvia that day or not. I know only that he didn't leave. I know only that he stayed.

★ ★ ★

I never saw Sylvia again. I don't know if my father ever did. There were times that summer and afterward when I'd hear him on the phone late at night, but I couldn't say who he was talking to or what was being said.

When he was not at work, my father spent hours cataloging my grandfather's possessions. His old oak clock now ticked in our living room. My grandmother's miniature spoons now dangled from the lemon-yellow wall of our kitchen. My grandfather's baby shoes, preserved in silver eight decades earlier, now sat on our living room shelf.

My father never mentioned Sylvia directly.

Together, we worked hard that summer to imagine that certain events had never taken place. The mind is a powerful force, two minds especially.

Sometime in June, the police report from my mother's accident arrived in our mailbox. It must have mentioned the pedestrian's fate — deceased — but I caught only one quick glimpse of the document as my father crumpled it up and tossed it into the fireplace among the newspapers he was using to build a fire. It was as if the two of us had learned to travel back in time to someplace simpler where the rules of chronology and consequence, of action and reaction, were different, more diffuse, less sure. He brought up Sylvia on only one occasion.

It was a clear black night, the moon three quarters full. We were walking down to the elementary school — his idea — to kick the soccer ball on the field for a while.

'I know not everything makes sense to you,' he said as we walked. A few streetlights showed the way. I was afraid of what he might say next.

'Do you know what a paradox is?' he said.

He paused and rubbed his forehead. A chain of nearby houses glowed in silhouette against the dark sky.

'Not really,' I said.

I recall the way my hands felt that night, curled tight in the sleeves of my parka. We could see our breath in the air. I was still getting used to it, how cold the long darknesses could be.

'A paradox,' he went on, 'is when two contradictory things are both true.'

He turned his head up to the sky. The tiniest bald patch had opened up at the back of his head; it was everywhere, I was realizing — the sharp evidence of time.

'Just remember that, okay?' he added. 'Not everything is clear-cut.'

We reached the parking lot and found an opening in the chain-link fence. I remember the crunch of artificial turf beneath cleats. Every outdoor plant in the neighborhood was dead by then.

The soccer ball shimmered in the glow of the auroras. My father stood in the goal while I took shots. As the months passed, it had gotten less and less satisfying to kick a ball through the air, harder and harder to make it fly across a field — it wasn't really gravity that was increasing but centrifugal force. The ball felt heavy on my foot.

'Did you hear they found another planet that might be kind of like Earth?' said my father, as we headed back to the street.

'Really?' I asked. 'Where?'

'A long way from here,' he said. 'Twenty-five light-years.'

A string of cars floated down the street, the headlights revealing momentarily a row of tree stumps at the front of the school.

'So it doesn't help us,' I said.

'No,' he said. 'No, not us.'

We walked in silence for a while. I zipped my parka up to my throat. My cleats clicked on the asphalt.

'I bet you'll make the traveling team this year,'

said my father. Streaks of green and violet flared across the sky.

'Maybe,' I said.

But I think we both knew that there would be no traveling team that year.

From every direction, the echoes of hammers were wafting through the air, the hiss of circular saws, the cutting of steel. Hundreds of radiation shelters were ballooning beneath the ground.

And still the days grew and kept growing. We hit seventy-two hours on the Fourth of July.

★ ★ ★

On dark days that summer, Seth and I roamed beneath the streetlights, pale creatures, still growing. Seth seemed healthy again. He seemed fine. We took turns riding his skateboard down the hills of the neighborhood. We bought candy at the liquor store, drank sodas on the cliffs above the beach. We stood vigil at the dying of the whales.

One afternoon Seth's nose began to bleed. A few drops landed on his T-shirt.

'It's nothing,' he said, wiping his nose with the back of his hand and pulling a tissue from his pocket. We were walking near the ocean, which was dark and loud beneath us. Seth tilted his head back, pinched the bridge of his nose. The blood quickly flowered through the tissue. 'It happens sometimes,' he said.

'It does?' I said. 'Maybe my dad should look at it.'

'It's not a big deal,' he said.

After a few minutes, the bleeding stopped. I noticed nothing else. He hid his symptoms well.

Sylvia's house remained empty. A for-sale sign stood in the yard, though the roof remained partially collapsed and draped in plastic. No buyers ever came to see it. Once, in our wandering, Seth and I peeked through a window. The wooden floor was slightly darker where the piano had once stood, and the wind chime made of seashells trilled lightly in the breeze. These were the only traces that Sylvia had ever lived there.

I sometimes wondered where she had gone. One of the networks aired a television special that year about the realtime colonies and their residents, and I searched it scene by scene for a glimpse of Sylvia in one of its shots, but I never spotted her.

In Circadia that same summer, three people died of heatstroke in one day, after forty-one hours of sunlight drove the thermometers to 135 degrees in the desert. The colonies would almost all close eventually. As the days grew longer, it proved less and less possible for the human body to adjust. The promise of slow time went largely unfulfilled. For real-timers, the consequences of long periods without sleep began to interfere with certain cognitive functions. Some gave up and joined the rest of us on the clock. Many of those who persisted in the colonies faded into madness. A group in Idaho was found close to starvation, delirious and hallucinating — the whole group had stopped eating, though their cupboards were full of canned food.

That was also the summer of food shortages and suicide cults. It seemed that every day a new group of people was found dead, poison floating in their bloodstreams.

Fresh produce was harder and harder to find. In July the government launched the Life Garden campaign to encourage individuals to grow their own food in covered greenhouses. Instructional kits were distributed, as well as packets of the hardiest seeds. We tried to grow carrots, but they came out sickly and small. What little light they got came from artificial lights. Mushrooms were the only abundance.

We swallowed mouthfuls of vitamins to make up for the lack. But soon the vitamins began to run low. My mother's collection of canned food grew rapidly that summer. The stockpile took over the dining room.

Seth and I spent a lot of time imagining what the world would look like after the humans were gone. We heard that everything plastic would outlast the rest, and so we pictured the houses on my street reduced to piles of PVC pipes and LEGOS, tupperware and beach pails, computer chips and cell phones and razors. Bottles of every variety would tower over everything else, the labels fading across the decades and the plastic cracking under the force of a harsh and lifeless sun.

'Think of all the toothbrushes,' said Seth.

Once we admired a mosquito landing on a porch light. 'Look,' said Seth. His eyes were large and watery. The mosquito fluttered away. It struck us, as it flew, as a delicate, elegant thing.

'Look! Look!' We were convinced for one moment that this was the last wild creature on earth.

We wandered the canyons with flashlights. We peeked beneath our curtains at the sun. We lay flat on our backs in the darkness and watched the auroras the way other kids had once watched clouds.

At night sometimes we'd kiss for a while in my driveway. I still remember the way his lips felt on mine, the sugary taste of his gum.

★　★　★

Sometimes it seemed that our memories were failing us. I found I could no longer recall clearly the contours of my grandfather's face or how my mother looked before she got sick — I was sure that her skin had faded some, turned rougher, but it was hard to say for sure. The sound of Sylvia's piano completely vanished from my head. Similarly went the sensation of sunshine on my face, the taste of strawberries, the squish of a grape in my mouth. It got harder and harder to recall those ancient mornings when the sun rose like clockwork, the slowly lifting layers of fog, the lovely light, the start of day.

But sometimes a bit of wind or a certain smell might remind me of the way it used to be. The horizon might seem stark again, and I'd wonder for just a moment what had happened to the trees. A sudden sense of silence sometimes rushed into my ears, and I'd remember what we had lost: the songs of all the birds.

On other continents, famine spread. We tried to remember that we were luckier here than most.

★   ★   ★

In August of that year, the power company dug up our street. It had something to do with the earthquakes, some related repair. Workmen in orange vests jackhammered a stretch of sidewalk to reach the cables that snaked beneath the street. A few hours later, when the work was finished, they poured two new squares of cement in the sidewalk to replace the ones they'd destroyed. The cement was still wet when the workmen drove away; it was guarded only by two orange cones and one strip of yellow caution tape.

Seth and I knelt beside it, eager to leave our mark but unsure what to write. I was aware of his body next to mine as we crouched beneath the streetlights and conferred.

'Whatever we write is going to last a long time,' he said. He stared hard at the cement and chewed his lip — this was one of his habits. I knew all his habits by then. He looked up at me. 'Maybe our whole lives.'

I felt a vague sadness then, the premonition of a future feeling.

The surface of the wet cement was as smooth as new snow, and it smelled like sea salt. We spent a long time deciding what to write, thinking only slightly faster than the speed at which wet cement dries in open air.

303

And still the earth turned, and the days passed, and the constellations wound across the sky. Gradually, we learned to sleep away the white nights in the radiation shelters we'd all dug beneath our yards, where the air smelled like dirt and like stone, so you never forgot you were under the ground.

Little by little — and then all at once — that summer slipped away.

*   *   *

What happened after that has been well recorded elsewhere. But I doubt that Seth's name has appeared in any account but mine.

He couldn't hide it forever. We were walking home from the beach one afternoon, headlights flashing past us. It was early in a stretch of darkness, and the moon was shining low in the sky, just visible above the rooftops of the neighborhood.

We were sharing a bag of sour candy as we walked. Seth was looking at the stars.

'If humans really could go to Mars,' he said, 'would you want to go?'

I loved the way he thought about these things.

'I don't think so,' I said. 'I'd be too afraid.'

'I'd go,' he said. 'I'd love to do something like that.'

It was only a few seconds later that I heard the sound of the bag drop from Seth's hand. I remember the slight smack of the plastic hitting the sidewalk as the candy spilled into the street.

As I turned toward him, I felt his body lean

hard into my shoulder. Then he jerked headfirst to the sidewalk.

I think I knew then that nothing would be the same after that.

I shouted his name. I looked at his eyes: they were half open and blank. His head was rolling forward and back. His whole body was shaking on the pavement.

I ran what felt a long distance from the sidewalk to the front door of the nearest house, at a pace that reminds me now of a dream I sometimes had at that age and do still, where the ground falls away wherever I step. Soon I was knocking on a stranger's door with two fists. Soon I was screaming at the woman who lived there. Then she was calling an ambulance, her voice as panicked as mine.

'Oh my God,' she shouted into the phone. 'There's a boy having a seizure in the street.'

I was grateful to that woman during those first few seconds, but then I wanted her to get away from us, and not crouch next to me the way she did while Seth rolled on the sidewalk, his head jerking, my young arms unable to hold his body still, my mind even more useless, those minutes too intimate for a stranger to see.

⋆   ⋆   ⋆

The seizure finally subsided, but Seth spent that night in the hospital. When he came home the next day, he called me to tell me what I had already guessed:

'They think it's the syndrome,' he said.

I could feel the words pressing down on my chest.

'I know,' I said.

We didn't say anything for a little while. I could hear him breathing into the phone.

'But I'm not that worried about it,' he said. I didn't believe him. 'I mean, doesn't your mom feel okay a lot of the time?'

'Kind of,' I said.

I didn't tell Seth then that his case already seemed much worse than my mother's.

He weakened rapidly after that. Soon he was spending most of his time in bed. After school, I'd rush over to his house, and we'd watch movies together or play cards, or just look at the stars through the windows of his room.

'When I get better,' he'd say, 'let's build a fort in the yard and set up your telescope out there.'

'Okay,' I'd say, nodding hard.

But it scared me how thin and wan his face began to look. Sometimes he'd close his eyes for a few seconds, riding out a sudden pain in his head. His nose would bleed and bleed. He talked less and less. His skateboard sat silent in the corner of his room.

Soon, he could barely walk. I felt him drifting away, like ice on a sea.

Seth's father never did develop the corn he was working on, the one that could live without any light. He gave up and closed his lab. One day that fall, he decided that he and Seth would move away — to Mexico where the radiation was said to be weaker.

I still remember the afternoon Seth told me

they were leaving, the way I hung, desperate, on the words he said afterward: 'But I bet we'll come back.'

I remember the day they packed the van, his father carrying Seth in his arms, the way Seth's legs dangled, spindly, where once they'd been strong. I'd helped Seth pack his things, and he'd given me his skateboard; he couldn't ride it anymore.

'Keep it for me,' said Seth from the passenger seat. I spent those last minutes crying so hard I couldn't talk. I remember Seth's father averting his eyes as he packed the van. 'It's just for a few months,' said Seth, touching my face with his hand. His skin had lost its color, but his dark eyes were as dark as ever. 'You'll see: We'll come back.'

I remember watching the van roll away from me, Seth's face receding in the distance. I stood in the dark street for a long time after that, clutching the skateboard to my chest and waiting, as if there existed some slim possibility that the van might change directions and begin to move backward in time instead of forward, while all around me life continued to proceed in only the one direction.

Seth sent me a short email the next day, a few precious words: *Mexico is weird*, he said, *and hot! I miss you!*

I read it over many times that day and the next. I could hear the echo of his voice in the words.

★ ★ ★

It was two days later that the whole of North America went dark, the largest power failure in history. For seventy-two hours, we lived by candlelight and rationed our supplies. All across the continent, crops were left without the nurture of artificial lights. We worried we would run out of food. Looters roamed the cities and the malls. For the first time in my memory, my father stayed home from work. The three of us huddled together in our radiation shelter. My father locked the doors with a chain. My mother worried we didn't have enough water, so we sipped it as slowly as we could. We counted hours, then days. In the middle of the second night, we heard distant gunshots in the darkness. We didn't sleep at all.

Finally, on the third day, the lights flicked on again.

But not everything returned. The massive servers that powered our computer networks and our email systems and most of our major websites were temporarily shut down to conserve electricity. All nonessential uses of power were put on hold.

And, as we well know, those servers never went back up.

I wasn't the only one who lost touch with someone they loved. I still remember the flyers that appeared in post offices and grocery stores; names and photos of people soon hung from the same signposts that had previously carried the news of lost pets. *If you see this woman, please tell her Daniel is looking for her. If you're out there, J.T., here's my number.* It was the newest relationships that were the least likely to survive — millions of new connections were cut off in midbloom. Think of all those potential loved ones lost once again on a planet of strangers. I didn't have Seth's phone number, but he'd given me a mailing address in Baja.

I started sending letters. I wrote one every day — every day for weeks.

Maybe it wasn't the right address. Maybe there was something wrong with the mail.

Sometimes the saddest stories take the fewest words: I never heard from Seth Moreno again.

34

It still amazes me how little we really knew.

We had rockets and satellites and nanotechnology. We had robot arms and robot hands, robots for roving the surface of Mars. Our unmanned planes, controlled remotely, could hear human voices from three miles away. We could manufacture skin, clone sheep. We could make a dead man's heart pump blood through the body of a stranger. We were making great strides in the realms of love and sadness — we had drugs to spur desire, drugs for melting pain. We performed all sorts of miracles: We could make the blind see and the deaf hear, and doctors daily conjured babies from the wombs of infertile women. At the time of the slowing, stem cell researchers were on the verge of healing paralysis — surely the lame soon would have walked.

And yet, the unknown still outweighed the known. We never determined the cause of the slowing. The source of our suffering remained forever mysterious.

★ ★ ★

I was twenty-three when plans for the *Explorer* were announced. A new kind of rocket, designed for high-speed travel, the *Explorer* would carry no humans with its cargo. This was a message in a bottle, a souvenir of Earth, perhaps our last communiqué. It would bring on its journey a gold disc containing information about our planet and its people, in case, in some distant realm of the universe, the ship crossed paths with intelligent life.

A special team was assembled to decide what to include on the disc. Among the final contents were the sounds of waves crashing on a beach, human voices speaking greetings from around the world, images of extinct flora and fauna, a diagram of the Earth's exact location in the universe. Certain basic facts were engraved in symbols on the outside of the disc, the goal to record in hieroglyphs the whole history of the twenty-first century, to convey in the fewest possible strokes the story of our time.

Not mentioned on the disc was the smell of cut grass in high summer, the taste of oranges on our lips, the way sand felt beneath our bare feet, or our definitions of love and friendship, our worries and our dreams, our mercies and our kindnesses and our lies.

The *Explorer* would eventually travel distances so great that only time could measure them. A patch of uranium in the middle of the disc would function as a radioactive clock so that one day — maybe 60,000 years from now, when the *Explorer* first floats near the nearest other star — some other beings might be able to determine the age of the ship.

They would also learn from the disc that at the time of the *Explorer*'s launching, the darknesses were deepening and our food supply was more and more at risk. Though the pace of the slowing had slackened over the years, it had never stopped. The damage had been done, and we had come to suspect that we were dying. But perhaps the disc will also convey that we carried on. We persisted even as most of the experts gave us only a few more years to live. We told stories and we fell in love. We fought and we forgave. Some still hoped the world might right itself. Babies continued to be born.

★ ★ ★

My mother continued to teach part-time at the high school until it closed a few years back, after too many kids stopped coming. Her sickness didn't progress the way Seth's did. My father works at the hospital to this day.

They live in the same house where I grew up, but it looks very different from the way I remember it. The grass and the bougainvillea are long gone, of course, and thick steel sheeting now coats the exterior walls to keep out the radiation. Sunproof shutters block the view I used to see from my old bedroom window. Across the street, Sylvia's house has been torn down. An empty lot sits where her porch once stood.

My mother says I spend too much time thinking about the past. We should look ahead, she says, to the time that's left. But the past is long, and the future is short. As I write this account, one ordinary life, our days have stretched to the lengths of weeks, and it's hard to say which times are most hazardous now: the weeks of freezing darkness or the light.

It's only a matter of time before the fuel that keeps us alive runs out.

I do try to move forward as much as possible. I've decided to try to become a doctor, though some of the universities have closed. No one knows what the world will be like by the time I finish school.

It's hard, I find, not to think of better times. Late on certain bright nights, during the long weeks of light, I lie awake, unable to sleep. My mind drifts, and I remember Seth. I sometimes find myself believing that he might come back to me someday. I've become a collector of stories about unlikely returns: the sudden reappearance of the long-lost son, the father found, the lovers reunited after forty years. Once in a while, a letter does fall behind a post office desk and lie there for years before it's finally discovered and delivered to the rightful address. The seemingly brain-dead sometimes wake up and start talking. I'm always on the lookout for proof that what is done can sometimes be undone.

Seth and I used to like to picture how our world would look to visitors someday, maybe a thousand years in the future, after all the humans are gone and all the asphalt has crumbled and peeled away. We wondered what those visitors would find here. We liked to guess at what would last. Here the indentations suggesting a vast network of roads. Here the deposits of iron where giant steel structures once stood, shoulder to shoulder in rows, a city. Here the remnants of clothing and dishware, here the burial grounds, here the mounds of earth that were once people's homes.

But among the artifacts that will never be found — among the objects that will disintegrate long before anyone from elsewhere arrives — is a certain patch of sidewalk on a California street where once, on a dark afternoon in summer at the waning end of the year of the slowing, two kids knelt down together on the cold ground. We dipped our fingers in the wet cement, and we wrote the truest, simplest things we knew — our names, the date, and these words: *We were here.*

Acknowledgments

Thank you to my teachers, all of whom were essential: Aimee Bender, Nathan Englander, Mary Gordon, Sam Lipsyte, Dani Shapiro, Mona Simpson, and Mark Slouka.

I am deeply indebted to Alena Graedon, Nellie Hermann, Nathan Ihara, and Maggie Pouncey, whose friendship, insights, and willingness to read my sentences so often over the course of a decade or so has shaped me as much as my work.

Thank you to Colin Harrison, for sage advice on life and literature.

Thank you to Rivka Galchen, Tania James, Susanna Kohn, and Karen Russell, for crucial readings and suggestions.

Thank you to Eric Simonoff, for your belief, patience, and vision. Thank you to Laura Bonner and Cathryn Summerhayes, for so brilliantly representing me to the rest of the world. Also at WME, thank you to Tracy Fisher, Alicia Gordon, Britton Schey, and Kate Hutchison.

Thank you to my wonderful editor, Kate Medina at Random House, whose insights and attention to these pages moved and amazed me at every stage. Thank you to the whole Random House team, especially Gina Centrello, Susan Kamil, London King, Lindsey Schwoeri, and Anna Pitoniak.

Thank you to Suzanne Baboneau, Ian

Chapman, Jessica Leeke, and the rest of the team at Simon & Schuster UK for your boundless enthusiasm.

For crucial assistance of various kinds at various times, thank you to Jonathan Karp, Alice Mayhew, Carolyn Reidy, Dan Scolnic, Michael Maren, Hannah Tinti, Antonio Sersale, and Carla Sersale. For consistently and entertainingly refining my ideas about books, thank you to Brittany Banta, Jenny Blackman, Meena Hartenstein, Paul Lucas, Finn Smith, Pitchaya Sudbanthad, and Devin McKnight.

For friendship and moral support over many years, thank you to Kate Ankofski, Shiloh Beckerley, Kelly Haas, Heather Sauceda Hannon, Sara Irwin, Samantha Martin, Carrie Loewenthal Massey, and Heather Jue Northover.

For love and enthusiasm, thank you to Liz Chu, Kiel Walker, Cheryl Walker, Steve Walker, and Chris Thompson.

Thank you most of all to my parents, Jim and Martha Thompson, for making everything possible. In particular, thank you for encouraging my interest in writing — even when it went against your better judgment.

And finally, thank you to Casey Walker, my first reader, whose intelligence, generosity, and love have improved not only these pages but also my days — in ways too profound to name. Thank you, Casey.

We do hope that you have enjoyed reading this large print book.

Did you know that all of our titles are available for purchase?

We publish a wide range of high quality large print books including:
Romances, Mysteries, Classics
General Fiction
Non Fiction and Westerns

Special interest titles available in large print are:
The Little Oxford Dictionary
Music Book
Song Book
Hymn Book
Service Book

Also available from us courtesy of Oxford University Press:
Young Readers' Dictionary
(large print edition)
Young Readers' Thesaurus
(large print edition)

For further information or a free brochure, please contact us at:
Ulverscroft Large Print Books Ltd.,
The Green, Bradgate Road, Anstey,
Leicester, LE7 7FU, England.
Tel: (00 44) 0116 236 4325
Fax: (00 44) 0116 234 0205

TELL THE WOLVES I'M HOME

Carol Rifka Brunt

Fourteen-year-old June Elbus, shy at school and distant from her older sister, has only ever had one person who truly understood her: Finn Weiss — her uncle, godfather, confidant and best friend. So when he dies, far too young, of a mysterious illness, June's world is turned upside down. At the funeral a strange man lingers beyond the crowd. A few days later, June receives a package in the mail. Inside is a beautiful teapot she recognizes from Finn's apartment and a note from Toby, the stranger, asking for an opportunity to meet. Then, as they spend time together, June realizes she's not alone in missing Finn, and if only she could trust this unexpected friend he might just be the one she needs the most.